I0763139

MARVEL

ENEMY OF MY ENEMY

Other novels by Alex Segura

Alter Ego

Secret Identity

Dark Space (with Rob Hart)

Bad Beat (with Rob Hart)

Shallow Grave (with Dave White)

Silent City

Down the Darkest Street

Dangerous Ends

Blackout

Miami Midnight

Encanto: Nightmares and Sueños

Araña and Spider-Man 2099: Dark Tomorrow

Star Wars Poe Dameron: Free Fall

MARVEL

LA TIMES BOOK PRIZE WINNER

ALEX SEGURA

ENEMY OF MY ENEMY

A DAREDEVIL
MARVEL CRIME NOVEL

HYPERION AVENUE
LOS ANGELES NEW YORK

For information address Hyperion Avenue, 7 Hudson Square, New York, New York 10013.

First Edition, March 2026
10 9 8 7 6 5 4 3 2 1
FAC-004510-25331
Printed in the United States of America

Designed by Amy C. King

Library of Congress Control Number: 2025946746
ISBN 978-1-368-09536-5
Reinforced binding

The authorized representative in the EU for product safety and compliance is Disney Trading B.V., Asterweg 15S, 1031 HL, Amsterdam, The Netherlands
email: DCP.DL-EU.bookscontact@disney.com

www.HyperionAvenueBooks.com

Logo Applies to Text Stock Only

For Ed, Brian, Dan, Annie, J. M., Karl, Marv, Gerry, Andy, Chip, Mark, Bill, Lee, Klaus, Frank, and Charles—creative heroes who became friends without fear.

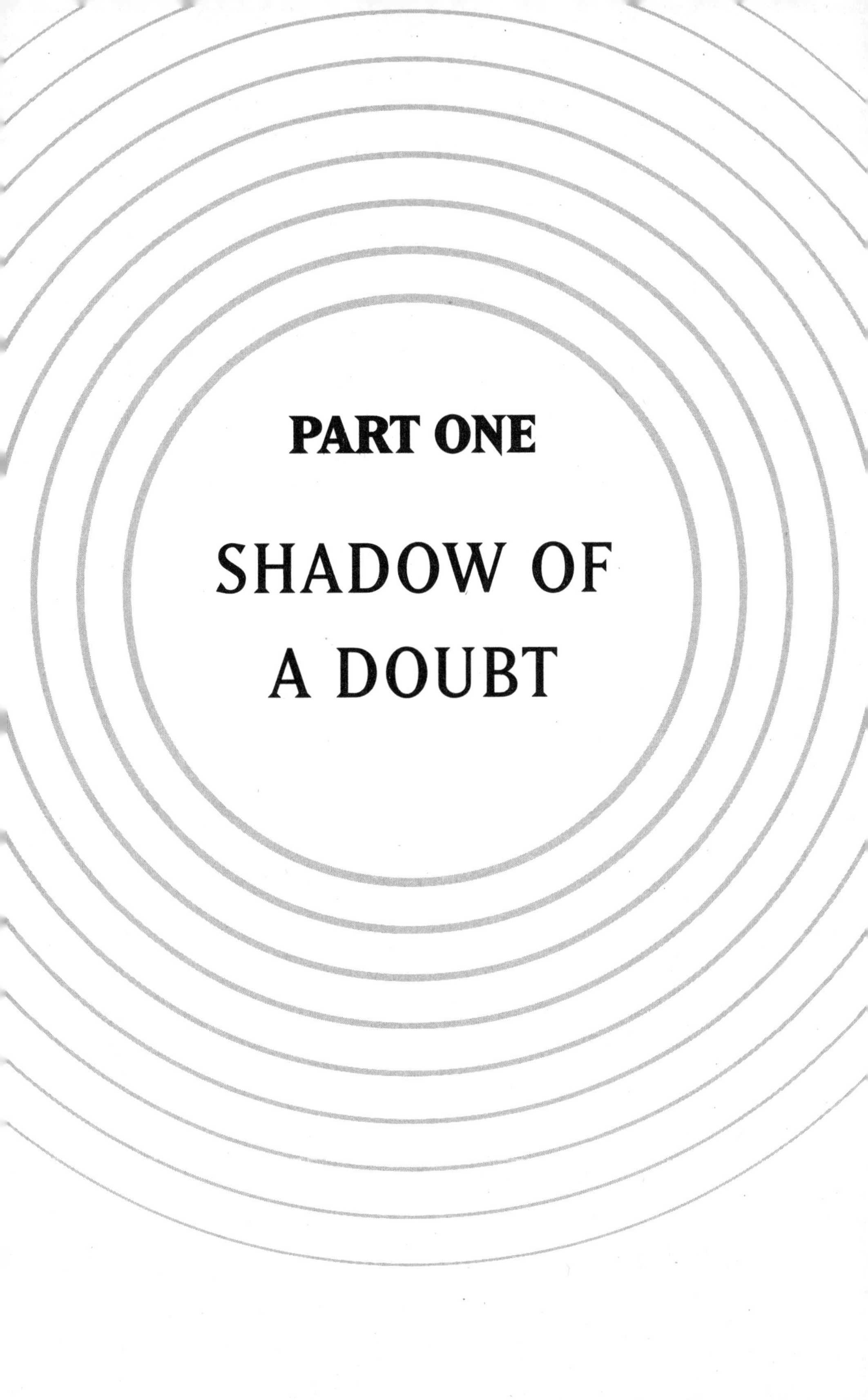

PART ONE

SHADOW OF A DOUBT

ONE

YOU COULD HEAR *a pin drop.*

The expression was apt, but it meant little to Matthew Murdock.

Not just because the words were clichéd, but because for Matt hearing an actual pin drop was akin to the crack of a baseball connecting with a wooden bat, or a car door slamming. Matt could hear a pin drop in the middle of rush hour traffic.

Still, Matt thought, a normal human *could* hear a pin drop in the Lower Manhattan courtroom where he made his way toward the jury box to present his closing argument in a case that had consumed his working hours for what felt like an eternity. Matt scanned his long thin white cane a few paces ahead of him and stopped a few feet in front of the jury box. Blind since childhood, he couldn't see the eyes of the jury on him, but he could sense their stares.

Matt was now a renowned New York City defense attorney, resident of Hell's Kitchen, and frequent gossip column target, but it was never clear that he would make it this far in life. When as a child he'd been blinded by some chemicals while pushing an elderly man out of a runaway truck's path, he had lost his ability to see in the traditional sense.

And even before the accident, Matt's world had been constrained. Matt's father—"Battlin'" Jack Murdock—was a local legend in the gym and in the ring and didn't want his only son to end up an addled bruiser like him. *No fighting, no roughhousing*: Those were the aging boxer's rules. Nothing mattered more to Jack than ensuring his son got out of the slums and made something of himself. And so Matt was forced to stay home—always studying, always reading, always stuck inside their tiny, cramped West Side apartment.

"People of the jury," Matt said, his voice echoing in the large courtroom. "Let me speak plainly. Jason Thomas is a criminal. That is a matter of record. He assaulted a man years ago. He stood trial. He was found guilty of *that* crime and served his time. But that alone is not evidence enough to prove that Mr. Thomas is guilty of *this* murder—of the brutal killing of Stephen Goldsmith. As a jury, it's your job to look beyond what Mr. Thomas has done with his life and focus on the evidence of the crime in front of you. The evidence is what matters most. Is Thomas a bad man? Has he done bad things? It's possible—but is it relevant to this case before you?"

Matt knew Jason Thomas was innocent. Unlike most defense attorneys—who would prefer not to know and just put up the best defense they could muster—Matt couldn't help it. A few minutes into their first conversation, in an NYPD precinct interview room, Matt knew. He could tell based on Thomas's demeanor, his heart rate, and how his breathing stayed focused. He left the meeting with Thomas knowing two things: that his client was innocent, and that Matt would have a hard time winning the case.

Matt's certainty about his client's innocence came from the unexpected benefit he'd gained as a result of the runaway truck and the toxic materials it carried. Nearly every sense Matt had was enhanced to a superhuman level. Which was why even from across a table, his client's heartbeat and breathing patterns told Matt the man was not lying when he professed his innocence and asked for the famed lawyer's help. While his vision was permanently lost in the accident, Matt had been "gifted" with a radar sense—a kind of 360-degree sensory experience that allowed him to picture shapes and figures if not their inherent visuals. Not distracted by certain details, he could read the body language of Mr. Thomas, and it backed up his sense that the man was truly innocent.

Abilities aside, innocent or no, Matt knew getting Mr. Thomas acquitted would be difficult. Matt had worked in the trenches of the New York criminal system for years. Certainly, the evidence against his client was slight: There was surveillance footage of a heated exchange between Thomas and Goldsmith outside a Hell's Kitchen bodega the night before the victim was found stabbed in his Midtown penthouse. A motive was nonexistent. However, Goldsmith was a beloved social media personality known for his glib takes on city life, whereas Thomas was an ex-con who lived in the Bronx. Goldsmith was white and rich; Thomas was poor and Black. Matt knew the odds created by the legal system, and they were stacked against his client. To many people, it was an open-and-shut case. In situations like this, Matt had to do a lot of work to overcome a jury's default assumptions and get them to see the facts at hand.

As Matt took another step forward, he could hear a woman in the public gallery mouthing an apologetic resignation email. He could smell the strawberry-flavored candy the security guard two courtrooms over was sliding into his mouth. Most importantly, he could hear the rhythmic, nervous pounding of juror number seven's heartbeat right in front of him.

Matt Murdock knew these abilities gave him an advantage. To be able to *hear* when someone was lying on the stand was certainly a benefit no attorney in their right mind would ignore. By registering a judge's metabolism rate, he could sense when they were having an unconscious reaction to something in their courtroom. Such powers came with great responsibility, and Matt knew this. Because Matt Murdock, first and foremost, was a believer in the justice system. He respected the rule of law. But if Matt could help an innocent victim beat a bad rap—or prevent an all-too-common systemic injustice from repeating itself—then he didn't see using his sensory powers as a cheat. He saw it as the scales of justice coming into some semblance of balance. He was a man with amazing abilities, and there was no law against him using them to make the world a little fairer.

But even that wasn't always enough.

One of the jurors in the back row cleared his throat, a loud, soggy sound to Matt's ears. He could sense the older female juror in front of him blinking furiously. Heartbeats were picking up speed. Breathing was coming in and out faster from the twelve bodies before him. It all told Matt one thing—they were listening. And they *believed.*

Matt turned his head away from the jury slightly, allowing him to pick up the sounds behind him. One sound in particular. His opponent, Assistant District Attorney Harry Tremins, was a nice enough guy—outside the courtroom. But when trial day came, he was a shark. Tremins was not afraid to push boundaries or a judge's patience; it seemed—to Matt at least—that his main goal was to anger the defense in the hopes that they'd show their cards and slip up in some way. He wanted to rattle his opponents, because rattled opponents made mistakes.

But Matt Murdock wasn't some fresh-out-of-law-school guppy. For years, high-profile cases like this had been his career.

Well, his *daytime* career.

Matt's life was conflicted, to say the least. By day, he was Matt Murdock, respected and capable defense attorney, willing to take big cases to help those less fortunate. Though paying rent for their Midtown Manhattan offices was a struggle more often than not, Matt and his best friend and law partner, Foggy Nelson, had built a reputation as the kind of lawyers you wanted on your side—the kind of attorneys big corporations and bad people feared. It was not rare for cases to be quickly settled once the other side discovered their opponents had put Nelson & Murdock on retainer. No one wanted a drag-out fight with them.

But the evenings were a different story, for Matt and for Hell's Kitchen.

Few stories of the dark side of Hell's Kitchen rang as true as that of his father. Battlin' Jack Murdock was a relic—an aging boxer who'd long ago dropped below the list of title contenders. Not nearly as quick as he once was, Battlin' Jack had become, to some, a joke. He'd lingered too long—a twisted and battered fossil who was barely hanging on. The promoters weren't calling. The fans weren't cheering. The fights weren't happening. Jack Murdock, despite the lies he told his college-age son Matt, was on the brink of losing it all.

The Fixer knew that. A mid-level gangster who spent most of his time managing his outfit's sports betting operation, the lanky, mischievous Fixer liked to put his finger on the scale of his bets to keep the money flowing. And in Battlin' Jack Murdock, he saw a big finger. People loved a comeback, and considering where Jack Murdock was, a comeback was all he had in him. He made Murdock an offer he had to accept.

Ashamed but also desperate to keep his son in college and his lights on, Jack said yes. And the Fixer's promise proved true—suddenly Battlin' Jack Murdock was back in the spotlight, winning some unexpected upsets and clawing his way onto the radar of local boxing gatekeepers. It was a story fans loved—an aging, washed-up fighter pushing for one last shot at the title. Even Matt remembered being in awe of it.

But it was a fraud. And all frauds soon come to light.

The call didn't surprise Matt when it came, around three in the morning. His father had been found dead—battered to death—in an alley near the ring where he'd just experienced his greatest glory. The police had no evidence or suspects, and didn't expect to get any—it was clearly a mob hit. As Matt processed what the detective was saying, he could almost see the man shrug through the phone.

What did surprise Matt was that he already knew what he was going to do about it.

Because, as a kid, Matt hadn't listened to Battlin' Jack or his rules. Sure, he'd studied and kept to himself, but on the frequent nights when his dad wasn't home, at a fight or off drinking or sleeping away a hangover, Matt *trained.* He trained at the very gym where Jack himself went. Though blind, Matt's gift of radar sense, and his heightened hearing, smell, touch, and taste, made him a formidable sparring partner, if he was able to reveal himself. Matt trained in secret—avoiding the fighters and tough-talkers that frequented the gym as he perfected the fighting skills he knew he'd need. But for what? He wasn't sure.

So when Matt got that three a.m. call—he was ready. He just hadn't known it yet.

Jack Murdock was dead.

But Daredevil had been born.

And a different kind of justice would walk the streets and corners of Hell's Kitchen.

"People of the jury . . ." Matt Murdock said again, shifting his weight from one foot to the other as he mulled over his next sentence. The speech Matt was about to utter in the courtroom was critically important. The wrong phrase could send his client to prison forever.

The right words could save this man's life.

((((( )))))

Matt took the courthouse steps quickly, scanning his cane ahead of him, dodging and weaving around the horde of reporters intent on intercepting him. He could still hear the judge's gavel, the loud *rap* echoing through his skull.

Not guilty.

Jason Thomas had been ushered away through the back exit. Matt had gripped his client's hand tightly, listening to his pounding heartbeat, like a bass drum being slammed over and over. His client couldn't believe it. In a way, Matt couldn't either.

"Don't make me regret this, Jason," Matt had said, feeling Thomas's hand, slick with sweat, pull away from his own. "Do some good with this next chance you've been given. We need you."

"You know it, Mr. Murdock—you know I will," Thomas had said as he was led away, down through the cavernous halls that would take him up streetside, away from the throngs of press that would be waiting out front. He should be happy, Matt thought.

"Keep fighting the good fight, MM," Thomas said, his voice

echoing through the long hallway. Matt winced slightly as the words throttled his overly sensitive ears. But something else—something bigger—was bothering him. A sense of dread he shouldn't have been feeling.

"—does Mr. Thomas plan to do now?"

"—surprised by the judge's decision, Matt?"

"—comments about the Wilson Fisk situation?"

It was this last question that sliced through the massive wave of white noise pelting Matt as he tried to dash to a cab waiting at the curb in front of the courthouse. Like a shock of electricity, it spun him around. Matt didn't need to see to recognize who was asking the question—his radar sense picked up the familiar shape of Ben Urich, the *Daily Bugle*'s longtime investigative reporter. He was lurking in the back—letting the TV clowns get close. Ben knew something the other journalists didn't—that the blind, crusading lawyer Matt Murdock and the two-fisted, justice-seeking vigilante Daredevil were one and the same. He knew he didn't have to yell to get Matt's attention. It was the words that counted. And two words counted above all else:

Wilson Fisk.

Matt had to stop himself from saying Ben's name—from revealing he could recognize his old friend not only by his voice, but by his smell and heartbeat as well.

"Excuse me?" Matt said, turning toward the sound of Ben's voice. He could sense the reporters parting, turning toward the grizzled print reporter.

"It's Ben Urich from the *Bugle*, Matt. I just wanted to know if you'd heard about Wilson Fisk."

Matt felt his own heartbeat jump before responding.

"Heard what about him, Ben?"

The sound of Ben's clearing throat—like a boot stepping on shattered glass—said so much. The old reporter's heart rate sped up with each word:

"Wilson Fisk is dead, Matt."

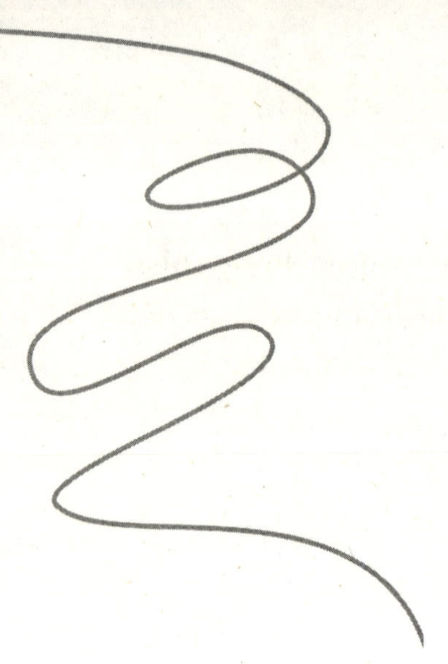

TWO

HE NEEDED TO feel the air. To pull away and be above the city—the sounds, the smells, the screams. To disconnect.

Ben Urich's words still rang through Matt Murdock's skull.

Wilson Fisk is dead.

But Matt Murdock was gone. Matt was Daredevil now, the dark red suit cloaking him from the world outside—protecting him. He needed that, too. Needed to think and mull over what Ben had told him. What the world apparently knew, having learned the news while Matt fought for the life of Jason Thomas in an out-of-the-way courtroom.

The crimson shape moved across the skyline, zigzagging from rooftop to rooftop, like a swerving bird avoiding any and all obstacles. Even as he swung stories above street level, Daredevil could hear the New Yorkers below.

"There he is!"

"Daredevil! Get 'im, buddy! We love ya!"

"Something's got old Hornhead in a tizzy this morning."

"Another menace, I think. Just like that Spider—"

Daredevil swung across the city, his body moving instinctively—his arm jutting out as his finger clicked a tiny button, the wind slapping his entire figure. He sensed the taut cord shooting out from his modified billy club, heard the *thwap* as it wrapped around a nearby balcony, his body arcing along the tension of the rope, swinging him forward as his free arm repeated the motion. Swing, shoot, swing. It felt good. It felt active and away from the noise below. He needed to think, he knew, but for now he also needed to *feel.*

Over his time as Daredevil, Matt had collected his fair share of foes. People who kept coming back to plague him, though he was sure they equally saw it as Daredevil haunting them. But Wilson Fisk was in a league of his own, a few tiers above the likes of Stilt-Man, the Jester, Gladiator, and the Owl.

Wilson Fisk, the man dubbed "the Kingpin of Crime" by the tabloid media and his frightened underlings, was the boss of bosses of the underworld. To the world at large, and to the law itself, he was a humble businessman who'd made his fortune importing foreign goods and reinvested his earnings into a multimedia empire that included a TV station, golf courses, real estate, and much more. But Matt knew better. The façade was a front for a much deadlier operation—one that ran the city's drug trade, numbers operation, human trafficking schemes, and more. Once upon a time New York was run by the Five Families of the Italian mob, with smaller gangs filling in the gaps. But those days were long gone. Today the Kingpin ran everything.

As Daredevil, Matt had crossed paths with the Kingpin so often it almost felt as if the two arch-foes took turns toppling each other. Kingpin was, like Urich, one of the select few who knew Matt and Daredevil were one and the same—which made their adversarial relationship much, much more complicated.

Kingpin had used that information to destroy Matt's life some years ago. Framed him for crimes he didn't commit. Broken the women he loved. All for revenge. Even then, Kingpin still held the truth in reserve—knowing he could hurt Matt more by striking at him at will instead of revealing Daredevil's secret identity to the world. It had taken Matt years to reclaim the broken pieces of his life. His law license. His home. His reputation.

Daredevil felt his boots hit the rooftop with a soft thud. He let his radar sense scan the Hell's Kitchen skyline. He could hear the buzz of the city. The thrum of the subway underground. A food cart vendor yelled that an order was ready. A woman cursed under her breath as she missed a bus. He could smell the bite of cleaning liquid as a display window was wiped down. The new Chappell Roan song blasted from a car driving past. The city was alive. Vibrant. Ever-changing.

And Wilson Fisk was dead.

Daredevil shook his head slightly. He didn't believe it. He didn't need to listen to the heartbeat of the city to know the truth: The Kingpin had cheated death so many times before, why should he believe this time was any different?

"Yo, yo—Hornhead? That you? Hey!"

Daredevil angled his head down and heard the squeak of a squeegee as it was pulled over the faded logo of Josie's Bar on a large stained window. The bar had never seen better days, Daredevil mused. It'd always been a dive—stinking of beer, stale bread, and overcooked hot dogs. It was barely dusk and he could hear the scrape of a pool cue on the worn-out table. The scrape of a mug sliding down the bar to an already-drunk regular.

But it was the voice that grabbed his attention. He recognized the throaty cry, the product of years of late nights and cheap whiskey.

Turk.

Turk, if Daredevil was being generous, was an informant. But the term implied some success rate to the information that the skinny, manic man trafficked in. Ostensibly, he was a low-rent criminal who spread rumors and misinformation to stay afloat. In reality, Turk was a fun-house mirror—reflecting back things that people didn't want to hear in the hopes they'd move on to look at someone else, forgetting Turk existed. Everything the man said had to be taken with a large grain of salt, if believed at all.

Daredevil shot his billy club down toward the street, hooking onto a nearby pole. He swung down and landed a few feet from Turk, who took a step back. That's when Daredevil noticed it: The informant's usual bravado and carnival-barker vibes were gone, replaced by something else. Something sharper.

Turk was scared out of his mind.

"Turk," Daredevil said, his voice lowered an octave—an intentional act, meant to differentiate this persona from the voice of the TV-ready lawyer Matt Murdock. "Is it true?"

Daredevil felt Turk's head move as he checked over his shoulder. Could hear the jagged intake of breath, like a thunderclap in Daredevil's head. Could smell the bite of well vodka on Turk's breath. Not only was Turk panicked—he was drinking himself into a stupor.

Daredevil took a step forward and repeated himself.

"Turk, is it true?"

Turk's head began swaying up and down so fast Daredevil could almost feel a breeze.

"He's gone, DD," Turk said. "News is everywhere. Streets are buzzing—everyone's plotting now. Trying to make a play for what Fisk left behind. Things are gonna get bad, man. Real bad."

Daredevil didn't need Turk to tell him that. Wilson Fisk's grip on the New York underworld was overwhelming. The joke among the criminal middle class was that the only checks that mattered were the ones signed by Fisk. Except it wasn't a joke—it was a stark reality. The Kingpin was in charge. No matter the inroads Daredevil sometimes felt he was making, Kingpin had everyone in his pocket. The judges, the city council, the unions. Sure, not everything landed exactly as Fisk wanted—but his money went far. And when it didn't, he had the muscle to ensure he got his way. Few dared challenge him, and the ones who did were either six feet under or speeding across Europe, desperate to outrun the hit men chasing them down.

Turk was wrong. Things weren't going to get bad.

They already were.

((((( )))))

The offices of Nelson & Murdock were swarmed as Matt approached the building lobby. There was no avoiding the crowd waiting outside now, even as Matt took pains to avoid the main entrance and make his way to the side door leading to the building's basement.

This wasn't a new experience for Matt. He'd been hounded by a handful of curious journalists for years. Though Matt's blindness seemed to stave off most reporters, some speculation about his dual role as lawyer and Daredevil was never far from the minds of those worth their salt. But this was also different. This wasn't just about him—or his alleged identity as a vigilante—it was about his greatest foe: Wilson Fisk, the Kingpin.

Matt needed to know what happened. And he didn't have time for anything else.

"Thought you could dodge us all, Matt?"

Ben Urich's words grabbed Matt. Somehow, the grizzled older reporter had figured out Matt's basement-entrance trick and was waiting for him inside. Matt was impressed. Urich was old-school. He pounded the pavement, used the phone, scrawled interviews in his tiny pocket notebook, and didn't suffer fools gladly. They'd been through a lot together. Ben knowing that Matt was Daredevil had put them at odds more often than Matt cared to admit, but Ben had promised him years ago that he wouldn't write that particular truth. It would do more harm than good, Ben had told him. Still, Matt knew that not every reporter was as trustworthy as that. All it would take was one thoughtless moment—taking his mask off a minute too early in his apartment, a slip of the tongue, a photo—and it'd be splayed all over the tabloids.

"Ben," Matt said with a nod as he walked toward the door, his walking stick tap-tapping a few steps in front of him.

"I've gotta ask," Urich said, taking a step closer to Matt, his voice echoing in the building's expansive basement. "Did you know this was coming?"

Matt turned slowly to face Urich. He remembered that sometimes a facial expression spoke more than words could.

"I—I just had to ask," Urich said, stammering. "Because this looks real bad, Matty."

Matt started to turn away.

"Wilson Fisk was a crime lord, sure—we all knew that, even if it could never be proven in court. Charges would get tossed, jurors ended up dead, judges changed, you name it," Urich said, his voice rising in pitch. Matt could sense him getting closer. "Remember what happened last time, Matt? Daredevil had *everything*—foreign criminal investments, DNA evidence—all pinning a murder on Fisk himself. And here we are again."

Matt stopped short.

"What's your point, Ben?"

Urich cleared his throat.

"I know you, Matt. I know Daredevil. I know your limits. But not everyone does. It's fair for people to ask . . . how much can one man take?" Urich had the decency to pause a moment before he continued. "How many times can he do the right thing and still lose . . . before he takes another path?"

((((( )))))

"You okay, Matt?"

Foggy Nelson's words seemed to boom in Matt's head as he entered the main office of Nelson & Murdock. They felt louder than the yelled questions he'd dodged getting inside. He could feel the concern in his best friend's voice. Foggy didn't know he and Daredevil were one and the same—though Matt was sure his friend had pondered it more times than he cared to admit. But Foggy understood the damage Wilson Fisk had wrought on Matt's life—how his machinations had robbed him of his law license, destroyed his apartment and reputation, and left him a shell of the man he once was.

He pondered Foggy's question. The reality was—Matt was not okay. But he needed to know more.

"What happened, Foggy?"

Matt could make out Foggy's stocky shape—could sense his shoulder shrugging, followed by a sharp intake of breath. His friend and law partner was speechless, and a little scared.

"Don't have a lot of details, just what we've heard on the news." Foggy motioned toward the television relaying updates at a low volume. "Looks like Fisk was gunned down in his own office—someone barged in blasting, took him out quickly."

Matt tightened his grip on his walking stick and moved toward Foggy.

"Do they have a suspect?"

Before Foggy could respond, Matt's attention was absorbed by the television. The volume was so low, Matt was certain a regular person would only be able to make out anything if it were deathly quiet. But to Matt, it was as if the news report was being blared through a loudspeaker.

". . . is Manoli Wetherell, CBN News 10. We have received confirmation from sources within the New York Police Department that a suspect has been named in relation to the murder of businessman and alleged crime boss Wilson Fisk, who was gunned down this morning in his Midtown penthouse office. . . ."

"Matt?"

Matt wasn't listening to Foggy anymore—he stepped toward the television and turned up the volume. Not for himself, but for appearances. Always appearances. He was but a blind lawyer, trying to do some good, after all.

"Listen to this, Foggy," Matt said, standing near the television but looking away from the screen.

". . . suspect is no stranger to New Yorkers—a controversial figure known for his own personal crusade against crime," the reporter continued. *"But after years spent evading capture and dozens of alleged murders tied to his name, we can finally say—"*

Matt felt his hand loosen. Felt the aluminum shaft of his cane slide through his fingers. Heard the slight snap as it hit the ground. But none of it mattered. Not as he heard the reporter continue.

"Frank Castle—the vigilante best known as the Punisher—was seen mere blocks from Fisk's office and has been charged with the murder of the alleged Kingpin of Crime. There is currently an all-points bulletin and reward for any information that might lead to Castle's arrest."

THREE

DAREDEVIL COULD SMELL the powerful mints first. Could hear the muttered curse words. Then the loud creak of the door that led her out of the city morgue and into the adjoining alley.

She hadn't noticed him yet. She wouldn't notice him, Daredevil mused, unless he wanted her to.

"Is it true?"

Daredevil's question bounced off the brick walls that surrounded Tamika Briggs, one of the top pathologists working for the city medical examiner. It was an educated guess that she'd be the one brought in to slice open Wilson Fisk.

Briggs looked up—surprised at first, then calm at the sight of Daredevil, standing a floor above, crouched on the edge of the fire escape across the alley.

"I'm not gonna yell," she said, looking back down at her feet. "So you'd better get your ass down here."

Daredevil complied, flipping down to the ground in a move that would make an Olympic gymnast jealous.

Briggs didn't seem impressed. In fact, she barely looked up.

"Is Wilson Fisk dead?" Daredevil asked.

"That's what I hear," Briggs said with a shrug.

"You're not performing the autopsy?"

"You think someone like Fisk—richest man in the city, pockets lined with money from all over—is gonna let just anyone put a scalpel to that big midsection?" Briggs said with a scoff. "Guy is dead and *still* having everything his way. He had his own specialists come in and do the work. Was in his will, apparently."

Daredevil could sense Briggs looking up at him. Her voice told him more than her expression ever could. She was tired. Defeated.

"How is that even possible?" he asked.

Briggs shook her head.

"You just get to the city, Hornhead?" She let out a dry chuckle. "Rich folks get what they want because they have the cash to make it happen—dead or alive. This news to you?"

"Did you see the body?" Daredevil asked.

Briggs nodded quickly, as if eager to speed past the topic.

"Oh, I saw it," Briggs said. "And he was dead—in my professional opinion. Dead as hell."

Daredevil didn't respond. He knew Briggs was burnt out. He let her vent. Over the years, he had learned that his job—or his side hustle, as a vigilante patrolling the streets of Hell's Kitchen—required more than fists and a thirst for justice. He needed information, and that only came from sources, from people he fostered and helped. People that, in turn, helped him. Briggs was one of the best. He needed her help now, whether she'd performed Wilson Fisk's autopsy or not.

"Anyway, I gotta bounce back inside," Briggs said, turning her back to him. "The cops get really touchy when it's one of their own."

"Wait, what do you mean, 'one of their own'?" Daredevil said, stopping himself from grabbing Briggs by the arm. "What are you talking about?"

Briggs's shoulders sagged.

"Eddie Sheehan? The cop? Castle gunned him down, too," Briggs said nonchalantly, as if she were reading from a grocery list. "Poor guy was two months away from getting his papers and retiring. Wanted to move up to Albany to spend more time with his grandkids. Not anymore."

Daredevil tried to speak, but couldn't form the words. When he raised his head, his radar sense told him the door had shut. He hadn't heard the sound.

Briggs was gone.

A second later, so was he.

((((( )))))

Daredevil didn't have to dig very far to find the intel he needed on Edward J. Sheehan. A quick late-evening trip to central headquarters did the trick. His radar sense guided him into the empty Internal Affairs office, and it only took a moment for his fingers to find a hastily hidden file cabinet key, which pointed him toward an array of manila folders, each one stuffed to varying degrees. Before long, he'd found Eddie Sheehan's record and background, pulling the details from the ink and paper as he ran his fingers over the documents.

Briggs had been right—Officer Eddie Sheehan was a few weeks away from cashing his pension. His record wasn't spotless, but far from the worst he'd seen. A few red flags. Some disciplinary actions. To Matt Murdock, defense attorney, Sheehan's sheet was a garden of opportunity when it camc to challenging his testimony and word on the stand—but there was little he could work with postmortem. Ed Sheehan had been a decent cop who seemed to be well-liked, and there was little about his personal life—living alone out on Long

Island, having few hobbies or friends, collecting guns—that pointed to anything overly suspect. Sheehan was boring. But he was also dead now, and Daredevil needed to figure out why.

Why had Sheehan been at Kingpin's penthouse office when the Punisher supposedly killed them both? What could have happened to drive Frank Castle to kill a cop—one of the few crimes that the unhinged vigilante had always avoided? Daredevil hated this part, where there were more questions than answers and time was moving too fast. Castle had a bounty on his head. The NYPD did not take kindly to losing one of their own. If Castle was cornered, all it'd take to finish him would be an errant shot.

Daredevil knew the only chance he had of getting answers—and the only hope Castle had of surviving the manhunt spreading across the city—was if Daredevil found him first.

((((( )))))

Wilson Fisk wasn't your typical crime boss. He didn't live in the shadows, ensconced in a social club deep inside Queens or the Bronx. When speaking to the press, he stuck to his story—he was just a simple importer who hit it big, nothing more, and certainly nothing illegal. He didn't try to hide his wealth—only a guilty man would. Wilson Fisk wasn't just some regular guy struggling to make rent. He owned a skyscraper that was a fixture of the New York skyline. He lived in the penthouse. He owned golf courses, TV stations, an airline, and had often been floated as a potential mayoral candidate. Wilson Fisk was a pundit's dream—always reachable for a quick, sharp quote, and always willing to throw money at the problems he wanted to solve. In some ways, he'd become an icon to the regular citizens of the city, who saw the bulky, dapper, and tough-talking Fisk as a sign that anyone could make it to the top.

But Daredevil knew better.

The entire high-rise was cordoned off, police swarming not only the crime scene itself but the interior of the whole building.

It took patience for Daredevil to wait out the officer stationed outside the office, who would eventually need a coffee or bathroom break. He lucked out about an hour in and dropped to the floor silently.

As he slowly opened the door to Kingpin's sprawling office, nestled atop the very skyscraper that bore his name, Daredevil thought hard about the endless con Fisk had been running on New York. How he'd fooled the city into thinking of him as the kind of guy who just lifted himself up by his bootstraps and carved out a fortune.

As he gingerly stepped into the dark office space, Daredevil let his enhanced senses sweep across the area. His radar sense bounced off the torn crime scene tape. The gentle ticking of a large clock behind Kingpin's massive oak desk added a metronome-like rhythm to Daredevil's search. He could still smell the bite of gunpowder, the coppery tinge of blood. The sounds of the city—the blaring horns, the bellowed curse words, the *thumpthumpthump* of crowds pushing up and down streets—were all muffled by the bulletproof glass that encased the Kingpin's inner sanctum. This was his most secure space, his throne room. Where he came to do business and give orders. Whoever got to him here—Punisher or otherwise—couldn't have done it alone.

Daredevil didn't have a lot of time. The cop on break would be back in minutes.

He leapt forward and spun in midair, landing in front of Kingpin's desk. Daredevil's fingers skimmed over the papers strewn across the wood finish, sliding over the pages, picking up the indentations of the printed text. Kingpin seemed pretty organized—there wasn't much clutter in his working space. Still, something jumped out at him.

It wasn't on the desk. Daredevil could barely pick it up. But it bounced back from his radar sense regardless. A small corner of paper jutting out from the only drawer the desk seemed to have. Daredevil slowly opened the drawer, which contained a few pens and a small piece of paper—torn from what seemed like a small booklet or address book. He ran his fingers across the pages. There were only a few numbers scrawled across it—five, to be exact. It wouldn't have meant anything if the numbers didn't match part of Sheehan's own phone number. Daredevil pocketed the scrap and left. He still didn't have any answers, but some of the questions were getting clearer.

((((( )))))

"Hello, David."

The man known as Micro wheeled his creaky desk chair around and looked up into the darkness of his tiny Queens studio apartment. Daredevil didn't move. Micro—real name David Lieberman—was a sometimes associate of Castle. A top-flight hacker who'd decided to join the Punisher's crusade against crime, no matter the consequences. If anyone knew where Castle was, it'd be Micro. But even that was a stretch, Daredevil knew.

"Who's there?" Micro said, a shiver of fear in his voice. Daredevil could hear the buzzing from the various screens surrounding Micro, the only light in the small space.

"Where is he, Micro?" Daredevil said, his voice low and almost guttural.

"I— Who's Micro?"

"Don't play games," Daredevil said, stepping closer. "You know why I'm here."

"Daredevil?" Micro said, his voice climbing an octave. "Look, I have no idea—I don't work with—"

Daredevil yanked Micro up to his feet jerkily, heard the cookie crumbs trickle down to the floor as he shook the portly computer tech. Could smell the stale day-old pizza on his breath, paired with cheap beer. That, mixed with Micro's natural odor—of a man who'd given up the idea of regular showers—led Daredevil, for once in his life, to regret his abilities.

"You may not work with the Punisher now, Micro," Daredevil said, pulling him closer, their faces inches apart, "but you have. You helped him for a real long time. Would be a shame if New York's finest found that out."

"There's nothing, no proof of that," Micro said hastily, shaking his head almost in an effort to convince himself. "I ain't scared."

Daredevil shoved Micro back down onto his chair, heard the sharp squeak of its plastic wheels grinding on the faux-hardwood floor. Micro's heart was pounding fast, like the bass drum of a good punk song.

"You should be scared, Micro," Daredevil said, looming over the man. If he'd had his sight, Daredevil would've been able to scan the various screens and monitors blinking and blaring behind Micro, but all he sensed was the heat and noise. He'd have to do it the old-fashioned way. "I've got a folder thicker than that pizza box, listing all the times you lent Castle a hand. Would be a real shame if it got into Ben Urich's hands at the *Bugle*—or, even worse, the NYPD. They don't like cop killers. They also hate the people who help them."

Micro took a long, exasperated breath.

"Look, Daredevil, I'm not lying—I haven't heard from Frank in months. We . . . well, we had a falling-out," Micro said, his voice lowering to a whisper. "I couldn't reach him if I wanted to."

Micro's heartbeat was consistent. As far as Daredevil could tell, he was being truthful.

"Falling-out?"

"It was strange," Micro said, shaking his head. "I mean, Frank and me—we were a team. Long time. I'd help him on the back end . . . I can't say any more . . . but we were helping each other. . . . Next thing I know, he cuts me loose. Barely a word."

"What did he say?"

Micro hesitated before continuing, each word coming out slowly, thoughtfully.

"He just said . . ." Micro continued. "Frank just said it was time to move up the timeline . . . and that I'd get myself killed if I stuck around."

FOUR

"MATT MURDOCK, you're allowed to smile."

Matt recognized the voice immediately—not just because it was the woman he was planning to meet, but because he could pick Melinda Torres's almost melodic lilt out of any crowd. Her tone was powerful but soothing, the sweet tang of her designer perfume another dead giveaway.

Matt did smile, slightly, as he pulled out a chair for himself at Serafina, the Midtown bistro Melinda had chosen for an impromptu lunch. His radar sense could make out her figure, could suss out the tilt of her head that told him she was kidding, and the speeding up of her heartbeat that told him she was happy to see him.

"Duly noted, Officer," Matt said as he took his seat.

Melinda reached out her hand and clasped Matt's tightly. He could hear the slight scrape of her shoes on the concrete as her body tensed up.

He smiled again. "Thanks for the invite."

In reality, he could've done without the social call—the need to find Frank Castle had consumed every waking moment Matt had to spare, in and out of the Daredevil costume. But if Matt had learned anything over his years as the Man Without Fear, it was that he had to at least play the part, lest people start asking questions about what lawyer Matt Murdock did with his time. Plus, it wasn't hard to convince himself to see Melinda.

"Of course," she said, leaning back in her chair. "I wanted to see you. I missed you. It's okay to say that, right?"

"I've missed you, too," Matt said. "And if it's not okay, then we'll both be wrong together."

Melinda let out a quick, machine-gun-fire laugh. Hearty but brief.

They'd been dating for little over a month—she the NYPD Internal Affairs officer who'd grown jaded and disillusioned by the job, he the passionate defense attorney who hadn't. He liked to think his optimism perked her up. He found her unflinching view of the world sobering, but not depressing. It was still early days, Matt knew, but he felt a balance with Melinda he hadn't experienced in a long time. Not since—

Not since Karen Page.

Matt shook his head gently, trying to shake the image out of his mind. Karen, the woman he'd wanted to marry, in his arms, dying. The maniac Bullseye looking on, eyes wide, mouth twisted into a terrifying grin—

Not now, Matt thought.

"You there, Murdock?"

Matt blinked under his thick glasses and looked toward Melinda—never at her directly. Matt knew that even though his radar sense could be as precise, if not more so, than the vision of most people, he still had to give the impression that he couldn't *see* anything.

"I am, just a little tired," Matt said, his voice cracking slightly. "I've become obsessed with this Fisk situation."

"You and everyone in the city, Matt," Melinda said with a quick shake of her head. "I can't escape it. The most powerful guy in the city, gunned down in his own office by the Punisher? I mean, I know the guy killed criminals, but how did he even *get* to Fisk?"

Matt could feel Melinda dancing around what the public knew and what she knew as someone on the inside. Matt didn't want to violate the tentative trust they'd built together, the understanding that they were sometimes on opposite sides of the legal process and that if they were to make this work, they'd have to respect that. But he was also desperate for any kind of lead—even the tiniest of breadcrumbs. That, coupled with his own exhaustion, led him to make a mistake.

"And the cop," Matt blurted out as the waiter came by with a pair of menus. Matt took the one he was handed and placed it gingerly in front of him.

"How do you know that?" Melinda asked without hesitation.

"I have sources," Matt said, trying to keep it light, but also realizing he was talking with his foot in his mouth. He'd pushed too far, too fast. "I'm hearing that a cop was on the scene and died, too—but the NYPD is keeping it under wraps until Castle is in custody."

Melinda looked down at the menu, but Matt could tell she wasn't reading it, she was thinking. Stewing over what to say. Suddenly the mood had shifted from friendly and flirtatious to tense and uncertain. Matt was okay with a little discomfort if it meant getting some intel, but he wasn't sure that was going to happen.

Melinda looked up. Based on her heart rate, Matt knew he'd overstepped before she spoke.

"I was hoping we'd have a nice lunch, fool around, and then I'd go back to the misery of my desk," Melinda said, her voice a hissing whisper. "I didn't expect my sort-of boyfriend to circle above me like some information vulture. If you have a question, ask me. But don't be surprised if I don't answer. And if I stop answering your calls or texts, period."

Matt sighed. He ran a hand across his face and could feel the wear and tear of long nights. He was tired. He was at a dead end. After visiting the Kingpin's office, Matt as Daredevil had scoured the city looking for Frank Castle—scoping out old hideouts, known associates like Micro, chasing rumors, and running himself ragged. He needed a lead, but he should have known this was not the way to get it.

"I'm sorry," Matt said, wincing. "I didn't mean it that way, but you have every right to be mad."

He leaned over and placed a hand on Melinda's arm. She tensed, but didn't pull back.

"Can we start over?"

Matt could hear her heart rate slow down. Could sense her body relaxing.

"You can start over, Mr. Murdock," she said. "And today, lunch is most definitely on you."

Matt laughed. On some level, he felt relief. Another part of him was elsewhere, thinking about how Melinda's heart skipped a beat when he'd mentioned Sheehan.

((((( )))))

He hated doing this. That's what he told himself.

Hated how he'd walked her to her train, hand in hand, only to find an alley and change into his red suit and follow her to the precinct. He didn't suspect Melinda of anything, but he did think she knew something. And, right now, Daredevil was desperate for any kind of knowledge that might help him find Frank Castle or get a sense of what an aging cop like Sheehan was doing with the Kingpin.

Wilson Fisk often kept cops on his payroll—he kept judges, lawyers, and politicians on there, too. It wasn't anything new for a man of his power. The easy explanation could be that Sheehan was a crooked cop, in the wrong place at the wrong time, and paid the price. And his record left space for that. He wasn't the perfect cop, and he had abused his power on more than one occasion. So why did Daredevil feel like he was missing something?

He perched himself on a rooftop adjacent to Melinda's office. He could barely make out her voice through the noise of the street, the office, and the city—it was like following soft piano music emanating from someone's phone in the middle of a crowded club. But Daredevil had spent years training to use and hone his powers—at first on his own but later under the tutelage of Stick, a martial arts master who understood Daredevil's gifts in ways that he still couldn't. He sat down cross-legged and closed his eyes. He let the sounds engulf his mind. The screeching of a truck's brakes. The blaring of music from someone's stereo. The heated argument a man was having with his partner. The jingle of keys as someone opened the front door to their store. The rustle of paper as someone stacked sheets together after printing them. A soft whistle.

There—that was Melinda.

He tried to hold on to her voice, her sounds, and felt himself following her—as if he were outside his own body. He could hear her footsteps walking through the packed Internal Affairs department. The pleasantries exchanged as she headed farther into the office. Her lips touching her coffee mug and slowly sipping on hot mint tea. The click of her door opening. Then something else.

"You got a minute, Torres?"

"Detective Gunderson—yes. I was about to hop on a call—"

"It's urgent."

"Then follow me."

Another click, then the sound of a lock. The scraping of chair legs being pulled back. A long sigh from Melinda.

Daredevil hated doing this. Hated it.

"We've got some intel on Sheehan," Gunderson said.

"I'm all ears," Melinda said.

Daredevil could relate. He took a long breath.

The ruffling of papers. The sound of one sheet being slid out of a pile.

"Looks like his brother, Terry—lives out on Staten Island—has been doing really well for himself lately," Gunderson said.

A pause. Daredevil visualized Melinda scanning a bank balance sheet or account snapshot.

"That's a lot of zeroes," Melinda said dryly.

"Pretty good for someone who works for sanitation."

"Where's it coming from?"

"That's the problem," Gunderson continued. "The company paying Terry Sheehan is a shell of a shell—Mezinis and Charleston. You hit their website and they claim to be a cleaning company, the people you hire to detox your office or clean big spaces. But there's no way to contact them and they aren't listed by the Chamber of Commerce."

Melinda cleared her throat before responding.

"Can you trace the site itself?"

"We tried. It's one of those CubeSpace deals—different company, Blue Fusion Enterprises. No site, no address, nothing," Gunderson said, exasperation seeping into every word. "We've hit a wall."

"You talked to the brother yet?"

"Not yet. We're trying to keep the Sheehan part of this under wraps, but the second we start sniffing around, the second we ask Terry what's up with his bank account, we'll see it on the internet. 'Police Officer Killed on Scene of Kingpin Murder, Unreported Until

Now.' Which, hey, it's the truth—but we need that info. We need to keep something to ourselves to help figure this out."

NYPD rarely kept the death of a police officer quiet—even if the perp was still on the loose, Daredevil thought as he listened. He filed the idea away. Another oddity complicating the bigger picture.

"I understand, Gunderson, but what do you want me to do about it?" Melinda said, her patience dwindling. "My investigation into Sheehan disappeared once he died."

Daredevil's mind seemed to freeze in place, wheels screeching to a halt. Melinda had already been investigating Sheehan? For what?

"Was he the cleanest cop on the force? Not by a mile," she continued. "But I never would've pegged him for a Kingpin goon. Now you tell me his little brother is raking in tens of thousands of dollars—and has been for months. That means I might've been wrong. But I don't have any *evidence*; this paper you just handed to me isn't it. You need to figure out a way to talk to his brother and figure out what the hell Sheehan was doing with the Kingpin and the Punisher. If this gets out, we're in an ocean of shit I don't want to have to swim out of. We may already be cooked. We need this fixed, yesterday. Understood? Make it go away."

Daredevil didn't hear Gunderson get up and leave. He was already swinging south—torn by the choice he'd made, and the information it'd given him.

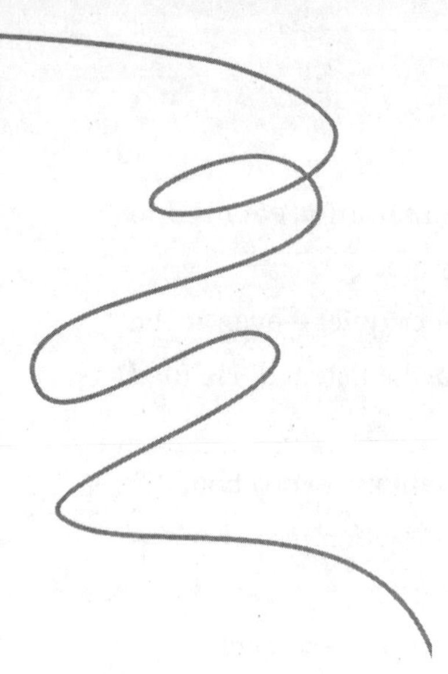

FIVE

TERRY SHEEHAN WAS already on the run by the time Daredevil found him.

He wasn't hard to pinpoint, even with the black baseball cap, flowing trench coat, and pharmacy-brand sunglasses. Daredevil knew that the size and shape of the ticket in Terry's sweat-soaked hand was for the Metro-North railway. Leave it to a lifelong New Yorker to think the Hudson Valley would give them enough cover.

Daredevil grabbed him on the lower level of Grand Central terminal, near the main food court, biting into a hot dog doused in ketchup and sauerkraut that did a number on his sense of smell. He reached out a red-gloved hand and yanked Terry into a closed-off corner, managing to cover the man's mouth before he could make a sound.

"If you scream, this is going to be much worse," Daredevil whispered as he pulled Terry farther into the shadows of the station's underbelly.

No one would bother them, if Terry stayed quiet. That was a big "if."

Terry nodded, and Daredevil slowly removed his hand. When it seemed like his target wasn't going to shriek and run, he spoke.

"Where ya headed, Terry?"

The older man shifted from foot to foot, his eyes darting around.

Daredevil didn't need to listen to his heartbeat to know he was going to deliver a whopper.

"Just takin' a ride, gonna see my cousin in Pelham." Terry gave a nervous shrug serving as a period to his sentence—as if that alone would exonerate him. "What's it to you?"

"You don't have any cousins in Pelham, Terry." Daredevil grabbed him by the coat and pulled him closer. He shifted his tone purposefully from friendly concerned citizen to something else. Something darker. "Your brother's your only family. Well, *was*."

That's when Terry changed. His temperature seemed to rise. His breathing got faster—and shorter. He tensed up in Daredevil's grip.

"Look, I don't know nothin' about my brother. . . ."

"C'mon, Terry, don't insult my intelligence, okay?" Daredevil leaned a few inches closer. "Now, I do know you have about five hundred thousand reasons to lie here, but let's just cut the bullshit, all right? Who was paying your brother? What was he doing?"

Showing a burst of unexpected strength, Terry pulled away, and Daredevil lost his grip for a moment—but it was enough. Terry had managed to turn around and bolt toward the light, the crowds. Daredevil didn't need a bunch of cell phones pointed at him as he tackled someone and dragged them away. Going viral was not on his to-do list.

He moved fast, tossing one of his billy clubs at Terry—connecting with the back of his head. His radar sense showed the shape of the man's lanky body slump to the ground, the loud groan letting Daredevil know he was still conscious. He walked slowly over to where the pronc body lay.

"That was a bad idea," Daredevil said, crouching down, his mouth close to Terry's ear. "There's no avoiding this. And honestly, you'd probably be better off talking to me than a cop, don't you think? Your brother was one of their own—it wouldn't be good for you to be implicated in his mur—"

"No! No!" Terry said, sliding up to a sitting position, his hands raised defensively. "I had nothin' to do with that, nothin', okay? I'd never hurt my brother—he was family. I loved the guy, we was tight. He was my best friend. I'd do anything for him—help him—"

"I bet," Daredevil said, grabbing Terry by the arms. "I bet you helped him. But now I need you to help me, all right? Your brother is dead. From what I can tell, he wasn't a bad cop, as far as that goes. He didn't need to die that way."

Terry looked down at his hands. Daredevil heard the muffled breathing—noticed the shuddering shoulders. He didn't need to see Terry's face to know he was crying. He placed a hand on the broken man's shoulders.

"What happened?"

"I . . . I don't know, really. I wish I did know, man. One day, Eddie comes to me—to my job, starts asking my crew chief to see me—asks to talk to me. Pretty normal. He comes by a lot. We're family. So we go in the back and he's—he's shaking—"

"When was this, Terry?"

"Not sure, I guess . . . I dunno, like a month or two ago?" Terry wiped at his mouth with his sleeve. "Eddie, uh, he looked bad. I was worried he was sick, cancer or something like that. But I wait and he tells me, he's shakin' and he tells me, 'Terry, I need your help,' says he's got a line on some serious money—life-changing money. But he can't take it himself. He can't, like, have it wired to his bank. People would notice. The wrong people. I thought he meant his bosses, like the cops, but now I dunno . . ."

"Who was paying him, Terry?"

Bloodshot eyes looked up at Daredevil.

"That's the thing, man. I have no damn idea. The wires came into my account and honestly, my eyes almost popped outta my head, y'know? Like I'd never seen so many zeroes in my life before. I thought it was a joke. Almost considered just riding off into the sunset, even though I love my brother."

"Mezinis and Charleston . . . any idea who they are?" Daredevil said, naming the company he'd overheard Gunderson mention in Melinda's office. He felt a pang of shame for invading her privacy. He pushed past it. "Did you recognize the name?"

"It could've been Minnie and Daffy, for all I cared, okay?" Terry said with a shrug. He was calming down now. "The money was there. So I tells him, 'Hey, bro, you're rich now.' I show him the numbers and ask him what he wants me to do. Then he got all weird."

"Weird how?"

Terry scoffed. "Well, how would you react to becoming rich, Mr. Daredevil? How do you think a normal chump should react, after working the beat for thirty years like a putz?"

"Happy?" Daredevil guessed.

"Yeah, happy. Like, my-life-is-locked happy. But you know what? Eddie wasn't happy. I don't know what set him off. The number. The name of the company, what. But when I showed him that slip? He looked scared out of his mind. Like I'd just handed him a death sentence."

"Did you know your brother was under investigation?" Daredevil asked. It was a bit of a long-shot question, another tidbit stolen from Melinda, another shameful act. But he needed next steps, and Terry Sheehan was close to becoming a dead end.

"Nah, no idea—I mean, how would I know? Eddie said he was rubbing his bosses the wrong way, but—"

Daredevil froze, turning his head away from Terry, who seemed to stop in response. He overheard the chatter—growing louder, more voices—coming from the main terminal area. Two Wall Street suits standing and sipping their tap beers as they waited for their train. Daredevil focused his hearing on them.

"Yeah, the *Punisher* . . . got him cornered in Queens somewhere . . ."

". . . Castle? Hope they blast that chump. . . ."

". . . say he's holed up on the 'Boulevard of Death.' Guy probably has hostages. . . ."

Daredevil ran.

He could hear Terry call after him, but there was no time.

He had to save a murderer from himself.

SIX

DAREDEVIL COULD HEAR the blaring sirens from miles away. Could feel the tremors from the speeding cars. The muttered curses under the breath of the armored SWAT team members inching toward their target. It was rush hour on Queens Boulevard in Kew Gardens, and a swarm of police and other vehicles were blocking the entire service road—surrounding Purdy's Fried Chicken.

The restaurant had only one customer: Frank Castle, the Punisher.

In the shadows, Daredevil was there, too.

"I hear you, Devil," the vigilante said, his low baritone startling Daredevil as he dropped from the ceiling onto the ground, between the tables and the register.

The restaurant had been evacuated by Castle. He'd made it clear he didn't want to have hostages, and he'd bought himself a few minutes with the gesture. But Castle wasn't the type to get cornered and have a conscience, Daredevil thought. Castle was a fighter. Why wasn't he trying to shoot his way out now?

Not wearing the familiar black bodysuit and white skull emblem, he was as nondescript as they come: Baseball cap pulled low, bulky shades, a puffy jacket—Frank Castle was in incognito mode, which was not his usual methodology. It even took Daredevil a moment to recognize him. He wondered how anyone else did. If Daredevil's hunch was right, Castle wanted to be able to walk into the restaurant and decide his own fate, on his own terms.

"What are you doing, Frank?"

Castle turned to face Daredevil. He took a few steps, the sounds of the sirens bouncing off his back. Daredevil felt overwhelmed. Every sense was overrun. He tried to focus on the figure approaching him.

"Isn't that the question, Daredevil? The big canyon between us, eh? 'What are you doing, Frank?'" Castle said with a high-pitched, mocking tone. "Aren't you the hero, Hornhead? Why don't you try and figure it out? Or do you have too many questions for me? Worried I might get mowed down before you get your nice, tidy answers, hero?"

Castle let the last syllable drag out, like an insult. Daredevil ignored him. He felt unsettled. Something wasn't right here—and he wasn't ready to throw down with the Punisher before he could figure it out. Frank Castle was a twisted man—someone who considered himself above the law, and someone who'd deputized himself judge, jury, and worst of all, executioner. In Daredevil's eyes, Castle wasn't a hero. Wasn't even close. But he knew that Frank Castle—the Punisher—believed in vengeance and defending the innocent, in his own contorted way.

So why is he here?

They'd fought more often than they'd helped each other. Daredevil couldn't get past Castle's ease with murder, how he preferred gunning down the people he deemed guilty instead of giving them the due process that Daredevil and Matt Murdock had built their life around.

The sirens kept blaring in Daredevil's head. The outline of Castle's body—the radar-sense shape—was blurring. He couldn't focus.

"Why'd you do it, Frank?" Daredevil asked, wincing slightly at the sound of his own voice. The downside of having enhanced senses was moments like this—moments that were too frequent in a metropolis. When you didn't get a second of silence, a moment without a strange smell or scent. He was overwhelmed. People talking. Sirens. The thick smell of burning animal flesh that couldn't be scraped off the grill. The radios blaring outside. It was too much. He had to—

"Daredevil, I thought you were smarter than this."

Another police car. Another blaring siren. Daredevil reached for his temples. Too loud. Too much.

"What . . . what do you mean?"

Castle was closer now. Daredevil crouched down—he could sense the Glock handgun in his right hand, his arms down the side of his body.

"I mean . . . c'mon, Daredevil—use that brain for once. Pull yourself out of what's right and wrong in your head and think about what's *really* wrong. What the big problem is," Punisher continued, squatting down now, their faces closer. "Wilson Fisk is dead. The Kingpin of Crime is gone—and you're here wondering whether I pulled the trigger or not. You ever think to yourself, Daredevil, that you might be missing the point, with your sick, holier-than-thou attitude? With that tone of yours? You think anyone cares about how the biggest criminal in the city finally ate it? They're just happy he's dead."

The large vigilante motioned to the street, to the sounds and lights dominating Queens Boulevard. "Look at them," he said with a scoff. "Waiting outside like a pack of hungry alley cats, desperate for the sound of an open can. You don't think I could leave any minute I want, Daredevil? You think I'm that easy—that these dime-store cops can take me down? The ones who weren't on Kingpin's payroll? They love me. The ones who were indebted to him? They're off the hook now, so they think I did them a favor. Meanwhile, you're sitting here, in your red pajamas, wondering if Kingpin maybe had a tough childhood, or had some undiagnosed trauma you could've workshopped with him, boo-hoo. Maybe he didn't mean to be as bad as he was."

The Punisher pointed one of the Glocks at Daredevil—the barrel close enough that he could smell the gunpowder, could feel a callused finger grating against the trigger.

"Tell me I'm wrong, Red."

"You gonna shoot me, Frank?" Daredevil asked. "For what? What's my crime? When you're the one who decides who lives and dies, when you're the executioner, you get to be the final word, right? Then tell me, Frank—what am I guilty of? What bad thing have I done in your mind that would merit a bullet in the head?"

Punisher stood up with a jerk and tossed the two Glocks to the ground. Daredevil stood as well and the two men sized each other up for a moment.

"You don't understand what's going on. I don't want this rap—I'm bigger than this. I'm not some cop killer. My crusade—my symbol—is more than that," Punisher said, shaking his head. "You've got it easy, Red. You just need to whimper and cry about how bad everything is, but you don't do anything to change it. Just keep feeding the system. Perps in, perps out, punch and kick and start again. Ever wonder who's playing who, Daredevil? Lemme know when you figure it out."

Before Daredevil could respond, Castle spun around, his hands folded behind his head in a sign of surrender. He walked toward the door. As it opened, the noises got louder—bursting into the greasy chicken restaurant and assaulting Daredevil's senses anew. He tried to follow, but a pair of cops—older officers who'd probably been at a dozen scenes like this one—approached the mythological Punisher and gently turned him around to handcuff him. Daredevil focused his senses on Castle as they gingerly searched him and patted him down. The man's heartbeat betrayed nothing. His breathing was calm, peaceful. Daredevil strained his hearing to catch anything as the cops started to lead him to their squad car. The only thing he picked up was Castle—a gruff, humorless chuckle.

It was then that Frank Castle turned to face Daredevil. It was then that Daredevil heard his parting words, whispered so softly no one else could even notice he'd made a sound.

"Fear the wild animal that willingly steps into its cage."

SEVEN

"WHY ARE YOU so surprised, Matt?"

Foggy's words were delivered between bites of a massive chicken parm hero, which Matt knew had been purchased across the street at the nameless sandwich spot Foggy frequented on his way to work. The added smell of the pepper oil the cook lathered on was a dead giveaway. So was the sound of Foggy's teeth tearing through the thick bread.

"The Punisher is a vigilante, Foggy—he can't exist if he's in prison," Matt said, shaking his head to himself as his fingers traced over the front page of the *Daily News*'s morning edition. "His entire reason for being—his calling card—is to murder criminals, to decide their fates himself. How can you do that from prison? The security they have on him—it's unheard of. They're probably logging every time he takes a breath."

Foggy took a long, loud slurp from his giant-size soda. "He's just not well, bud." Foggy wiped at his mouth hastily. "You can't predict what he's gonna do. Maybe there's someone in the joint he has his sights on? Or, I dunno, he saw the light? Can't we enjoy the quiet week and—"

Matt sighed.

"Have a little empathy, Foggy—I agree, the Punisher is unwell, but

I'm just pointing to his behavior." Matt tapped the newspaper gently. From what he'd heard Foggy say as he tossed the tabloid on his desk, he knew a scowling Frank Castle was on the cover—with the headline FROM PUNISHER TO PUNISHED? accompanying it. "He was cornered, then surrendered without putting up a fight. The man is wanted for one of the biggest murders in the history of New York City."

"Are you really sad about it?"

Foggy's words seemed to land between the two friends like a loud thud. It took Matt a moment to process them.

"Sad?"

"I mean, Matt, he killed Wilson Fisk. That guy had it out for you in the worst possible way," Foggy said, dabbing at his tie—now stained by a glob of marinara sauce—with a napkin. "He ruined your life, bud. Destroyed your home. Had you disbarred. Tormented Karen. It's okay to be glad he's gone, you know. I know I am."

Matt didn't respond immediately. He was surprised—by the casual ruthlessness of Foggy's comment, but also by something else. Something more primal that Matt couldn't shrug off. A feeling that he'd long buried but one that scurried up to the top of his mind at the mere mention of Wilson Fisk's crusade against Matt—and Daredevil.

Matt agreed with Foggy. He wasn't sad the Kingpin was dead. He wasn't sad the man who'd made it his life goal to destroy him and his alter ego was dead.

But that didn't matter.

"Castle's gonna need a lawyer," Matt said softly—almost as if he were speaking to himself.

Foggy responded with a slow choking sound, the bite of chicken parm struggling to get down his throat. Foggy let out a few quick coughs before responding.

"You gotta be kidding, Matt," Foggy said, exasperated. He stood up from his seat and started pacing in front of Matt's desk. "You think we should take on Castle's case? Why not just let the man take the L and move on? It's a done deal. They found casings that match the Punisher's weapons. It's also, uh, the freakin' Punisher, Matt . . . killing criminals is his whole deal. What's the win aside from playing for the cameras here?"

Matt started to respond, but Foggy interjected. "And please, before you start ranting about how it's the right thing to do—remember the one thing you always told me, about us, about this partnership . . ."

The two friends said the words in unison:

"We will never play the media game."

Foggy leaned forward, his palms on Matt's desk. Matt could smell the greasy sandwich on his friend's breath, could feel the heat of his body close to his own. Foggy was getting riled. For anyone who knew Foggy—knew the jovial, agreeable, and friendly man he was most of the time—this was a rare moment. Foggy would much rather have a laugh or crack open a good book than argue. But Matt, as was his wont, had hit a nerve. *You'd think Foggy would be used to experiencing this by now*, Matt thought.

"There you go," Foggy said, his voice a low growl. "Now, please, explain to me how defending Frank Castle for a murder he clearly committed doesn't fall under that umbrella. I am all ears, pal o' mine."

Matt cleared his throat, then said, "The cop, Sheehan."

"What about him?" Foggy stood back up. Matt didn't need to see his face to know he was scowling. "So he was a little crooked. So what? You know how many cops are on Kingpin's payroll? Or Hammerhead's? Or the Owl's? We don't even know for sure what kind of money he was making, if anything. According to his record—"

Matt stood up and faced his friend. Now it was his turn to be stern.

"Franklin Nelson, let me finish," Matt said.

Foggy straightened his posture and backed up a step.

"All right, all right," Foggy said, his hands up in a sign of surrender. "Sorry."

"It's fine, just listen to me," Matt said with a soft smile. "It's not that Sheehan wasn't a good cop—which, from what I can tell, he was at least a little off. But it's the fact the Punisher killed a cop at all. While Castle hates criminals, he's always gone above and beyond to not get police or other city workers caught in his personal war on crime. Unless they were extremely corrupt to the point of working directly for the criminals he was hunting. Are you following me?"

"I think so," Foggy said, rubbing his chin. "So, Sheehan was definitely corrupt? Castle had reason to kill him?"

"Maybe," Matt said. "Or maybe that's how someone wanted it to look."

Foggy let out a long sigh.

"Oh, Matt, are we really doing this?"

Matt reached for the phone by his desk and dialed a number by heart.

As Matt spoke to someone on the other line, he could pick up Foggy's confused and frustrated mumbling as if it were playing on a radio a few feet away.

"Frank Castle. Geez. You wanna defend the freakin' Punisher? So much for a quiet week."

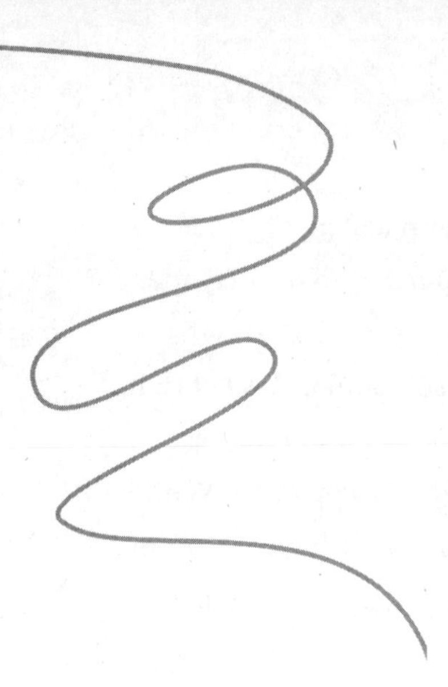

EIGHT

MATT TRIED TO ignore the loud, echoing clang of the massive metal doors, drew on his years of training, and let the waves of sound flow past and through him. After a moment, he felt a tap on his shoulder from the prison officer, an older gentleman named Kolakowski nudging him forward.

"No touching, no giving of anything, no funny business—all right? He's gonna be chained to the table because those are the rules. Frank Castle isn't your usual perp, Mr. Murdock. I know he's your client, but—"

"I understand, Officer," Matt said with a friendly nod.

He heard the whoosh of a smaller door opening and stepped inside. He could make out Castle's figure—tense, rigid, poised, like a giant cat waiting to pounce on unsuspecting prey.

The vigilante would be disappointed, Matt thought, if he saw him as a meal—or a victim.

"Need me to stick around?" the officer asked.

Matt waved Kolakowski off and walked toward the table where Castle was seated. He dropped his briefcase on the table and clicked it open, pulling out his phone. He instinctively selected his recording app and tapped the large red button at its center. Then Matt sat down across from the Punisher and smiled in his direction.

"Matt Murdock." His voice was gravelly and sharp—like rocks being ground to dust. Matt thought he could feel the killer's eyes boring into him, but he shook the sensation off. "You here for any particular reason? Wanna ask me how I murdered Fisk? Wanna get off on the death of one of the worst people to walk the planet?"

There it was. Subtle. Small. But it was there. A slight hiccup in Castle's heartbeat. A little pivot that let Matt know there might be more to this than he first thought. Had he missed it when they'd faced off inside the chicken joint? Matt wondered. His mind flashed back to the noise, the sirens, the yells, the sounds of the city seemingly concentrated just outside the restaurant doors.

Or was Frank Castle's story more complicated than even Matt could see right now?

Either way, it wasn't any kind of evidence. Matt couldn't walk up to the judge and explain that the truck had contained chemicals that not only blinded a young Matt but also gave his remaining senses a powerful boost so that he could generally figure out whether someone was lying or truthful by listening to their heartbeat. No, that wouldn't stand up in court.

Sorry, Your Honor, but I heard a slight skip when I questioned my client, which means he was probably lying. Can we toss the case—

"Why are you smiling?"

Castle's low growl of a question shook Matt out of his daydream. He tried to replay what he'd just heard. Had he imagined the skip? He was sure he'd heard it. Or did he just want it to be there?

Matt ignored the question and tilted his head up a few inches above the killer's scalp before he began to speak.

"Mr. Castle, I'm going to assume you can probably guess why I'm here," Matt said flatly. "The charges against you—in the Fisk murder alone—are enough to send you to prison for life. Not to mention the file cabinet full of cases the city, state, and federal courts can toss your way if they feel like it. I'd also imagine being housed with dozens of men you've put away—or harmed irrevocably—won't increase your chances of living a long, albeit boring, life behind bars. On top of that, killing a police officer won't endear you to the law enforcement officials you'll be dealing with until you die. The ones who are responsible for keeping you safe."

Matt noticed a sudden uptick in Castle's heartbeat at the mention of the cop. What it meant, he couldn't determine. Not yet.

"I don't need an attorney," Castle said, placing his palms down on the table and looking at his fingers. "The system is broken. I won't get a fair shake. I never expected one. And I don't kill cops."

Matt licked his lips. He didn't know what to say—how to convince a literal sociopath to take his one best shot at getting a fair defense. Castle didn't seem suicidal, but he did seem uninterested in the legal process, already resigned to whatever fate the law had planned for him. Matt understood that—could feel an aching need to just let that be in this case—but he also knew that these were the moments clients needed people like him most. An advocate. A defender who understood what options people had in these situations. And someone willing to protect them even if they were no longer interested in protecting themselves.

"You do need a lawyer, Mr. Castle," Matt said, moving his chin down toward the recording app on his phone. The first recording always signaled a new case for Matt—a place to begin to brainstorm, generate ideas, strategize. There was hope in that first recording. Hope that maybe, just maybe, Matt Murdock and Foggy Nelson could pull another victory out from the jaws of defeat.

But even Matt wasn't deluding himself. *People of the State of New York v. Frank Castle* was about mitigation, not exoneration. He had to try to ensure his client got the best deal possible—even if it meant bargaining with chips he wasn't even sure he had. But this wasn't a singular act. Frank Castle was a spree killer with dozens of bodies tied to his name. He was also a vigilante with intel about crime organizations up and down the East Coast. Perhaps a few downloads of his intelligence would be worth Castle's time, as opposed to dying in solitary on Riker's, being eaten alive by rats, or shivved by the cousin of a criminal he'd obliterated with machine-gun fire. Defending him was not a task Matt was going to relish—but it was something he had to do.

Matt cleared his throat.

"You may not want one," he said. "You may just think this is the end of the line, and that you'd rather go out in a blaze of glory. But let me assure you, Mr. Castle—there's a lot of work to be done. There's a lot of time if you want it. You may not care if you get tagged as Wilson Fisk's killer—hell, it'd probably help your rep—but do you also want to be known as a cop killer? You said yourself you didn't do it. But do you think the DA is gonna treat these as two different cases, or look at it closely enough when there's an easy win in his sights? You're a fly on a window, Frank—and the city is tossing a brick at you. There's no nuance here. You have to ask yourself how you want this to end."

A low, groan-like sound infected Matt's ears. He sensed Castle's shape shaking violently. It sounded like a wild animal dying—a grazing creature being mauled by a surprise predator.

He was laughing.

"You're a special case, Murdock," Castle said, wiping his eyes, still chuckling to himself. "You lawyers think you know it all, when there's so much out there we don't know—so much *you* don't know. You think it's so clear-cut, huh? What's that like, Murdock? Living in a land of rainbows, of good and bad, of birds and unicorns? What's it like feeling like you can actually change things? As if that giant ax of fate isn't hovering over all of us, waiting for the right time to slice and dice everything we love?"

Castle's heart was beating like a bass drum, his breathing fast and ragged. Matt had hit a nerve.

Matt had interviewed all kinds of clients. White collar criminals. Abusers. Thieves. Housewives. City employees. Shop owners. Hustlers. He prided himself on one thing—that he could tell almost immediately if the person asking for his help had done the crime they were being accused of. It wasn't just his super-senses, either. Sure, they came in exceedingly handy to listen to a client's heartbeat, but that wasn't infallible—and there were other tells. Shifting postures. Inconsistent stories. Defensiveness. None were foolproof. There was a holistic alchemy to Matt's approach, and while he had been wrong from time to time, each guess had been informed by Matt's tried-and-true formula.

This time, he felt none of that.

His senses weren't helping him. Castle, when not laughing at Matt, seemed completely blank. If Matt took him at his word, he would have to assume Castle wanted to die in prison, bleeding out from a kitchen-made shiv to the heart delivered by a nameless thug let into a secure area by a prison guard who'd just been made a few thousand dollars richer. But that couldn't be right. The Punisher was a stone-cold killer, the kind of merciless murderer who made Hannibal Lecter look like a Care Bear. But it wasn't just a blood hunt for Castle. It was strategic. He hadn't survived this long, avoiding capture for years, by just accepting his fate.

There was something deeper happening—but Matt didn't understand it yet.

So he rolled the dice.

"I know you think I'm an idiot, Frank, and I honestly don't have the desire or the energy to debate you." Matt looked up at Castle, which seemed to disrupt the killer's cool posture for the first time. "But the bottom line is, you need some help. You tell me you didn't kill Sheehan. I believe you. But you're not going to be able to convince a jury of that alone. Let me try to keep you away from the people who want you dead—and there are *a lot* of them. I can stall and delay the tidal wave of legal pain that is about to rain down on you. . . . I can make this bad situation a little better. Think it over. You're a smart guy. I think you should consider hiring me. Have one of your friends on the outside hand me a dollar and we'll call it even, too."

Matt slammed his briefcase shut and stood up. He didn't expect an answer from Castle now, if ever, but he'd said his piece. He felt the sleek faux-leather fabric of the briefcase handle slide over his fingers as he stepped back and turned toward the exit. He tapped the glass with his walking stick.

Matt could make out Kolakowski stomping toward him. The door swung inward.

"You all done, Mr. Murdock?"

"All done."

"No, not all done."

Matt turned at the sound of Castle's voice. He could hear his own heartbeat thumping faster, harder.

"Excuse me?" Matt said.

"If you're my lawyer, we're gonna have to talk details," Castle said, each word coming out like a growl. "Isn't that right, Counselor?"

NINE

A HARSH WIND slammed into Daredevil as he leapt from rooftop to rooftop, his modified billy club pulling him along between buildings, his body running on automatic—arm stretching out, arm pulling back—like an aerialist practicing before a big show. He should've been paying more attention to what was going on, he thought, but his mind wouldn't let him.

What have I done?

The question boomed in his skull every few seconds. Matt Murdock was now defending Frank Castle, a murderous vigilante, against first-degree murder charges. Had Castle killed Wilson Fisk, Daredevil's greatest enemy? Matt wasn't sure. And that bothered him, too. The Punisher was sharp—a cagey fighter and strategist. But did he know Matt Murdock and Daredevil were one and the same? And if so, would he use that against him at some point?

Daredevil shook his head as his boots landed on a rooftop a few blocks from the brownstone home of Matt Murdock.

He was spiraling, he thought. He was letting his anxiety get the best of him. Daredevil was a mysterious, larger-than-life vigilante—a name that sparked fear when heard by the underworld. But Matt Murdock was a man, and a man versed in the law. He trafficked in *facts.*

As he walked across the grimy rooftop, Daredevil pondered them.

Wilson Fisk was dead—gunned down in the penthouse office of his Midtown skyscraper.

Also dead? Ed Sheehan—an unremarkable NYPD police officer with a smudgy record, but no obvious strikes.

The main suspect was none other than Frank Castle—also known as the bloodthirsty vigilante the Punisher. All evidence pointed to him. In a surprising move, the Punisher surrendered to police.

Though vague on everything else, Punisher was adamant he didn't have anything to do with Sheehan's death—so adamant he was willing to become Matt Murdock's client.

Which led Daredevil to believe there was something else—something percolating below the known facts. Something deadly that pointed more clearly to the "why" of Wilson Fisk's death—and the person behind it.

Daredevil wasn't yet sure what had driven him to meet with Castle and to even take his case. He knew it was the right thing to do. Even a murderer like Castle deserved a good defense. But this case already felt more complicated than just mitigating charges against an obviously guilty defendant.

He had to admit to himself that he was *intrigued* by spending time with the Punisher, in conversation and not just in battle. The killer was up to something—

Daredevil felt a change in the air around him and immediately recognized what was coming. He swung right to avoid the sai speeding toward him. Heard the soft *thunk* as the tri-pointed blade stuck into the faded brick of a nearby chimney.

She was here.

Elektra.

Daredevil turned around. He didn't sense her—couldn't make out her shape or hear her. But Elektra Natchios wasn't your typical super hero or street-level brawler. She was a ninja, trained by the magically imbued dark cult known as the Hand.

She was also Daredevil's college ex.

Years ago, before the death of his boxer father "Battlin'" Jack Murdock, Matt had found himself in a passionate romance with Elektra, then a classmate and daughter of a Greek diplomat. But around the time Matt's father was killed by gangsters for refusing to throw a fight, Elektra's father was also killed by underworld assassins. The couple drifted apart, coping with their grief in different ways. Matt sought vengeance by using his enhanced senses and fighting skills on the streets of Hell's Kitchen as Daredevil. Elektra became enveloped by darkness. The next time they met, years later, it was not as lovers.

What would it be this time?

The sai had been a warning shot—otherwise she wouldn't have missed. Elektra knew Daredevil intimately—his powers, his tells, and his disdain for extreme violence. In another life, Elektra had been a hired killer. For a brief time, she'd also worn a version of his costume. Right now, though, they were just two people who needed to have a conversation.

"Come out, Elektra," Daredevil said, standing up straight, his body projecting that he wasn't afraid. And he wasn't. If Elektra had wanted him dead, he would be already. "Let's talk."

"What are you doing, Matthew?"

Her ethereal voice seemed to catch and wind into Daredevil's ear like a mystical whisper. But it was enough, and he found her—perched above him on a fire escape, looking down—the long belts of her uniform flapping in the wind. A moment later, she was leaping down to the roof and standing a few inches in front of him. He could smell her perfume—salty and tangy. Could recognize the cadence of her breathing, calm and confident. His instinct was to hold her—to pull her close. But those days were long over.

"I'm going home," Daredevil said. "What should I be doing?"

"Castle. I heard you're defending him. Are you unwell?"

"I'd say I'm being pretty consistent," Daredevil said with a scoff. "He needs an attorney."

"He's a mass murderer," she spat. "A deceptive idol for weak-willed men everywhere."

"Are you really going to cast stones in that department?"

The slap came fast—precise and strong. Daredevil felt Elektra's open hand connect with his cheek, the contact like a gunshot. He stumbled back and sensed her unmoving form as he struggled to regain his balance. She wasn't the type to react in anger. But she would also not be insulted. If he hadn't experienced the slap, based on her posture he would've thought nothing had happened.

"I didn't come here to explain to you the nuanced art of death, Matthew," Elektra said, her voice low and sedate. "I come with a warning: Stop what you're doing, before you lose yourself in a darkness of your own making. Be wary of everyone—even me."

Daredevil stepped forward, as if to strike—Elektra sidestepped him easily, but the message was clear: This could devolve into a brawl in a minute if she let it.

"Elektra—I am not in the mood for veiled threats," Daredevil said. "If you know something, tell me."

Then she smiled. But it wasn't a happy expression. It carried the inert sadness and pain that had marked Elektra since the death of her father.

"I know what the public knows, Matthew, which is substantial as of today," Elektra said. "The cop—Sheehan. It's no longer a secret. You have to wonder why it took so long for that news to come out."

Daredevil could feel his patience dissipate.

"What are you talking about, Elektra?" Daredevil almost yelled. "I don't have time—"

Elektra interrupted him.

"Why don't you ask the Internal Affairs officer?"

Daredevil started to respond—but by the time the words started to form, Elektra was gone.

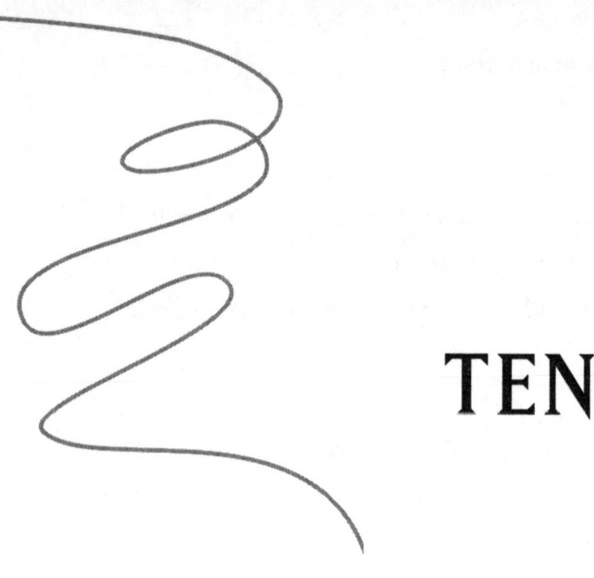

TEN

FROM HIS PERCH on a rooftop across the street from a massive skyscraper, Daredevil slid his fingers over the evening edition of the *Daily Bugle*. The headline was impossible to ignore:

COP SLAUGHTER:

VIGILANTE CASTLE HELD IN DEATH OF NYPD HERO

But it was the byline that Daredevil was most interested in.

Daredevil felt his radar sense reflect the large building that faced him. He could hear the small television squawking in reporter Ben Urich's tiny office.

An office. A rarity in the fading newspaper industry. Most of Urich's colleagues—ten, fifteen years his junior—toiled away in cubes spread out across a cramped newsroom floor. A pale echo of a bustling *Daily Bugle* newsroom that once occupied three floors and a printing press. From Daredevil's vantage point, it seemed like a year didn't go by without a visceral round of layoffs—cost-cutting measures meant to keep profits in the black while the management focused less and less on the quality of the paper and the information it relayed to its dwindling subscriber base. Somehow Ben Urich survived, even as his style of deep-dive investigative reporting dwindled in print, replaced by independent newsrooms, podcasts, and Substack newsletters. Yet here the reporter was, Daredevil thought, sipping another diet soda as he typed away on his obsolete MacBook, his tiny office barely lit by the desk lamp Urich had inherited from his father. This meant something, Daredevil thought. To be the last one. To be a survivor.

The news was playing a brief profile of Sheehan, which hastily credited Urich's original reporting, and celebrated the "beloved" officer's now-sterling track record to its own dwindling viewership. It was the puffiest of puff pieces, ignoring the truth as Daredevil knew it—that Sheehan was a crooked cop. Not as bad as the worst, but certainly not the angel of justice being portrayed by the blank-faced correspondent.

Daredevil leapt from his rooftop perch to the window of Urich's office and rapped on the glass gently. He could sense Urich's shape turning in his chair to face him. The way Urich's heart rate sped up told him plenty: the reporter was surprised.

Urich stood slowly, then stepped toward the window—which opened with a low whine.

"It's late," Urich said, stepping back to allow Daredevil in. "My wife is gonna kill me."

"How many times have you uttered those words, Ben?" Daredevil walked over to the television and turned it off with a soft click.

"That's marriage, isn't it? You have the same three arguments over and over again until one of you gets sick of it, or you die." Urich returned to his seat, swiveling to face Daredevil as he propped a foot up on his rickety desk. "But you didn't come here for Ben Urich's treatise on marriage, did you?"

"How'd you find out?"

Urich let out a quick cough. A delay tactic. Daredevil could hear the thumping of his heart picking up even more.

"Guess you mean about Sheehan?"

"Bingo."

Urich took off his glasses and wiped them with his shirt. Another delay.

"It was a matter of time," Urich said. "If it was buried any longer, you'd have everyone in the damn city screaming cover-up. Even now, it doesn't look good. But the second I called NYPD media relations the flack seemed almost relieved—like he'd been grappling with it himself. Ten minutes later, I get a release about a press conference. I had to type my piece and get it up on the site before then just to hold on to the news."

"You're evading my question, Ben," Daredevil said. He knew Urich would never reveal his sources, but that didn't mean he couldn't ask.

Urich let out a humorless laugh.

"I'm a reporter," Urich said. "My people gave me intel that didn't match what the NYPD talking points were. So I reported what I found out—that Sheehan was on the scene and he was killed, too. The big question remains unanswered."

"What's that?"

"Why?" Urich said. "What was Sheehan doing in Fisk's office—and why would the Punisher—a complete monster, sure, but not one who is prone to killing law enforcement—gun Sheehan down, too, crooked or not?"

Daredevil pointed at the television set. "Seems like the press is coming out full force for Sheehan."

Urich nodded. "It's strange. There was a time you couldn't avoid the bad-cop narrative. Now it seems like everyone is backing away from this one," Urich said, looking off into the distance, past Daredevil—past the *Bugle* offices. "Hell, even Jonah buried my piece on Sheehan, didn't seem to care about it for breaking news. Got a few inches, interior page of Local, and barely a mention online. Quiet enough that most people got the news from the NYPD's mouth."

"Why do you think that is?"

Urich shrugged. "Jonah—his myriad faults aside—is a newspaperman. I don't think he tanked the story intentionally," he said. "But he's also a man who understands the tone of this city. He watches the news and reads his competitors obsessively. If he thought this story had legs, he'd push it through. But I think he sees where the tides are rolling."

"It's not worth a fight?"

Urich turned toward Daredevil. "Who are we fighting, Matt?"

The use of his real name was a sharp reminder that Urich could be trusted. Not every journalist would sit on the scoop of the century.

Urich grabbed a manila envelope from his desk and tossed it to Daredevil, who caught it.

"As far as anyone knows, the TV narrative is true—Sheehan was a good cop. The Punisher is a bad, bad man—for killing a good cop and a maybe-gangster. It's convenient," Urich said. "And who could dispute it?"

"Terry Sheehan—" Daredevil started.

"Check out what I tossed you before you start talking about his brother."

Daredevil let his fingers scan the top page—a newspaper clipping from this morning's *Staten Island Daily Gazette*. It was a news brief, the third of three, on the back page of the local section. The headline said it all:

BROTHER OF SLAIN OFFICER FOUND DEAD

IN STATEN ISLAND APARTMENT

Daredevil looked up at Urich. "He's dead?"

"Seems like it," Urich said, turning his chair toward his computer. "Cops say it's a suicide. Guy was so broken up about his brother, he offed himself."

"You don't buy it?"

"Do you?" Urich asked without looking up.

"I just spoke to him a few days ago," Daredevil said, crossing his arms. "He was scared, sure. But he didn't seem like he was despondent. He was more worried about the police figuring out where his money was coming from and what the penalty would be."

Urich sighed.

"Here's the thing, Matt—I think you're right about one thing. Guy was scared. But I don't think he was scared about the cops. Not *just* the cops, rather."

Finally the reporter looked up at Daredevil. "I think he was scared of the people his brother was in business with," he said. "Because Terry is the only link out there—the only person who can legitimately connect his brother to some other group. Now that he's gone—what does anyone have? Hypotheticals. Theories. The bad guys get to fade into the shadows again."

Urich reached for the pack of Marlboro Reds on the other side of his desk. He tapped one out as he spun around.

But when he looked up, Daredevil was gone.

ELEVEN

"YOU'RE LATE."

Matt ignored Foggy's comment as he sidestepped him and went into Judge Sonia Porras's chambers. Foggy was, of course, right. Matt was ten minutes late for a meeting that could decide the fate of their newest client. But it couldn't be helped. At least from Matt's perspective.

"Mr. Murdock," Porras said as Matt approached her in her large office. "Nice of you to join us."

"I'm sorry, Your Honor, it couldn't be helped," Matt said as apologetically as he could muster on a few hours' sleep. After his talk with Urich, Daredevil had made a beeline to the morgue to learn what he could about Terry Sheehan's death. But he'd gleaned very little beyond what Urich had already told him. On the surface, the evidence that Sheehan had taken his own life held up. But it didn't fit for Matt. Not yet.

He took a seat to the right of Assistant District Attorney James Sprenger, a lifer on the city side whom Matt had crossed paths with a number of times, including during his own short stint as an ADA. They nodded to each other politely as Foggy took the open seat on Matt's other side.

"Mr. Murdock, considering you had us sitting here wondering if you were even going to show up, I think we deserve more of an excuse than that," Porras said.

In most situations, Matt respected the hell out of Judge Sonia Porras. She was fair, she was direct, she was honest. But in this instance, she was annoying—and Matt was struggling with how to wiggle his way out of this one.

"I'm feeling . . . under the weather, Your Honor," Matt said. It wasn't totally untrue, and it was his job as an attorney to find those little gaps of truth and navigate them to his client's benefit. Or his own. "I wasn't sure I was going to make it."

He didn't need enhanced senses to feel Foggy's stare boring into the side of his head.

Porras nodded. She was willing to let this go in the name of moving things along.

"Well, I'm glad you did," she said, shuffling some papers on her desk, not looking up. She grabbed her reading glasses and put them on before continuing. "If I'm reading this correctly, Mr. Murdock—and Mr. Nelson—the defense would like to strike any mention of your client's alleged past crimes?"

"Yes, Your Honor—we believe any mention of other crimes Frank Castle has been accused of, or alleged to have committed, would be prejudicial to his chances for a fair trial," Matt said, his tone flat.

"You mean, the fact that you're defending a serial killer, Matt?" Sprenger said, his words thick with sarcasm. "Not only are we gonna have a hell of a time finding a jury of people who don't know who Frank Castle is—or the Punisher for that matter—but now we can't even explain to them why he's on the stand? If his past crimes aren't relevant, I don't know what is. The guy wears a damn skull on his shirt—he's killed people who haven't even had their day in court. Maybe you can rationalize why you're defending him, but people deserve to know who's on the stand. It's context. This isn't Frank Castle stumbling into Fisk's office and accidentally setting a gun off—it's murder. You need to convince people otherwise."

Sprenger capped his rant with a loud scoff.

"Mr. Sprenger, remember you're in judge's chambers, please," Porras said, not looking up. Porras continued, talking over Sprenger's brief and terse apology. "Now, Mr. Murdock—your motion is very well-crafted, as I've come to expect from your firm. You lay your case out thoughtfully, but that doesn't mean you're right, does it? I'm hard-pressed to—"

Matt felt the wave hit him. Of pure exhaustion. His double life was never easy. Even on a good day, he was usually running on a few hours' sleep, a gallon of coffee, and a handful of missed appointments and plans. But ever since Wilson Fisk ended up dead, everything had seemed to ratchet up sharply. He needed something to fall in his favor, and just listening to Porras's tone—and the sharp intake of her breath—he knew where this was going.

And he couldn't stand it.

"Your Honor, if I may interject," Matt said, interrupting the judge. He could hear Foggy cursing under his breath, could hear Sprenger's surprised chuckle. "You'd be sentencing Frank Castle to life in prison if the jury is allowed to hear about his past—about allegations that have not yet had their day in court. Whatever my opponent thinks about Frank Castle is not relevant—what matters is whether it will skew the perspective of an impartial jury. The second you validate his track record in a court of law, the second you introduce rumor and allegations to the jury, he'll be as good as dead. Do you really want that on your—"

"That. Is. *Enough,*" Porras said through gritted teeth.

Matt knew he had gone too far. Way too far. It was then that he noticed Foggy's hand on his arm, holding him back. Had he been getting up from his chair?

"You are completely out of line, Mr. Murdock," Porras seethed. "I have the power to penalize you into next year if I wanted to."

"Your Honor, I'm so sorr—"

Porras let out a long sigh, cutting Matt off.

"You've said more than enough, Mr. Murdock," Porras said, shaking her head, the disappointment clear. "I'll do you—and your partner, who seems like he'd rather melt into his seat—a favor. Let's pretend this moment didn't happen."

Matt let out a long sigh of relief. Porras was tough, but she was human. He felt a sheen of cold sweat covering his body.

"Thank you, Your Honor."

"Don't thank me yet. I haven't made a ruling," she said. "I've set a pretrial hearing for next week on your motion, Mr. Murdock. I suggest you get some sleep before then. I won't tolerate another outburst like that. Especially in my courtroom."

Porras motioned for them to leave, and Foggy's tense body language as he rose made Matt think twice about speaking again. He hung his head and followed Foggy and Sprenger out the door.

"Really nailed that one, Matty," Sprenger said under his breath. "You trying to make this case even harder for your team?"

"Get bent, Sprenger," Foggy said as their opponent turned down the long hallway. Foggy looked at Matt. "What the hell was that?"

"Foggy, I—"

"Have you lost it?" Foggy said. He pointed toward Porras's office. "That woman is the only hope Frank Castle has. If she grants us that motion, we're on even footing with Sprenger. Castle becomes just a man who might have killed two people, not a serial murderer with a reputation across the city. And you choose today, of all days, to suggest she might be responsible for it all? Matt, I don't know what to say."

"Say nothing, Foggy, okay?" Matt said, exasperated. "I made a mistake. I'm exhausted. Let's move on—she granted us some grace, can you grant me some, too? Let's get to work."

"Matt, all I've ever done is grant you grace," Foggy said with a hiss. "But you keep this up and I'm not sure our firm—or our friendship—can survive."

((((( )))))

Matt knew Melinda Torres was inside his apartment before he turned onto his block. He could smell her perfume. Hear her nervously humming a Beach Boys song. This wasn't Elektra, Matt reminded himself. Melinda wasn't one of them. She was a normal person. And she seemed very anxious.

He walked down his street slowly, mulling over how to play what was to come. But this exercise rarely helped. People were wild cards, Matt had learned. And more immediately—Matt was tired. After his visit to the morgue, Daredevil had scoured the city for more than six hours, most of it spent just . . . patrolling. He wasn't sure how much the action of hopping from rooftop to rooftop across Hell's Kitchen actually helped in terms of the crime rate, but it certainly helped him. Kept him focused on the action—like working out. But the streets were quiet—and the few times Daredevil caught an armed robbery or break-in, the assailants immediately went quiet when he brought up the Kingpin.

It was unsettling. Normally, when a mob boss dies, it's impossible to keep a lid on it. The buzz on the street becomes more about how he died and even more about who is going to step in. But they hadn't hit that phase yet, Matt realized. It was as if someone had put everything on pause somehow.

Even a quiet night had cost him, as he'd learned sitting in the judge's chambers a little while ago. Daredevil was wiped out, which meant Matt Murdock was, too. He needed a long shower, a warm meal, and silence. He wasn't sure he'd get any.

Matt slid his key into the door and turned the knob slowly. He stepped in, eyes glancing up and around. "Is—is someone there?" Matt asked, his voice raised. He knew she was there, of course, but appearances had to be maintained.

"It's me, Matt."

Melinda's voice sounded curt, dry. Yup. She was upset.

He remembered sleeping over at her place the week before. How he'd handed her his spare key. It felt like the beginning of something more—something serious and potentially meaningful. Her using the key for the first time—for this—seemed to dispel that.

"Oh, I wasn't expecting you," Matt said, taking a few more steps into the apartment. "Is everything all right?"

Melinda walked toward him, her hand wrapping around his arm and guiding him farther inside. She knew he could get around; this was an intimate, knowing gesture. She might be mad, Matt thought, but she still cared.

"I think so," Melinda said as they entered the apartment's large living room area. She led Matt to the wraparound couch that shadowed the outline of the room. He sat down on the far corner and looked up as if to say *Well, what is it, then?*

"I heard you're defending that killer," Melinda said, unable to hide the disdain in her voice.

Matt was getting tired of the people he cared about asking him why he was defending the Punisher, but he did his best to hide it.

"I was going to—"

"It's fine, I know you've been busy," Melinda said, sitting next to him—placing a hand on his leg. "It was just a surprise, is all."

Matt placed a hand on hers. "Every person deserves a good defense."

His radar sense tracked her head nodding up and down slowly.

"I guess so, Matt, but . . . but Frank Castle isn't like everyone else," Melinda said. "He's a monster. He killed a cop."

Matt didn't respond. He flashed back to Castle, in the dank interview room—adamantly denying responsibility for Sheehan's death. If he let his mind linger over her words, he'd have to agree. Frank Castle *was* a monster. Did he merit the same defense Matt would spare for an innocent shop owner, or someone entangled in a criminal enterprise beyond their control? For actual innocents or conflicted people who didn't hurt anyone along the way? Frank Castle was a killer—Daredevil had witnessed it himself. Why did he deserve a chance to skate by when so many others were ground to dust by the gears of justice?

They should both be dead.

The thought burst into Matt's mind like a wrecking ball, so hastily it jolted him. No, that wasn't right. He knew the truth—Frank Castle deserved the best defense the system could offer. No matter what, he was innocent until proven guilty. And even if Wilson Fisk was also a murderer a dozen times over, no one deserves to be slaughtered in cold blood.

They should both be dead.

Matt shook his head. Brought himself back to the present. He couldn't dwell in that darkness for too long. It would destroy him.

He tried to figure out what Melinda was getting at here. Did she feel betrayed because her almost-boyfriend hadn't told her he was taking on the biggest murder case since OJ took his white Bronco for a ride?

"And you're not safe," Melinda said, taking in a sharp breath, her grip tightening on Matt's hand. "You're not safe here—who knows who will come after you, Matt? We don't know who's stepping in to fill Fisk's seat. And I know a lot of my own officers idolize Castle. That skull is everywhere. They might just want him out—not on trial for a murder they see as a righteous kill. It's messy. The things I'm hearing . . . the temperature is high. I'm worried about you."

There it was. Not anger at Matt being cagey—but fear that someone might strike out at him for his job.

He gave Melinda a wry smile. "I'm a big boy. I've been through this before. Don't worry about me."

"I can't help it," she said, moving her hand up his arm, resting it on his shoulder. "I care about you."

"I care about you, too," Matt said.

As he leaned forward to kiss Melinda he heard it—a familiar clicking sound, from the next building over.

A rifle bolt lifting.

Matt turned his slow lean into a shove, grabbing Melinda and pulling her down as the large windows across from them shattered into a million pieces and a barrage of bullets pounded into the wall right behind where they'd been sitting, the sound echoing through his apartment.

"What the—?" Melinda yelped as they hit the floor.

BUDDABUDDABUDDABUDDA!

Matt covered his ears as he placed his body over Melinda, who was struggling against him, trying to crawl away from the firing line, her cop instinct taking over. The sound was overpowering Matt, each shot like an earth-shattering explosion in his skull.

"Matt, Matt—are you okay? We have to stay down, you hear me?" Melinda yelled, finally pushing Matt off her and crawling toward the window, her gun suddenly drawn.

Matt tried to follow but felt himself being tugged back and up. The sound of metal grinding against flesh was familiar. The clawed hand gripping him spun Matt's body around. The cacophony of the bullets was still hammering in his head as he struggled to make out the shape of the invader in his house. But he already knew who it was.

The Owl.

A low-rent crime boss who could glide on air and would sometimes augment his feeble physique with cybernetics, the Owl had never been a dire threat to Daredevil, but he had been a nuisance on many occasions. The kind of enemy who just kept coming back, never learning their lesson and somehow finding a way out of prison and into the good graces of whoever was in power. Last Matt heard, the Owl had carved out a little piece of territory on Long Island, with the Kingpin's passive blessing. He ran numbers, had a few places paying him protection money, and seemed to be biding his time for something else.

Maybe this was something else.

Matt could feel the Owl's claws start to dig into his shoulder and arm. Felt the sting of their nails breaking skin. He winced, trying to hold back any sound. He wouldn't grant him that. Couldn't grant him that. The Owl didn't know Matt and Daredevil were one and the same, but that didn't mean Matt Murdock had to give in to fear, either.

He felt the Owl's free hand reach up and point a clawed finger at his neck. Not drawing blood yet, but letting Matt know he could—very quickly—if he wanted to.

"Matt Murdock," the Owl hissed. The smell of fast food and cheap cologne wafted through Matt's nostrils, almost making him gag. "I need your help."

Matt could hear other footsteps, two pairs. The men were surrounding Melinda. Her gun clattered to the floor as she grunted in frustration. Matt could sense her being restrained on either side by the men. They weren't here for her. They seemed calm. Just doing a job. No, the target was Matt—and the Owl was on that case.

"Who—who is it?" Matt asked, turning his head, trying not to crack a smile at the thought of saying such to a man named the Owl. "What do you want?"

The absurdly garbed villain pulled Matt closer. Matt could feel his warm, rank breath on his face. There were times he hated his abilities. The villain's voice irked as he intoned, "The Owl seeks your attention, lawyer. I need to know about your client—about the Punisher. . . ."

"There's nothing to know," Matt said, trying his best to sound scared, desperate—but what he was really doing was something else. Letting his enhanced senses zoom out, go wide. Trying to listen or smell or feel an opportunity to get out of this, like he had so many times before, red togs or not. "I just agreed to represent him, that's all. We haven't even had a chance to go over the evidence—"

The Owl shook Matt violently.

"Don't toy with me, Murdock! You're not some green paralegal—this is your bread and butter." Mechanical claws dug deeper into Matt's arms. "I want the truth. I want answers. Why did the Punisher do it? Who gave the order?"

As the Owl trailed off Matt realized why the green-cloaked never-was had shown up here, had rolled the dice on attacking a civilian. He wanted to know if he had a new boss, same as the old. Or if, by luck, he might have a path toward becoming the boss . . . himself.

Matt tried to stifle a laugh and failed.

"You scoff at me?" the Owl asked, indignation soaking every word.

Matt could hear the sound of fabric slipping loose from a sweaty grip. Melinda was getting free. This was his chance.

He let out a long, hearty laugh. "I—uh, well, I just can't help it, Leland," Matt said, trying to hold back another chuckle. "I'm just amazed you think you've got a shot."

The Owl shoved him backward. Matt stumbled but stayed on his feet. Melinda was about to pull away.

"You dare mock me, as I hold your meaningless life in my hands?"

Matt stopped pretending for a second. Stopped pretending he couldn't sense where his opponent was. Stopped pretending he was a mild-mannered attorney. The villain, his hair shaped in two embarrassing points—like some low-rent Wolverine—seemed shaken by the stare. Matt let it last for a millisecond. Just enough time to keep him off-balance.

Then he said, "Oh, I dare, Owlsley."

Before the Owl could leap toward Matt, a scuffle broke out. Matt turned to sense Melinda grabbing one of the thugs by the back of the head and sending him toward the other—two skulls connected with a soft thud. Without hesitation, she picked up her gun and sent two bullets into the Owl's legs, and Matt took a hit of pleasure as he sensed the avian-themed criminal bend over in pain.

"Aiiieeeerrrgggh, what— How could you?"

Melinda backed up toward Matt, standing in front of the wannabe villain, gun trained on him and his two men, now dazed and stumbling toward their fallen boss.

"Get the hell out of here, all of you," Melinda said, her voice loud and in command. "There are units on the way right now."

Matt knew she was lying. There was no way she could've gotten a call off that fast, and the NYPD's response time to Hell's Kitchen was anything but prompt. But she said it with such fervor he almost doubted himself. The Owl let himself be dragged by his goons toward the front door. The low, whimpering sound coming from the costumed attacker would stick with Matt for a long while.

"Murdock, you and your friend will regret this," the Owl hissed, between groans of pain. He was clutching his legs—both bleeding from the shots fired by Melinda. "When I rise to power . . . when the Owl rules over this city . . . you'll be my first target."

"Keep yapping, bird-boy," Melinda said, taunting the trio as she stepped closer to them. "You touch a hair on the lawyer's head and you'll be spending your life in a dirty birdcage on Riker's."

Melinda's heartbeat was pounding like a steel drum, the *thump-thump-thump* almost drowning everything else out. It wasn't until Matt's front door slammed that she relaxed and spun around, grabbing him by the arm.

"Are you hurt? Did he do anything to you?" she said, sliding her hands over him like a pat-down, checking for injuries. Her touch felt professional, not intimate—but then she stopped, her hands on each of Matt's shoulders, and pulled him in close. He could feel her breath on his neck. The tear sliding down her face and onto him.

"Oh my God, Matt—that was insane. . . . What the hell just happened?"

"Just part of the job," Matt said, tightening his arms around her. He felt her mouth move toward his—the kiss brief but passionate.

"Glad you were here," Matt said with a nervous laugh, the press of her lips—hot and powerful—still lingering on his mouth. "Not sure how I would have gotten out of that one."

She took a step back and ran a hand over his face, tilting her head slightly to get a better look at him.

"You're a lucky guy, Matt Murdock."

"So I hear."

She led him to the couch and started pacing around the living room, taking a mental inventory of the damage. Matt knew cops did this—writing their report in their head, long before pen hit paper. After a few minutes, she sat down next to him. Her body was tense—as if Matt was going to collapse at any moment.

"Melinda, seriously, I'm fine," Matt said, trying to wave her off.

"You're not fine, and that's normal," Melinda said, placing a hand on his leg. "You were just attacked in your own home by a dude who likes to dress up like a bird of prey."

Matt fought the urge to explain to Melinda that he'd made a career of punching the Owl in the face—had tossed him into prison more times than he could remember. But instead he let her help him.

"Why in the hell is the Owl busting into your apartment?" Melinda asked, her tone shifting from concerned girlfriend to investigator. She was looming over Matt now. He couldn't make out her expression, but he also didn't have to guess. She was curious and worried—but also intrigued, like a cat catching movement on the edge of its vision.

Matt shrugged.

"I'm a defense attorney, Melinda. It could be anything. You heard him—he was tipped off about me defending Castle. Also, a lot of these guys think I have some special connection to Daredevil—so they come for me," Matt said, not looking up. "I kind of wish I did. It'd make my job a lot easier."

The lie hung between them for a few moments, the sound of the kitchen clock's ticking second hand the only sound.

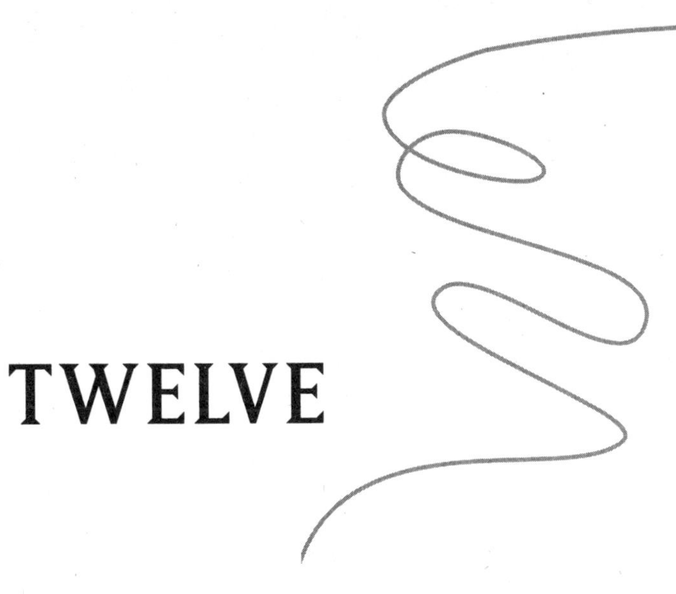

TWELVE

TERRY SHEEHAN'S DILAPIDATED studio apartment was tucked behind a shuttered hair salon right off Victory Boulevard in Staten Island. Daredevil had made his way here a few days prior—but it had been crawling with NYPD, the crowd so dense that it was impossible to get a look at anything. The place was nondescript and gray. The kind of building you'd walk by for years without thinking twice about. You might not even know there were apartments there, Daredevil thought, as he looked down at the entrance from the two-story building's battered roof.

This was where Sheehan killed himself. That's what the police and the press and the city wanted you to believe. What helped make the story tidy. Ben Urich, the best reporter New York City had to offer—and the man who broke the story of Ed Sheehan's death—felt different. Matt trusted Ben. Something had scared Terry Sheehan—sent him into a panic he never got to shake.

Daredevil climbed down carefully, reaching a window on the far end of the worn-down structure. He gave the window a tug. With little struggle, it opened. He slipped in, his feet landing on rough, old carpet. The room—a generous description of the space—was in shambles. A small bookshelf flipped over. A sofa mattress torn to shreds. Glasses and plates shattered near the tiny kitchen area. If this was where Terry Sheehan had taken his own life, his final moments had been violent, desperate.

"Who wrecks their apartment before they take their own life?" Daredevil muttered to himself as he scanned the detritus.

He'd hoped to come to Sheehan's apartment to look for evidence—anything on the company Terry said was paying off his cop brother, which could in turn give some insight into why the Punisher had allegedly decided to gun him down alongside the Kingpin. He hadn't expected to find a crime scene. A crime scene that implied someone had attacked Terry Sheehan—not that he'd killed himself. A crime scene the NYPD had overlooked. Who had been in here with Terry when he met his end—and what were they looking for?

From the looks of it, they hadn't found what they wanted. Daredevil tiptoed around the cluttered apartment, which reeked of mold, cheap beer, and things he didn't want to think about. He thought of Melinda—and how he'd used his powers to violate her trust. That's what it was, he'd come to accept. A violation. He had tried to reason it out. To rationalize that he would've done it to another officer if given the chance. But he was *dating* Melinda Torres, not just trying to get intel from her, and it was wrong.

He crouched down and let his senses reach out—absorbing the sounds, smells, and texture of the ramshackle apartment.

Why wasn't anything simple anymore? he wondered.

Had it ever been?

His memory drifted back to Karen Page. To the woman he'd loved. The partner who had stood by him during his darkest times and forgiven his greatest failures. But Karen's memory also brought up thoughts of another woman.

Typhoid Mary, who had come out of nowhere.

Years ago, she'd stormed into Hell's Kitchen without a care, slicing though the underworld with abandon, just two blades and pyrokinetic abilities that could compel most anyone to fear her. Eventually, she'd become something else—the Kingpin's newest and deadliest enforcer. But she did the most damage in a quieter way.

As the meek and shy "Mary," she'd slithered into Matt Murdock's personal life. Still reeling from the Kingpin's complete dismantling of his professional and personal identities, Matt had opened a legal clinic where he and his partner Karen Page could help the poor and disenfranchised with substantive legal advice. It was a workaround—Matt had lost his legal license and was struggling to reclaim it. The operation connected him to the law, and to his neighborhood. He was helping despite being broken.

And it kept him close to Karen. The only person who'd believed in him. There was no Nelson & Murdock. No high-rise apartment. No press conferences. Matt Murdock had been swallowed by the city and the system.

But then "Mary" appeared. Matt felt drawn to her immediately—first out of a sense of protectiveness, but then eventually out of raw attraction. Before long, the fleeting glances and hands brushing past each other became stolen kisses and illicit meetings. Despite his best efforts, Matt was being unfaithful—and he couldn't stop himself. He was drawn by the potent mix of pheromones and power Mary seemed to give off with ease—perhaps a byproduct of her fire-based mutant ability. Matt was lost to her, and nothing else mattered.

But as Matt fell for "Mary," Daredevil grappled with Typhoid, the newest player on the scene—violent, sadistic, brutal—and Typhoid Mary beat Daredevil to the brink of death, laughing all the way. It was then, on his hospital bed, as Karen held his hand and prayed for his recovery, that he'd muttered her name. Mary's name.

And so the Kingpin's destructive impact on Matt cratered out even further. And it would be some time before Karen would return to him, forever changed.

Karen was gone now, and since her death at the hands of the Kingpin's chief assassin, Bullseye, Daredevil had struggled to find balance—between his life as the vigilante Daredevil and Matt Murdock, the man. Sure, he could do the lawyer bit in his sleep. And it fed into his quest for justice. But Matt—the person beneath both sides, the man who'd loved and lost and suffered, had been stifled. Daredevil could sense that now, in this dank apartment, as he mulled over the lines he'd crossed.

But how do I get back to the man I was?

The question hung over Daredevil as he gently rapped his knuckles on the flimsy hardwood floor. He felt a slight imbalance—an emptiness—in the floor. But just in this one spot. Otherwise, the floor sounded full, packed, like you'd expect. But there was something strange here, in this spot. A space.

He took a few steps forward and rapped again. There it was. An echo. There was a space under him. A small one, but it was something.

Daredevil tapped again. He was over the space now.

"What were you hiding down here, Terry?" Daredevil asked as he raised his arm up. His elbow shot down, just above the open space. With a loud, satisfying crack, the wood under him gave. He moved debris off to the side and felt under the loose board. Wiping some dust off the top of the box, he reached for it.

That's when he heard the ticking sound. It was low and methodical; no normal ears could hear it. But it was there.

Tick. Tick. Tick. Tick. Tick.

Daredevil focused his senses on the box—could hear the small machinery in the device working, could feel it begin to vibrate.

He stepped back—trying to push past the shock to create as much space between him and Sheehan's dumpster apartment as he could.

That's when the entire floor exploded—the decrepit building overtaken by a wave of fire, stone, and ash.

THIRTEEN

"I JUST CAN'T believe it, Heather," Foggy Nelson said into his cell phone as he barged into the offices of Nelson & Murdock. "We're defending the Punisher of all people—the *Punisher.* It's insanity. There's no way Porras sides with us on the motion, not to mention the damage this does to our reputation—"

Foggy froze a few moments after stepping inside, chilled by the expression on Becky Blake's face. Becky was the only other lawyer working at Nelson & Murdock aside from the partners. She'd climbed the ladder slowly—first as their executive assistant, then their paralegal, and now their peer. When she was in the office, she was usually smiling and cheerful. Not today.

Today she looked like death warmed over.

"Becky, what— Heather, let me call you back," Foggy said, hastily placing his cell phone on the nearest desk. He approached the other attorney cautiously. "Becky, what is it?"

"It's . . . it's *Matt*, Foggy," she said haltingly. Her eyes were red. She'd been crying.

These were the words Foggy had always dreaded. He knew Matt was brave. But Matt was also fearless and hotheaded. He didn't think about his own safety. It served him well as a defense attorney. He would charge right into battle without a care for himself, his reputation, or the risks. It was what made him a great lawyer. But it also put him on the radar of very angry, very mean, very dangerous people. Foggy often worried about what would happen if one of them lashed out. He'd dreaded it. Melinda Torres, Matt's latest girlfriend, had let Foggy know about the Owl attack just the night before. What had Matt gotten into now?

"Becky, take a breath—what happened?"

Becky rubbed her eyes and moved her wheelchair around the desk. She reached for Foggy. He took her hands in his.

"He's in the hospital—they said he stumbled in, looked wrecked, like he'd been in some kind of explosion. Collapsed in the St. Vincent emergency room. He's still out. They're not sure—"

Foggy didn't wait for more details. He spun out and ran through the office doors.

Matt needed him.

PART TWO

THE NIGHT OF THE HUNTER

FOURTEEN

KAREN.

Matt could see in his dreams. Could visualize everything. His senses were still powerful—but sometimes, when he dreamed, he could see. Her blond hair. Her smirk. The way the ponytail would hold up her hair, leaving a few strands framing her face.

Karen, where are you? Come back to me.

"Matt, you need to get over it," Karen said, tapping her plate with a fork.

They were at a restaurant. A diner. Somewhere on the Upper West Side. He could remember it now. They'd come to grab a bite after consulting on a case. They had a clinic open—to help the people of Hell's Kitchen.

Before.

Before he made a mistake. Before he'd betrayed Karen. Before he'd lost his mind, his memory. Before she'd forgiven him.

Before she was killed.

He reached for her—his hand stretching for hers. She pulled back. Her face confused, then surprised, then . . . then something else. Something angry. Dark. Her features morphed into something deadly and demonic—her teeth, her fangs growing, her hair turning a dark shade of red, her eyes morphing into black puddles with a red center. Her fingers became long, sharp nails—talons even. For a second, Matt thought he recognized her—this creature. Karen Page was gone. But the woman in her place was oddly familiar.

"Matt Murdock . . ." the creature said, its voice gravelly and low, like a hoarse old gatekeeper struggling to speak. "I can't save you. . . . No one can. . . . You owe me a debt. . . ."

The diner started changing, too, the off-white walls turning into a dark, fluid black. The black ooze, first a dusting, then a sludge-like coating, began to spread. First over the walls. Then the tables. Suddenly, Matt could feel it inching over his hands and arms until it consumed everything—including him.

He tried to scream.

FIFTEEN

THE BEEPING WAS the first thing he noticed. The loud, throbbing beeping sound.

Matt Murdock felt like he'd been wrapped in a thick, wet towel—his senses dulled and distant. But they were coming back. Slowly and surely.

He could feel the rough texture of cloth—bedsheets, cheap and washed roughly. Clean but overused. The smells—disinfectant chemicals, generic and unappealing food. But the sounds. The sounds dominated. The beeping. The slow drone of television news. Plastic and metal connecting, the buzz of conversation, rubber soles squeaking on the linoleum.

The pain. The pain cut through everything else. A dull ache all over his body.

Then a voice. A few of them. Familiar. Distant.

"I think he's . . . he's waking up. . . ."

"Did he say . . . who . . . who's 'Karen'?"

"Matt? Matt? Can you hear us?"

"Just step back, folks—I need to—"

Then his radar sense kicked in. The shapes took form in front of

Matt's face. Three figures. He knew two of them almost immediately—Foggy Nelson and Melinda. The third, a woman, was directly in front of Matt, speaking in a low, calm, and soothing voice.

"Mr. Murdock—you've had a bad accident. You're safe now."

Linda Carter. Matt knew her now. Had known her for a long time. He pieced it all together slowly. Vignettes of what had happened over the last few days.

The visit to Sheehan's apartment. The bomb. Rushing to get away. The explosion. Struggling to get to Linda, the Night Nurse.

Linda Carter wasn't your typical nurse practitioner. She was a special figure, helping super heroes like Matt, who couldn't exactly waltz into a hospital, bruised and battered, and get treatment without their identities being revealed. Matt was still piecing together what happened after the explosion, but he'd apparently had enough sense to make his way to the Night Nurse's location. He'd figure out the rest in due time, he assumed. For now, he was glad to be alive.

Matt winced as he tried to prop himself up. The pain was sharp but not as bad as he'd expected. Melinda rushed toward him.

"Slow down, big guy—you just woke up," she said, her voice heavy with concern. "You need to rest."

"How long have I been out?"

"A little over a day," Foggy said matter-of-factly. "You had us really worried there, Matt. I'm just glad you're okay."

Matt extended a hand and gripped Foggy's. He could feel Foggy's form slouch a bit at the contact—relief pouring over his friend.

"I'm okay, Foggy," Matt said. "I'll be okay. I'm still—still not sure what happened."

Melinda stepped forward, closer to Matt, her mouth near his ear.

"You were doing something risky, Matt—I know it. I don't know the details. But I know you," she said, begrudging respect coating every sentence. "You need to protect yourself. There are some bad people gunning for you, and I need you safe."

She leaned in. He felt her warm lips press against his.

The kiss was brief, powerful. Matt didn't want it to end.

"We all do," she said, pulling back and breaking the embrace.

Linda Carter raised a hand toward Melinda and Foggy. "Matt needs to rest," she said flatly.

Foggy started to protest but Linda shook her head. He understood and turned to follow Melinda out. As the door clicked shut, Linda slid a chair close to Matt's bed and spoke in a low, hushed tone.

"You really pushed it there, Daredevil."

Matt hoped she was smirking.

"Thanks for your help, Night Nurse," he said with a pained smile. "Not sure I would've made it out of that one. What story did you give them?"

"I find that when lying it's best to hew close to the truth," she said, looking out toward the hospital floor—watching people milling around. "I said I found you outside, and it seemed like you'd been attacked. Once your cop girlfriend got involved, she was quick to layer onto it. Guess you'd been attacked by the Owl not long ago?"

Matt nodded.

"So, it fit. And maybe it really fits. You muttered something when I found you . . . about a bomb. What were you doing in Staten Island of all places?"

"Following up on a lead," Matt said. He suddenly felt very tired.

"Looks like the lead knew you were coming," Linda said. She stood up and patted him gently. "You're lucky they know me here. It wasn't so weird for me to drag your body in. The police all seemed agreeable, too. Just stay light on the details and blame your head being fuzzy."

"My head *is* kind of fuzzy," Matt said, gingerly rubbing his forehead.

"For your own sake, the less you say the better," Linda said. "Oh, and one more thing."

Matt could sense her figure turning at the doorway.

"Don't say your dead girlfriend's name when your current lady is within earshot."

SIXTEEN

"YOU DON'T LOOK TOO HOT, Matt."

Ben Urich's words were delivered in his usual raspy monotone, but Daredevil could sense there was some concern there, too, as he crouched outside Urich's office window. Though Daredevil's training and enhanced senses gave him a healthy advantage in the super-hero vigilante game, he was still in many ways just a man. His punch was a punch. He couldn't fly. He couldn't shoot energy from his hands. A serious concussion—like the one he suffered trying to escape Sheehan's building—still required some time to fully heal.

And so, a day after being discharged from the hospital, Daredevil was far from the top of his game. His entire body ached. He battled bouts of dizziness and imbalance. But he couldn't sit at home, he knew. Part of being Daredevil, the part he rarely thought about directly—like a secret shared with a few friends—was the thrill. The jolt of adrenaline he got while swinging between skyscrapers. The buzz of energy that coursed through him as he pounced on a mugger or disabled an attacker. It wasn't just power—it was a challenge. To himself and his body. He felt stronger and powerful. He dreaded a time, if he lived for another decade or two, when he wouldn't be able to do the things he sometimes took for granted now. What would being Daredevil look like then? he often wondered. In the past, he could shrug and kick that particular can down the road. Lately, it'd become harder.

"I'll get by," he said as he began stepping into Ben's claustrophobic apartment. The window screeched as it opened fully and Daredevil felt the shape of a medium-size cat scurrying into the tiny space. "Got a minute?"

"I do now," Urich said, motioning for Daredevil to step inside. "You see Owlsley on your way out?"

Daredevil felt a tingling in the back of his skull.

"The Owl? Why?"

"Was hospitalized last night," Urich said, looking back at Daredevil. "Brutally attacked in prison. Stabbed all over. They weren't sure he was gonna make it."

Daredevil paced around Urich's small office area. "Another prisoner?"

"That was my first thought," Urich said. "But they ruled that out. The Owl was in solitary, for various reasons—one being they didn't want him riling the 'regular prisoners' up. Second, they were worried some of Wilson Fisk's ex-goons might try to take revenge on him."

"For what?"

Urich frowned.

"You sure you got your head checked, Matt? The Owl was making a play—like many—for the Kingpin's old territory. Didn't he come at you directly?"

Daredevil nodded.

"He did, but he seemed—on edge. Different. I figured it had to do with the Punisher more than anything else," Daredevil said. "Leland has never been a serious player in the underworld."

Urich sat down at his desk and let out a long sigh.

"These guys aren't self-aware, Matt," Urich said. "They think they're one step away from being 'the Guy'—the big boss. When someone like Fisk falls, the rats come scurrying to take his place. But what they don't realize?" Urich took a long beat before continuing. "They're trying to replace a lion."

SEVENTEEN

MATT MURDOCK'S DOOR chime cut through the quiet evening. He let out a long, dispirited sigh. He'd just returned home from visiting Ben Urich—for a quick bite, then back out to pay Owlsley a visit—when the door buzzed. Matt could identify the visitor by their heartbeat. It wasn't the *who* that worried him—it was the hour.

Why was Foggy at his apartment this late in the evening?

Matt opened the door and could tell by his best friend's slouched posture that he was tired. His suit was rumpled and disheveled, and Matt was certain Foggy had come directly from their office—perhaps making a pit stop at the local deli for a late meal. Matt knew this wasn't a friendly check-in. Foggy glanced at the windows Matt had repaired in his apartment after the Owl's attack. He looked distracted, angry.

"Foggy, hey, listen—"

Foggy stormed in, sidestepping Matt as he entered the apartment.

"I know it's late, Matt, believe me," he said, his voice low and choked with emotion. "But we need to talk." Foggy spun around to face his friend. "What the hell were you thinking? Did you know we lost the motion? Porras is letting Sprenger bring up Castle's past. We're defending a spree killer, Matt. You couldn't even show up to the hearing—"

Matt shrugged.

"Foggy, I've been in the hospital—"

"Look, Matt, I know," Foggy said, shaking his head, as if the words weren't coming out of his mouth in the right order. "It's more than that. It's this whole Castle business, Matt. It's a disaster. We're getting threats—bomb threats; the press is brutalizing us. You missed most of it, but we're getting cooked out there. People are saying we're defending a cop-killer."

Matt cleared his throat.

"You know as well as I do, Foggy, that—"

"Yes, yes, innocent until proven guilty, but tell that to the guy on NY1—or Jameson before he writes his columns. We're getting obliterated, our case is dead in the water. Hell, we even lost a few clients," Foggy said, his tone growing more and more exasperated.

"We'll restock, we always do," Matt said, trying to keep his voice calm.

He wanted to leave. Wanted to suit up and feel the sharp wind of New York City on his face. Why did life always throw these things in his path when he was already full up? He didn't have the mental space for Foggy right now.

"Foggy, we just have to stick to what we do, which is the right thing—"

"But *is* it right? And even if it is, we aren't able to wait, Matt," Foggy said, his eyes wide. "We're not getting any new clients. We're not going to be able to pay Becky for much longer, much less ourselves. She's not a secretary, Matt—she's an attorney, too. On top of that, this client you brought in? The serial murderer known as the Punisher? He's not doing anything. He's not talking during our interviews. He's refusing to give us any details on what happened that night. The preliminary hearing—which you missed because you were in the hospital—was a circus. Press everywhere. The courtroom packed with the families of Punisher's various victims, not to mention every kind of goon . . . It was a nightmare. Porras was a complete hard-ass. She seemed to enjoy giving Sprenger what he wanted. We're not getting anywhere with this case. . . ."

"We've had tough cases before. . . ."

"This is not just a tough case!" Foggy yelled, his voice booming through Matt's empty apartment. Foggy never screamed. Never raised his voice. Matt often took Foggy for granted—his loyal, lovable friend. The comic relief. Smart but a bit silly.

Matt took a step back.

"You're upset."

"Hell yeah I'm upset, Matt," Foggy said, his voice still elevated. "You did this. You decided, unilaterally, to defend a psychopath—sure, we chatted about it—but did you sit down and agree with me, your partner, or our employees that this was the right plan, or even think, for a goddamn second, that maybe this would be a bad idea?"

Matt started to respond, but Foggy kept going.

"The sign on our door says *Nelson* and Murdock. Not Murdock and *Associates*. Not Murdock and *Whoever He Wants to Talk To*. We're partners. Hell, my name is first. My dad put the money down for us to get that office, all those years ago. When we made this dream, the fantasy we talked about in law school, into a reality. But it's never been that, Matt. The dream never came true. It's just been me chasing you around, hoping you'll wake up one day and give this the care and attention it deserves."

"Foggy," Matt said, reaching for his friend.

"Don't 'Foggy' me, Matt," he said, shaking his head. "This is *your* mess. This is *your* problem. You need to fix this."

"What are you saying?"

"Frank Castle isn't a client of Nelson and Murdock, Matt. If you want to defend him, you do it on your own, on your own time, using your own resources. But as far as I can tell, I didn't sign off on this and I'm not supporting it."

"We're a team—"

"We are a team, when it suits you," Foggy said, spittle flying out of his mouth as he sped through his response. "But when you need to decide something unilaterally, I disappear. Do you think that's fair?"

"Foggy, you don't understand," Matt started, but froze up. He was right, though—his friend didn't understand. Couldn't understand.

"Understand what, Matt?"

Matt could change it all now, he realized. Could admit to his lifelong friend that, sometimes at night, he liked to dress up as a giant devil and punch criminals. That he knew they were just part of a bigger, more complicated strategy—that Matt knew he was seeing Kingpin's own succession plans play out, and he needed to dig into it deeper to keep them all safe. That Frank Castle, the Punisher—and what he knew—was the key to it all. But that would be the easy path. And it would put his dearest friend, one of his few living friends, in more danger than before. So he just stalled, stammering and shrugging. But also realizing that his partner was right, and that while Matt may have been trying his best to be a hero to Hell's Kitchen, he was failing in a very important role—as a friend to Foggy.

"You have some serious thinking to do," Foggy said, shaking his head. "You're putting everything we've built in peril. And it doesn't seem like you care."

Matt didn't have a response.

"This is on you," Foggy said as he turned around. "But I'm gonna warn you—I don't want this case anywhere near our office, or our partnership. Assuming you want to keep that."

He didn't wait for Matt to respond. Foggy slammed the door shut with a finality that sent a chill through Matt Murdock.

EIGHTEEN

"YOU'RE TELLING ME you're not working for Nelson and Murdock, but that's who I have down as Castle's attorney," the uniformed prison desk clerk said, not looking up at Matt.

"I have an appointment. I'm Matt Murdock," Matt said through gritted teeth. "I'm here to see my client."

"I understand, Mr. Murdock, and I know this is frustrating," the officer, who was named Waldman, continued. She tried to give Matt a polite smile. "But Frank Castle isn't our typical resident here, and we need to make sure every person that comes to see him is on his list. We gotta keep him safe, you see? It's a short list—just representatives for Nelson and Murdock. But you're telling me—"

"All I said was that I was representing Castle myself, independent of my firm," Matt said, impatience echoing through every word. "I'm still Matt Murdock."

Waldman looked up at Matt, a wry smile on her face. It wasn't every day you got to tell a fancy-schmancy attorney to stick it, even in a nice way.

"Oh, I know who you are, Mr. Murdock. I read the news. I see you on television," she said. She motioned behind her. "And I know you're defending a guy who gunned down a police officer. A good cop, by every account—"

"You can't keep me from seeing my client—"

"Oh I wouldn't dream of interrupting *justice*, Mr. Murdock. I'm just following protocol and not about to bend over backward to ignore the rules. I suggest you give your friend, *Mr. Nelson*, a call, and then both of you can talk to my boss, or my boss's boss, and figure out how this should go. But for now—I'm only letting people representing him from your firm in here, and you told me that's not what you're doing."

Matt opened his mouth to respond but thought better of it.

He wheeled around and yanked his cell phone out of his pocket, speaking into the mic. "Call Foggy Nelson."

The phone rang, over and over. Then it was Foggy's jovial voicemail message. Matt hung up and cursed under his breath.

He needed to make things right with Foggy. He was taking that part of the process for granted, as he'd done so many times before. Just assuming his loyal bestie would come around, and he could continue as he always had. But he'd felt it in his apartment last night. Something had changed. A line had been crossed. And Foggy, a pillar of reliability, was gone. Matt knew he needed to fix that.

He waved at Officer Waldman and walked back toward his Dryve. Yes, he had to make amends. He had to repair things with Foggy.

But first, he had to scare a bird.

((((( )))))

Daredevil stepped gingerly down the dark hospital hallway. He could hear the guard's slow, methodical breathing—he was asleep. This wing, reserved for prisoners in need of medical attention a prison infirmary couldn't provide, was particularly desolate. The one nurse who should have been stationed behind a desk across from the snoozing security guard had left. Daredevil wasn't sure how much time he had. So he'd make the most of it.

He slipped by the guard and listened intently as the door slowly swung open, pausing for any squeaks and sounds that might disrupt the officer's slumber. He closed it cautiously as he let his radar sense fall over the room. On the bed, the patient's chest rose and dropped methodically. Daredevil could make out the man's shape. The frail, almost birdlike frame. The pointed hair. Daredevil had exchanged blows with Leland Owlsley—the man who would call himself the Owl when wearing his wings and green costume—more times than he'd care to admit. But he'd never seemed so weak. So close to death.

Daredevil walked toward the Owl's bedside and listened. The breathing was labored, jagged. He hesitated for a moment before talking. Was he hurting this man by interfering with his rest? It didn't matter, Daredevil thought. He needed answers. The city needed answers. Someone had killed the Kingpin of Crime, Wilson Fisk. Daredevil needed to figure out what was happening—and how it tied into Frank Castle—before it was too late, before the New York City underworld exploded in the kind of violence one man could not contain.

"Leland, wake up," Daredevil said, his voice low. "You have a lot to answer for."

The figure didn't move.

"Wake up, Owl," Daredevil said, more forcefully now. He jostled the villain with his hands, felt the rough, paper-like texture of the man's hospital gown.

The wounded man's eyes fluttered, closed, then fluttered open again. His hoarse, dry voice shook Daredevil.

"You . . . you dare to come here?" the Owl said, turning his head to look up at his visitor. "What, you're a killer now, too? Here to finish what they did to me . . . ?"

Daredevil leaned forward, his voice quiet but direct. "I'm not here to kill you, Leland, I'm here to save you." He placed a hand on the villain's shoulder. "You tried to make a play for the Kingpin's turf, right?"

The Owl sighed.

"Who wouldn't?" he said. "If I have to spend another year stuck like this—in and out of prison, getting beaten up by morons like you and Spider-Man . . . I might as well give up. I needed to make a move. I was a loyal thug for Fisk. Did as he asked. Did his dirty work. Whenever the Arranger would come calling, I'd jump at the chance. . . ."

Daredevil's ears perked up. The Arranger. A name he hadn't heard in some time.

Oswald Silkworth was Wilson Fisk's right hand. His assistant, organizer, and hatchet-man. A smarmy, smooth-talking suit who could fit in at a business lunch or violent assault. He was nondescript, half butler and half notary. Silkworth was invaluable to the Kingpin because he formed the connective tissue between the boss's mandates and their eventual execution, without implicating Fisk himself.

If something needed doing, you wouldn't hear from Fisk himself—and if you did, you were in deep shit. No, most of the time, it was Silkworth who paid you a visit. And he didn't mince words. Daredevil made a note to check in on "the Arranger"—to see what he'd been up to of late.

"But then you jumped at another chance," Daredevil said, his words falling out in sharp whispers. He could sense the Owl stiffening at his voice. "Did you really think you had what it takes, Leland? Did you really think you could be the next Kingpin?"

The Owl emitted a low sputtering sound, like a toddler trying to formulate an excuse for spilling something.

"What do you want, Daredevil?" he growled.

"I want to know who did this to you," Daredevil said. "Because whoever they are, they're after people like you, Leland—people trying to make a grab for power before Fisk's body goes cold. And my guess is you got really lucky. If I were you, I wouldn't get too comfy in this bed, on those meds they've got hooked into your veins. No . . . I bet whoever took a swing at you is really mad they didn't finish the job."

Daredevil sensed Leland's heart rate quickening. Felt the villain's hands clench the railings on either side of his bed.

"What do you mean?"

"Think about it," Daredevil continued. "You threatened the golden goose. They tried to take you out. Somehow, you managed to get away—why leave that dangling, Leland? You're a lesson to all who would dare step up and defy the order of things."

"Fisk is dead," Owl snapped. "It's fair game."

"That's the thing," Daredevil said, standing up and looming over the Owl, who was shaking now. "That's where you're wrong, Owl. Nothing's going to be fair in this. And if you don't think the Kingpin had some kind of plan for his succession, you're out of touch."

The Owl let out a low, gurgling cough.

"I'll ask you again, Daredevil," he said weakly. "What do you want?"

"Did you get a glimpse of who attacked you?"

The Owl shook his head.

"Nothing. I was meeting with my lieutenants—we were strategizing. Small warehouse out in Mincola. The only way they'd know I was there was if they had a mole—a spy—in my gang. But that must be it. One of those pricks sold me out. But I was planning. I wanted to reach out to the others in the Fisk org—let them know I was in charge now, or moving into that space. But before I could get very far, the lights got shot out and I was attacked. Not a bullet, not a knife—some kind of sharp spear, poking and stabbing me, cutting me open. Before I knew it, I was in the air, barely alive, but away from whatever was trying to slice me to death. I collapsed a few feet outside the hospital. I woke up a few days later."

Daredevil waited a beat. He went over the Owl's story in his head. The man had no reason to lie. He knew as well as anyone the game he was playing. He knew it was fraught with risk. But the attack sounded more covert than the Kingpin or his underlings preferred. When you stepped out against the boss, the boss usually made a point of knocking you down visibly and loudly. Whoever was pushing back against a new Kingpin didn't seem to want to be known. Yet.

Daredevil patted the Owl's chest lightly.

"Get well, Leland," he said. "And turn that head around as much as you can."

The Owl made a confused sound.

"Even owls can be prey."

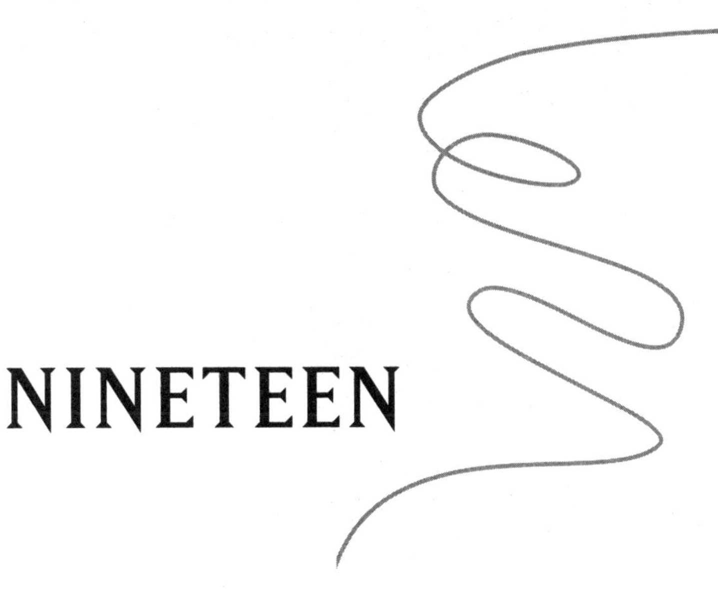

NINETEEN

"HEARD YOU'VE BEEN having some trouble lately."

Matt grabbed the receiver on his side of the glass and looked in the direction of his client, Frank Castle. It'd taken some doing, but Matt had been able to clear up the red tape blocking him from seeing his client. If only the rest of his life could be streamlined so easily. He tried to remain calm, but his frustration was impossible to ignore. They were in a room off from the main prison visiting area but still divided by security glass "for your own safety," Matt was told.

"You could say that," Matt said. "We've hit some snags, Frank."

"Are you telling me, Murdock, that our justice system might not work like the glorious, well-oiled machine you seem to think it is?" Castle said, feigning shock. "Well, color me surprised."

"Porras won't block discussion of your past crimes," Matt said, ripping the bandage off. He needed to get through the bad news to start strategizing, even if his client wasn't up for that part. "And I'm defending you on my own."

"Oh? What—that pudgy jellyfish Nelson can't hack it?" Castle said, genuine disdain in his voice. "Not a surprise. Maybe the Owl scared him off, too."

Matt wasn't surprised that Castle managed to stay up to date, even behind bars, but the speed with which he got his information was impressive. Even in jail, Castle needed to know what was happening on the outside.

"You get cable news in solitary?"

"I hear things," Castle said as he cracked his knuckles. "Like how you stumbled into a hospital, saying you got attacked. But my friends tell me it looked more like you were caught in some kind of explosion. Funny that you'd say otherwise."

Matt swallowed hard. The last thing he needed was Frank Castle figuring out that he and Daredevil were one and the same. But like any good investigator, Castle seemed to be poking and prodding, giving the appearance of knowing the answer to his comment, all in the hopes of finding it. Matt wouldn't give him the pleasure.

"We don't have a lot of time," Matt said, setting his briefcase on the small shelf in front of him. He pulled out a few manila folders. "Everyone but us wants this trial to happen yesterday. We need to figure out your defense, or we're cooked before it starts."

Frank Castle leaned forward, his eyes glaring at Matt.

"News flash, Counselor—we *are* cooked," he said, no trace of humor in his voice anymore. "You're the only person deluded enough to think we're gonna see a fair trial. Or that we have a chance for one. Maybe this'll teach you a lesson."

There it was. The core difference between not only Castle and Murdock, but the Punisher and Daredevil. Whereas Matt believed in the system—flaws and all—and in its mechanisms, Castle was a nihilist. He trusted his own contorted sense of justice above all else—even if it meant ignoring or flouting the laws he claimed to uphold. He'd sidestepped justice to enact his own, while Matt did everything he could to keep some semblance of order. It was a marked difference—a gulf neither could traverse, nor wanted to.

Matt cleared his throat.

"We're on the clock," Matt said. "I need an alibi. I need something, anything, that can place you somewhere that isn't Wilson Fisk's office—something that explains the shell casings and why they match your gun. Give me anything. I can make it work. But we're sitting ducks now."

"Quack," Castle said flatly.

Matt lifted his glasses and rubbed his eyes roughly.

He felt himself coming apart. Felt the control dwindling. Why was he here, he wondered? Helping a man who didn't seem interested in that help? Would it be so bad if Frank Castle went to prison? Would Matt shed a tear if Castle had the life choked out of him in some dreary, isolated prison washroom? Could it be, Matt thought, that the one good thing the Punisher ever did was murder Wilson Fisk?

Matt winced.

"You're not making this easy, Frank."

His words seemed to bounce off the thick glass between him and Castle, who sat on the other side, unflinching.

He flashed back to two nights before, and Foggy's heated visit. He'd never seen his friend like that—so worked up and agitated. Matt mused it was only a matter of time. It was a testament to Foggy's patience and caring that it took years for him to fully snap at him. But the timing couldn't be worse. Now Matt was defending Frank Castle out of his own pocket—using his own resources and doing every aspect of the work himself. It made an already hard job almost impossible, and his falling-out with Foggy wasn't helping.

"Nothing's easy," Castle said, not meeting Matt's eyes.

"I've asked for another bail hearing, since I couldn't make the initial one, and Foggy isn't your lawyer anymore," Matt said, shuffling papers in front of him. "I doubt very highly we'll get bail. No one seems to want you outside."

"No one decides that."

Matt looked up, confused. "Excuse me?"

Castle emited a short, low growl. Raspy and sharp—like a cornered animal.

"No one decides whether I'm in here or not," Castle said. "Understand?"

Matt swallowed hard.

He took a long, deep breath and laid his hands on the table.

"Listen, do you want me to help you or not?" Matt said. "Do you want to rot in prison forever? Because that's where we're headed. We're going to have a hell of a time finding an impartial jury—everyone in New York City and the five boroughs thinks you're guilty. It's too easy for them. 'Psychotic killer kills someone else who happens to be a mob boss.' The pieces fit. It's my job to figure out that they don't, and then convince a jury of your peers of that beyond a reasonable doubt. But, Frank, if you don't help me—it won't matter. And you might as well get another attorney—a public defender, maybe—to ride this out and send you on your way."

Castle shook his head.

"Those tricks don't work on me, Murdock," he said with a dry laugh. "I'm not one of your perps desperate for absolution or a technicality to get them out of prison. I've been on both sides of this glass. I know why I'm here. And I know when it'll be time to come out."

Matt slammed a hand down on the table. Castle didn't flinch. But Matt didn't do it for him. He did it for himself. It was all getting to him. He could feel it—could see the different strands dangling before him. But he couldn't make out what they were. Sheehan's death. The bomb. The Owl's attack, the attack *on* the Owl. There was a shadowy force lurking just out of Matt's range.

But this was something else. A wild card Matt hadn't even anticipated. His mind cut back to that moment in the restaurant, as he watched Castle turn himself in. Remembered the words he uttered, a whisper only Daredevil could hear:

Fear the wild animal that willingly steps into its cage.

Matt stood up abruptly and walked toward the door.

"Giving up already?" Castle said as the door closed behind Matt with a loud clunk.

No, he wasn't giving up. But there was only so much Matt Murdock could do alone. And if Frank Castle had a personal Get Out of Jail Free card, things just got a lot more complicated.

He grabbed his cell phone from the security desk and walked outside, feeling the slap of wind on his face, a relief after hours indoors. He tapped the number out on his display from memory.

"Hey, Matt," she said, her voice low and familiar. "Wasn't expecting to talk to you today."

"I need some help," Matt said. "My friend does, too."

TWENTY

DAKOTA NORTH PACED around Matt Murdock's living room.

"That's a lot," she said, sliding her hands into the pockets of her leather jacket.

"You're telling me," Matt said. "But I don't know where to start. Foggy isn't talking to me. Ben Urich is still digging. The Punisher is acting like his incoming life sentence is a vacation. . . . What am I missing?"

Dakota knew what this meant. Whenever Matt Murdock hit a wall, which was rare, he'd reach out to someone. She was part of a small group that understood Matt Murdock and Daredevil were one and the same. She also understood the complexities that created.

Dakota let herself flop onto Matt's couch. She was a private investigator. One of the best. When Matt's friend Jessica Jones couldn't take a job, she'd refer people to Dakota. She knew how to get her hands dirty and had a sharp mind—meaning she could cut through the bullshit and see the bigger picture. It was why Matt called her. But a few hours into her visit, they'd still gotten nowhere.

Matt let out a sigh. His life was complicated. He glanced at Dakota's familiar figure. His mind flashed back to the handful of nights they'd shared together not long ago. He liked her—she was funny, disarming, sporting a dry wit that kept Matt on his toes. She was also stunning—with a carefree beauty that was natural and impossible to ignore. But they'd gotten together at a bad time for both of them. Matt was reeling from Karen's death and Dakota was struggling with her own case of impostor syndrome. She'd handled the end well—with a shrug and a smile, which only made Matt like her more. She didn't hide her feelings when she had them. She was direct and warm. A unicorn on the mean streets of Hell's Kitchen.

"You're missing everything," she said, crinkling her nose. "Let's talk it out. Fisk is dead. Who benefits? Who's in charge—and who doesn't want anyone else to be in charge or know about it?"

"The list is long," Matt said. "Owl was the first to step in, but there are a ton of two-bit gangsters eager for more power. Where do I start? Silvermane, Hammerhead, Chameleon, Tombstone, Jigsaw, the Maggia, Fisk's own son. We could be here all night. It's a fool's errand."

Dakota let out a long, playful sigh.

"Matt, you're not listening. Those are the people who hope to benefit. But who benefits *immediately*? Who runs the kingdom when the king is slain, before a new one is crowned? Think about it."

The name appeared in Matt's mind almost immediately.

"The Arranger," Matt said. "He was Fisk's main guy. He knows where all the bodies are buried. That's power. He could do whatever he wanted as long as he had the Kingpin's blessing."

"So maybe he's having a hard time giving that up," Dakota said, leaning forward. "Maybe he wants to be the boss for once. Maybe that's what Fisk wanted, too."

Matt nodded. That tracked. But something felt wrong. Incomplete. His mind went back to his aborted meeting with Castle.

"But why is the Punisher just sitting idly by?" Matt asked. Now he was the one doing the pacing.

"Matt, listen to yourself. When has Frank Castle ever sat idly by?"

Matt rubbed his chin. His pacing picked up some speed.

"It's connected," Matt muttered to himself.

"What's connected?" Dakota asked, rising from the couch and stepping closer to Matt to place a hand on his arm.

"I'm not sure of the details yet, but it has to be—Castle is waiting something out, and it ties into Fisk and his empire," Matt said, staring off toward the opposite wall. He could feel his senses tugging at him, overwhelming him. Dakota's perfume. The sound of her voice. The rhythmic beating of her heart. He was tired. But he couldn't stop now. "Dakota—you know the Punisher. This is the kind of guy who has been captured before. I'm not saying he can escape whenever he likes, but he doesn't seem . . ."

"Worried?" she asked.

"Right, it's like he's sitting around, waiting for the other shoe to drop."

They stood in silence for a few moments.

"I think the Arranger has some explaining to do," Matt said.

Dakota stood up. "Need an assist?"

Matt shook his head.

"No, not now—but this has been really helpful," Matt said. As he turned around, he sensed Dakota in front of him, closer than he'd expected.

"I'm happy to help you," Dakota said, her volume lower, more intimate.

Matt reached out and pushed a strand of hair back from her face. "I can't do this," he said.

Dakota tilted her head slightly and smiled.

"Do what, Matt Murdock?" she said. "I'm just an old friend visiting. We're just talking shop. I'm just offering to lend you a hand—"

He felt her finger slide down his chest, stopping above his belt buckle.

"I can't."

Dakota let out a quick laugh before taking a step back. "You're *seeing* someone."

Matt nodded.

"That's never stopped you before," she said, turning to the couch to gather her things. "So it must be serious."

Matt scratched the back of his head as she moved toward the door.

"It is," Matt said. "I think."

Dakota nodded.

"Good. Don't screw it up this time," she said before closing the door behind her.

Matt sensed her leave through the main windows—the same windows that had been shattered by the Owl just a few days before. He closed his eyes and tried to center himself.

His life was always complicated, he reminded himself. So why did it feel like things were unraveling at a much more dangerous clip?

Dakota's presence continued to hover over Matt as he walked toward his bedroom and pulled his shirt off. In another life, he might have kissed Dakota—no matter who he was with. But he wanted to be better than that now. Better than the Matt Murdock of not that long ago. The Matt Murdock who didn't know how to process the pain of loss. A pain so familiar. A pain he tried to replace with lust and distraction. To avoid thinking about the losses that never seemed to disappear.

First Elektra. Then Karen.

Never again, he muttered to himself as he placed the red cowl over his head.

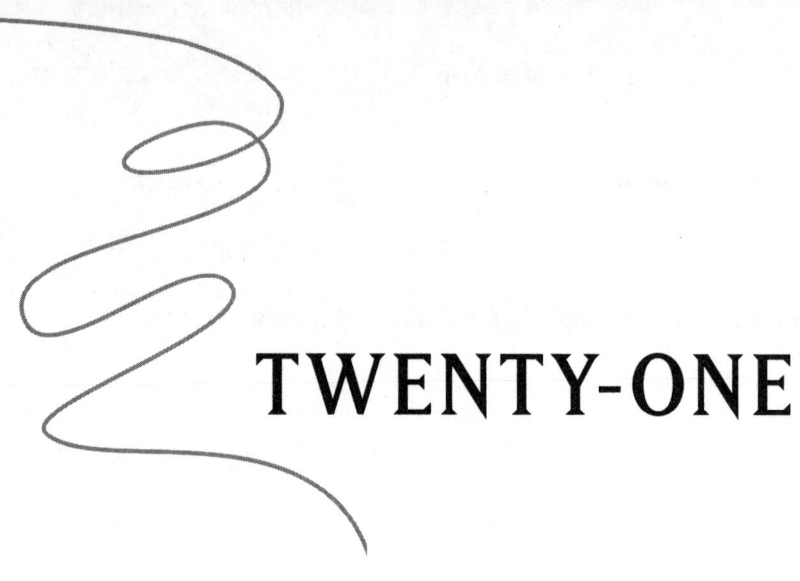

TWENTY-ONE

DAREDEVIL DIDN'T BOTHER with subterfuge. It wouldn't serve him here. He walked up to the security desk that took up the bulk of the lobby of the Fisk building, home and office to Wilson Fisk.

At least previously.

The lobby was a wide, open space—silver and white everywhere, including the two sets of sofas and chairs on either side of the main security desk, which was staffed by a single, confused-looking attendant. Guess it wasn't every morning that a dude dressed like the devil waltzed in.

"Um, can I help you—mister?" the attendant asked.

"Daredevil," he said as if he were ordering a bag of popcorn at the movie theater. "I'm here to see the Arranger."

The attendant, a young kid nowhere close to thirty, seemed to lose their breath for a second. Daredevil wondered if this kid was a temp, filling in for a staffer who saw the writing on the wall and gave notice after Fisk turned up dead. If he was, the temp agency needed to improve its screening process.

"The Arranger?"

"Silkworth," Daredevil said.

"Oh, uh, Mr. Silkworth? Uh, well—"

Daredevil leaned over the counter.

"Let him know it's urgent."

The attendant nodded and wandered to the other end of the security desk. Daredevil heard him nervously ask his colleague what to do. The colleague, an older woman who looked very unhappy to be here, suggested he called the Arranger himself.

The attendant took in a deep breath and picked up a phone nearby. Daredevil didn't bother eavesdropping anymore. He could predict the rest.

The attendant made his way back to Daredevil a few moments later.

"Mr. Silkworth will see you now."

((((( )))))

Daredevil couldn't remember the last time he'd walked in so casually to the Kingpin's office. Often, he'd arrived by crashing through one of the floor-to-ceiling windows, or sneaking through a shaft. Wilson Fisk's office was seemingly endless—a testament to the grandiosity and power of the man who owned the building. A massive oak desk ran the length of the far end of the room, where Fisk usually sat.

But today was different.

The man Daredevil was here to see didn't dare seat himself behind such a desk.

The Arranger waited, next to the desk, a pad in hand. Silkworth was unremarkable in his appearance. Frumpy. A bit of a nebbish. His thick glasses, bald head, and pallor gave him a vampiric air. This was not a violent mob boss. This was not a leader of men. But for now, Daredevil told himself, he was. If anyone was running the remains of the Kingpin's empire, it was the Arranger. And he wanted to confirm it.

"Well, I'm surprised it took you this long," the man said calmly. "At least in terms of formal, approved visits."

Daredevil didn't respond. He understood what that meant. The Arranger knew he had been in the room since the Kingpin's death—and that he'd rummaged around. Daredevil didn't care. For him, the difference, the big difference, between Fisk and his aide-de-camp was clear: He didn't feel threatened by the Arranger. As smart and conniving as the Arranger might be, he was a single punch away from a hospital visit. The criminal's hold over the underworld was tenuous at best, if he even wanted to have one.

"Nice to see you, too, Silkworth," he said, grabbing a pen from the Kingpin's desk and rolling it over his palm. He could sense the Arranger's temperature rising. Could hear his heartbeat quickening. "I won't waste your time. I know you're busy cleaning up after your dead boss. I just have a few questions."

"You are . . . already wasting my time." The Arranger plucked the pen out of Daredevil's hand and pocketed it. "And it doesn't take a law degree to understand why you're here."

The word choice hit Daredevil hard. He hadn't expected that.

Law degree.

Had Wilson Fisk passed on his knowledge of Daredevil's true identity to his lieutenant? Or was it just a coincidental choice of words? Daredevil felt his own blood pressure increase. Felt the emotions and fear of the last few weeks start to coalesce inside him. He pushed it back. But he was also just one man.

Daredevil stepped toward Silkworth and grabbed his designer shirt. He yanked him toward the desk and slammed him down atop it. A jolt of pain shot up his arms as he did so—residual effects from the bomb explosion. It would be a while before he felt like himself again, if ever.

Daredevil leaned over the older man—their faces close. He could smell the cheese Danish he'd just wolfed down. Could hear the fast, rhythmic beating of his anxious heart, and the pacemaker that tried to keep it under control.

"Now—now, there's no need for this. . . ."

"Listen to me, Arranger," Daredevil said, each word coming out slowly. "I don't have time for some three-dimensional chess match. I want answers. Last I heard, the underworld said you were gone—retired. But now you're back, standing in Kingpin's office like you own the place. You knew Fisk better than anyone aside from his wife, Vanessa. You're keeping the lights on here. That tells me you're in control in some way. So you must have some idea—some clue—about who took down your boss. And why."

Daredevil stepped back, allowing Silkworth to slither out of his grasp.

"There's no need to resort to violence," the little man said, straightening his shirt and tie, his tone akin to someone complaining about the wrong milk in a latte. "As you can imagine, we're all grappling with Mr. Fisk's sudden—and tragic—death."

Daredevil took a step toward the Arranger. He couldn't lie about the jolt of pleasure he got watching the man back away in abject terror.

"Who did it, then?" Daredevil said, taking another step. "Who had the means to get in here—to gun Fisk down?"

Arranger moved around to the other side of Fisk's old desk—putting the giant slab between him and Daredevil.

"You know as well as anyone, Daredevil," Arranger said. "It was that madman, Castle. He killed Wilson and that police officer, Sheehan. Very sad."

Daredevil let out a quick laugh. The sound seemed to unsettle the Arranger, who stepped toward the phone.

"Don't even think about doing that. Like I said, I have some questions."

The Arranger moved his hand back to his side.

"Mezinis and Charleston. Who are they?"

The Arranger didn't move. His heart rate didn't skip. Stoic and frozen. "Never heard of them. Some kind of musical act?"

"You're lying." Daredevil's senses were a great advantage, but they were not foolproof. If he dealt with a serial liar, a person who'd honed the skill of telling falsehoods well, it'd jam him up. The Arranger was hiding something, though, he was sure of it. It just meant he'd have to find out a different way.

He moved forward again, but stopped as the older man raised a hand up.

"Do you think I'm without resources, Daredevil?"

A soft clicking sound let Daredevil know that the bookish mob capo had pushed some kind of secret button.

"Do you think I'd allow you into this space without taking the proper precautions?"

Daredevil heard the doors behind him swing open. He knew who he was up against even before he his radar sense bounced off them. Recognized the familiar, lackadaisical gait—and the hoarse, monstrous tinge to the dry laugh the figure released as he entered the room.

"Mr. Bullseye," the Arranger said perfunctorily. "Please show our friend . . . out."

TWENTY-TWO

"GOOD TO SEE YOU, Daredevil," Bullseye said as he slowly stepped into Wilson Fisk's office, his air casual and light. "Been a minute. Shame it all has to end so fast."

Daredevil swallowed hard. He wasn't ready for this. Had expected to scare some information out of the spineless Arranger and be on his way. He wasn't in top form, either—his body was still recovering from the bomb in Staten Island. He was in no shape to go toe-to-toe with one of the deadliest assassins on the planet.

Bullseye wasn't just a well-trained killer. That would be a problem on its own. He had the ability to make anything a weapon—a pencil, a pebble—*everything* he touched was a deadly tool in his hands.

He also killed Elektra—and Karen Page. Through the mystical work of the two clans who'd warred over control of Elektra, she was brought back. But Karen wasn't so lucky.

Daredevil knew he wasn't up for this fight. His entire body ached just from manhandling the Arranger. He had to get out.

Bullseye had often been on the Kingpin's payroll—stepping in for Elektra when she left his employ as his main killer-for-hire only to be replaced by Typhoid Mary. Had he been working for Fisk before his death? Did that contract carry over? Or was something else going on?

"This explains your bravery, Arranger," Daredevil said, his radar sense still locked on Bullseye. "Easy to talk tough when you're holding a machete behind your back. Or rather, when someone else is holding a machete *for* you."

"Aw, I'm flattered, Devil," Bullseye said. He'd stopped approaching now. He stood a few feet away, his body relaxed. Even his breathing and heartbeat felt calm and collected. "You do like me. After all these years—after all these bodies . . . glad you don't hold your dead girlfriends against me."

Daredevil felt something snap. Like a hot poker stabbing his brain. He knew he would regret this later—if he survived. But he acted on impulse. It was most definitely what Bullseye wanted, but in that moment, he didn't give a shit.

He leapt backward, doing a flip midair. He landed behind the Arranger and wrapped an arm around the older man's neck. He tightened his grip until he heard Fisk's bookish consigliere yelp in pain.

Rage boiled through Daredevil. He could feel the sensory overload of Elektra and Karen's final moments. Karen's final, desperate breath as he held her in his arms. He'd felt her breathing stop, heard her heartbeat go. Even now, Daredevil could feel her fully—her sharp smile. The way she'd walk down the hall while putting her hair up. The knowing look she'd give him when they worked together, when they heard or read about something that she knew Matt would have to handle as Daredevil. The shared life that bonded them into one thing, for a short, brief while. The relief and release of finding each other after years apart. All of it yanked away by the man who stood in front of him now.

This *monster.*

Would the world be a lesser place if Daredevil took Bullseye's life? Would he be less of a hero if he threw a billy club straight into his eye, piercing his brain? Or would that just erase him as a hero at all—make him a vigilante killer like the Punisher, no longer the defender of justice, but his own judge, jury, and executioner? Could he be said to be serving justice, or just his own bloodlust?

Daredevil knew the truth.

Knew it wasn't his place to decide who lived or died. If he did, he'd be just like the vile creature in front of him, and the one biding his time in Riker's. Justice had to mean something—he had to stand for the rule of law, or there wouldn't be any law left.

Not that he had to be nice about it.

Daredevil picked up the Arranger and tossed him in the air halfway to Bullseye. The act was a question as much as anything. If the assassin was on the Kingpin's payroll, he'd leap to save the man signing the checks. If he didn't care, that would answer that.

Either way, it'd leave him open.

Bullseye hesitated for a moment as the Arranger yelled midair—but eventually pitched himself forward and caught his boss on the descent. As he did that, Daredevil backflipped over the desk and sent a kick into Bullseye's chin.

Bullseye groaned in pain and surprise, but Daredevil knew this was only the opening salvo—any brawl with the man was to the death, and he couldn't hack that now. He didn't have a death wish.

Standing up behind his foe, he sent a barrage of punches into the back of the villain's head, sending him reeling forward, causing him to drop Silkworth with a low thud. Daredevil sensed the crime lord scrambling away from the brawl as Bullseye turned around. The black-clad assassin stepped backward and grabbed for something. Before Daredevil could get a clear sense of what it was, Bullseye had launched the Arranger's pen toward his gut.

Daredevil tried to dodge left, but he was a half second too slow.

He felt the sharp end of the pen slice the side of his midsection. A moment later, blood was seeping out of the wound and a sharp pain overtook the area. Daredevil clutched the gash and stepped back.

"You're not moving so well, Hornhead," Bullseye said, smiling. "I'd hate to take you out under less-than-ideal conditions."

He stepped forward and swung at Daredevil. The punch barely missed. Bullseye was right. He was off. His reflexes—even if augmented by his radar and enhanced senses—were dulled somehow. But it wasn't just the cut. His senses were not clicking at the right pace. His radar sense felt fuzzy and unclear. Had he spiked the pen tip with something?

"Need a break . . . Daredevil . . . ?"

Bullseye's voice sounded distant. Hazy.

He needed to get out, fast.

Daredevil took a step back and stumbled slightly. He straightened himself up and braced for impact—arms raised. But Bullseye wasn't moving toward him. He was watching. Waiting.

It was a question of time, then, Daredevil thought. Whatever Bullseye had laced the pen with, it would act fast. Why brawl with Daredevil at half power when he'd be done in no time?

Daredevil pivoted to his left and ran.

He heard Bullseye's surprised curse, but only for a second. The sound of crashing glass—as his body careened through the windows that formed the far wall of Wilson Fisk's former office—dominated his senses only to be immediately replaced by the whooshing wind as he fell down, story after story.

His senses were sluggish. He felt the air tighten around him. On instinct, his hand went to his side. He felt himself clutch his billy club. The click of a button. His arm jerked out. The familiar hiss of sound as a rope detached.

He prayed it connected.

Then his body jerked to one side, the familiar tightness and cold as he swung between buildings. He registered the basics—that he was moving away from the ground, that he might be okay.

But then his mind went black and he let go.

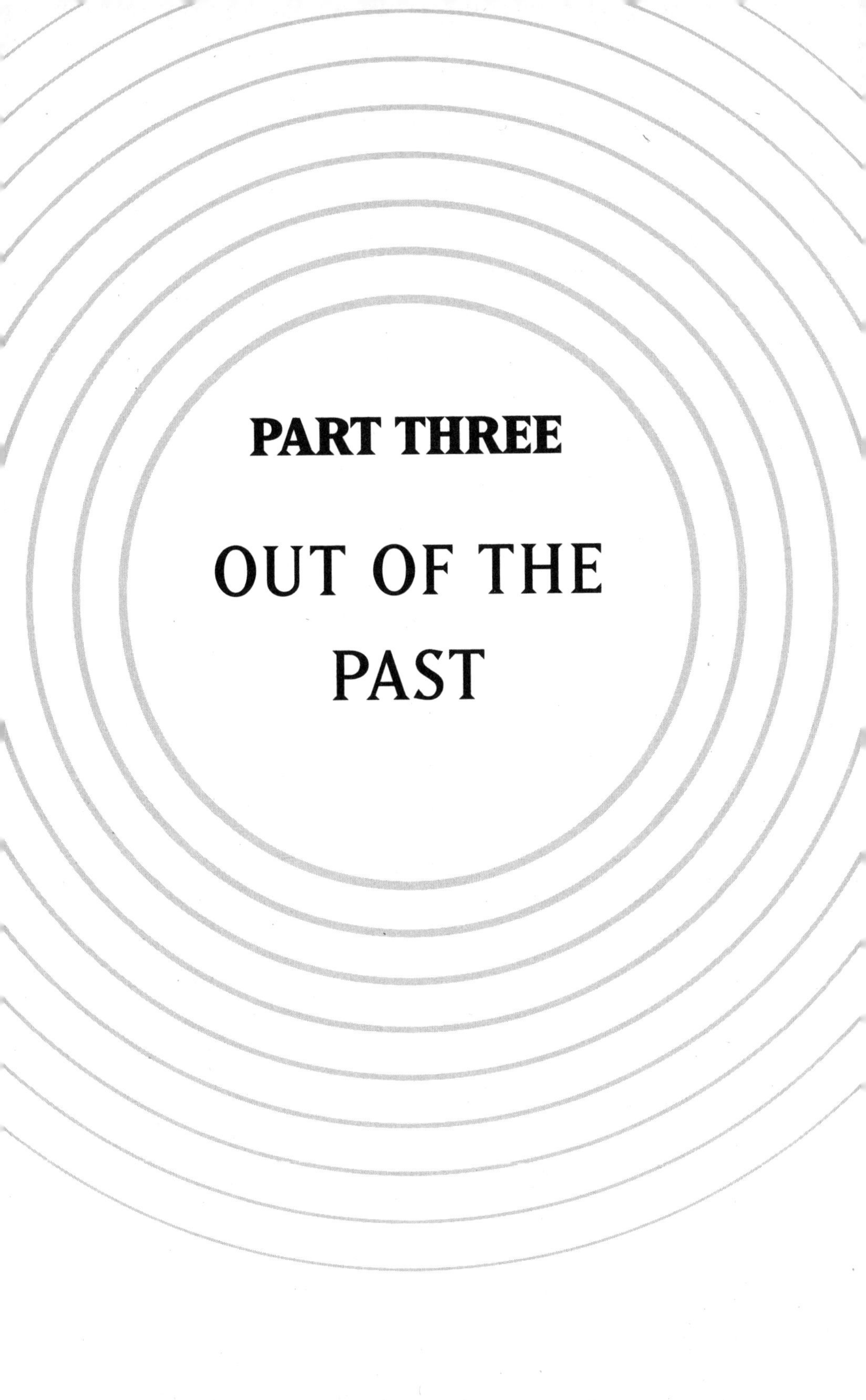

PART THREE

OUT OF THE PAST

TWENTY-THREE

BEN URICH FELT A CHILL. But it wasn't the weather.

The reporter was inside a diner located in Midtown, just a few blocks north of Hell's Kitchen proper. He was seated near the back, his hands cradling a lukewarm mug of coffee.

It was late afternoon. He needed to file a story in a few hours or his publisher, J. Jonah Jameson, would have his hide. He wanted something meaningful and in-depth about the New York City underworld—and where things stood now: just a little over two weeks since the death of Wilson Fisk, and the sudden attack on the Owl. But Ben had nothing. Until this morning, when he'd received a brief, untraceable call from someone purporting to be Richard Fisk—Wilson Fisk's only son, and a mob boss in his own right, albeit as a middling, purple-masked villain named the Rose.

Perhaps that should be qualified as past tense, Ben thought. The Rose had raised a viable challenge to his father's empire a few years back, but when the Kingpin stomped him out, the junior Fisk had scurried away, eventually ending up in his dad's employ, managing what was left of his old gang as a semi-independent fiefdom that still answered to Daddy. It was an ego blow to the young man, but also the kind of off-ramp Fisk's other enemies probably dreamed of. The benefits of being the flop kid to the deadliest mob boss in the history of New York.

But then, in the wake of his father's death, why hadn't Richard stepped into the void?

Ben rubbed his chin. He had a few thoughts.

The first was simple: Richard wasn't Wilson Fisk. He wasn't up to the task. He wasn't loyal, and his father's men just didn't respect him. In every conversation Ben Urich had had where Richard Fisk came up, he was treated as a joke—a failure. The son who could've unseated his father but flubbed it. At best, he'd be a hard sell as leader. Ben doubted the Kingpin would name Richard his heir apparent. If anything, he'd exiled his son to oversee operations as far from Hell's Kitchen as possible. Last Ben heard, Richard Fisk was the "capo" of Staten Island. Not exactly a prime spot with which to take the top rung.

But Richard Fisk wasn't stupid. Ben knew that much. So why talk to a reporter?

The door chime jangled as a nondescript, middle-aged white man with a stubbly beard entered. He scanned the diner before making his way toward the back of the restaurant. If there was cosplay for "Person Trying to Hide in Plain Sight," this would be it. Big coat, collar turned up, cheap drugstore sunglasses, and the skittishness of a veteran alley cat. Aside from being a fashion eyesore, it told Ben Urich something else: Richard Fisk was scared.

The fading mobster slid into the booth across from Ben and looked down at the menu, avoiding eye contact.

"Thanks for meeting me," he said in a hurried voice. "Almost didn't make it."

"Happy to chat," Ben said, pulling a notebook out of his back pocket.

"Though I can't say I wasn't surprised to get your call. Figured you'd be pretty busy these days."

Fisk looked up at Ben. That's when Ben could see the fear in its purest form—panicked and desperate. Richard Fisk's eyes were bloodshot and he was sporting every nervous tic Ben could imagine. Licking his lips. His eye twitched. It seemed like Fisk had been tossed into a blender for too long and left to piece himself together.

"Busy?" Fisk scoffed. "Busy trying to stay alive, man. That's what's keeping me busy."

"So you called *me*?"

Fisk inhaled deeply before running a hand over his tired face. "I'm a dead man walking, Urich. Everyone is in denial about it except me."

Ben raised a pencil.

"Before you continue—"

Fisk waved him off.

"Yeah, yeah, I'm on the record—I don't care. Like I said, dead man walking."

"Okay, well, about that."

Fisk gave Ben a blank stare.

"Your father is dead . . . gunned down, allegedly, by Frank Castle—who your ilk call 'the Punisher,' because he murders people he sees as criminals, before they're given a fair shake," Urich said, leaning forward slightly. "That leaves a pretty big hole to fill. I think some pundits, if there is such a thing when it comes to the underworld . . . thought you might try to fill that void."

Fisk laughed. An empty sound. The laugh of someone who hadn't really chuckled in years.

"You think I could do that, Ben? Or are you just puffing me up for your story?"

Ben hesitated before responding.

"I'm giving you a chance to talk," he said finally, tapping his pad with the eraser end of his pencil.

"My father was at the height of his power. He wasn't thinking about succession. He didn't need to. Every gang was under his control. The Maggia? Answered to him. He'd turned his enemies, like me, people like Owl, Hammerhead, Tombstone . . . into lieutenants. And lieutenants not driven by fear, but by some passionate love for the Kingpin. And he didn't have to give a single order. It all came through Silkworth."

"The Arranger."

"Right, my father's right hand. Every order, you knew it was legit if Silkworth called you," Fisk said.

"So is the Arranger in charge? I thought he was gone?"

Fisk shook his head. "You met Silkworth? He was gone, but not forgotten. The list of people my father trusted is short, and Silkworth was on the top. He was never a threat to him. Guy looks like an adjunct professor at some New England college," he said, scorn soaking into his voice. "He's never held a gun. Never choked someone out. Never shoved a knife into someone's midsection. He's a white collar criminal. The kind of errand boy my dad needed to keep his hands clean. But in a fight? Worthless. All of my father's men know that, too. No one's scared of him."

"So what are they scared of?"

Fisk waited a second, then looked around the table. He didn't meet Ben's gaze.

"Bullseye."

Ben's eyes widened. "He's got Bullseye?"

"Yeah, somehow he lured him back to the business," Fisk said, his voice lower than before. "Not sure where he'd been. But the last time I talked to my father . . . they'd been on a break. You know as well as anyone, my father likes to rotate his top guns. Elektra. Bullseye. Typhoid. He doesn't believe in letting them get comfortable. Bullseye wasn't on the outs, but he was gone. Could've been bad, could've been nothing."

"So the Arranger has him in the fold? How does that argue against my point?" Ben asked. "It seems like the move the new boss would make—"

"Or a move someone terrified for their life would make," Fisk interjected. "You notice how I walked in here? I got two of my guys outside, scoping everyone inside, outside, and anyone who wants to come in."

"You think someone's gunning for you?"

"I know someone's gunning for me," Fisk said, tapping the table between them. "Put that in your paper. Before long, there's gonna be a bloodbath in the streets of Hell's Kitchen. Someone is taking out all the guys who'd dare or even might dare to be the next Kingpin. Owl was the opening salvo. That bird ain't ever gonna flap his wings again."

Ben swallowed hard. Fisk's words rang true. Part of him, a small voice in the back of his mind thought, *So what? What if these criminals kill each other? Let them die.* But the reality was, gang wars didn't just affect the gangsters. Innocents always managed to get caught in the cross fire. He could read the headline now:

HELL'S KITCHEN HEADED TOWARD GANG WAR,
ORGANIZED CRIME BOSS PREDICTS

And it'd be a cautious headline, too. Because if Fisk were to be believed, the war had already started.

"You're not counting on Daredevil," Ben said, without really thinking about it. But the words came out anyway.

"No one is," Fisk said, shaking his head. "How do you think I found out about Bullseye, reporter man?" A smile spread across Fisk's face. "Silkworth told me himself. Told me Bullseye loaded that red-suited freak with so much poison he'd be dead in an hour," Fisk said. "Besides that, he fell out of my dad's window. No one's worried about Daredevil anymore, man. Daredevil's as good as dead."

TWENTY-FOUR

ELEKTRA WATCHED THE WOMAN, Melinda Torres, buzz Matthew's bell again.

It was late in the afternoon. Elektra assumed Matthew's current lover had checked in with Foggy or his office first. He wasn't there, either. Normally, Elektra would move on, keep looking for Matthew on her own terms, but something intrigued her about this moment—this chance to speak to this woman who so bedeviled Matthew. Why was that?

She laughed dryly.

Oh, Matthew. Always falling in love, even when you're really just in love with the past. Still mourning Karen Page, still mourning the love Elektra shared with you, and yet, ever willing to fall into bed with someone else. Some things never change, Elektra thought.

Another thing that never changed? Matthew's innate ability to get himself into trouble. To put his mind and body at risk in his Quixotic quest for justice.

That was why Elektra was here, in the middle of the day, perched on a rooftop, looking down at his luxurious loft . . . wondering if he was dead.

She hated the way her heart jumped at the thought, terrified. Hated how this man still took up space in her mind. But she also understood why—and had come to accept it. They had meant so much to each other for so long, it was only natural.

And Elektra had to remind herself that it was okay to be human. She was more than just a killing machine. More than just a "super hero." She was a person with vices and problems, no matter what Stick's or the Hand's training had done to her. She was more than just a weapon.

But if someone hurt Matthew, she thought, she would become a weapon. And would rain destruction down on whoever was responsible.

"He's not here," Elektra said as she landed a few feet behind Torres. The Internal Affairs officer, who seemed fit, smart, and pretty in her own way, spun around—gun drawn. Once she realized who was behind her, she sighed and reholstered her weapon.

"You could get shot doing that."

Elektra straightened up and walked over.

"You'd miss."

"You're Elektra, right?" Torres said, looking her up and down. "Don't you get cold in that outfit?"

"I don't get cold, period." She understood the tactic. Sarcasm was a useful defense for people like Torres. It gave others—people who were not trained ninja assassins—pause. "Are you looking for Matthew?"

"Matthew? Matt, you mean?" Torres asked. "Yes, why are you asking? What's with you tights people? You keep coming here—"

Elektra stepped forward.

"Did someone else come here before?"

"Yeah, that bird-freak, the Owl," Torres said, checking her phone. "He crashed through Matt's window and attacked us after they announced he'd be defending Castle in the Fisk murder trial. Not sure how they're related."

"I'm not like the Owl. Or Kingpin," Elektra said. "I knew Matt. Before."

Torres tilted her head slightly. She was absorbing everything.

There was something about her that sent Elektra's mind whirring. She couldn't put her finger on it. She was capable. Clearly fearless. Strong-willed. Did Elektra . . . *like* her?

She'd always shrugged off Matthew's other lovers. Karen had been kind-hearted but physically weak. Heather Glenn troubled. Even the Black Widow, as capable as she was, never felt like a real match for Matthew. She didn't think about the rest. What was it about this woman that piqued Elektra's interest? She filed it away for later.

"Like I said, he's not here," Elektra said. "I'm assuming you checked his office."

"Yeah, Foggy said he hadn't heard from him."

"Since when?" Elektra asked. She found it strange that Torres, an officer of the law, hadn't pressed Foggy harder.

"I'm—I'm not sure," Torres said, looking down at her hands. "I should have asked for more details, but—"

Her voice caught at the end. She was worried.

"He will be fine," Elektra said.

She wasn't sure why she was trying to comfort this woman she barely knew, but then she realized it was for Matthew. She only seemed to extend these kindnesses in relation to him. It was a bad habit she would have to remedy.

"Matthew is stronger than he seems," she added.

"I'm starting to realize that."

Elektra yanked Torres's phone from her hand and started tapping the display.

"Hey!"

"I'm giving you a contact," Elektra said. "Call this number when you find him or he appears. Don't say anything specific. Just let me know. I won't respond. But I would appreciate word as soon as you know. I will return the favor if I'm able."

Torres watched carefully as Elektra handed the phone back. She waited a second and spoke. "How do you know Matt?"

Elektra looked at Torres, her hand still on her phone, as if they were about to tug at each end like temperamental children.

"We dated in college," Elektra said. "We were both very different then. At least, I was."

"You still care for him?"

Elektra let go of the phone and backed away. "We all have our weaknesses."

As Torres started to dart away, Elektra turned her head back and called out, "Stay safe, Detective. Things are about to get very complicated."

TWENTY-FIVE

"THE ARRANGER?"

Elektra's question hung in the air between her and Dakota North. They were on a Hell's Kitchen rooftop, above Josie's Bar—Elektra's next target in her increasingly stressful hunt for Matthew. Before she could make her way down to the dive's entrance, though, she'd gotten a call. Only a handful of people knew how to reach her. Dakota North was one of them.

They weren't exactly friends. She knew they shared an affection for Matthew, though Elektra assumed hers was a bit more complicated. Dakota was no-nonsense, a relatively free spirit who wanted to keep a roof over her head, investigate interesting cases, and do some good. Admirable, Elektra thought.

"The Torres woman," Elektra said. "Did she tell you I was looking for Matthew?"

"No, Foggy did," Dakota said. "And honestly, I'm tired of talking about Matt, but if the guy's missing—well, that can't be good."

Elektra pulled out a sai and spun it on her fingertips. More habit than threat. Dakota didn't flinch.

"Matthew can take care of himself," she said. "But I would like to think I know when he's really in trouble."

"This feels bad?"

"It does," Elektra said with a slight shake of her head. "But you saw him last. What was on his mind?"

Dakota smirked.

"Beyond the usual," Elektra said, a slight tinge of annoyance in her delivery.

"He was trying to figure out who was climbing onto the Kingpin's throne," Dakota said with a shrug. "Which, hey, it could be anyone. But he seemed focused on the Arranger."

"Silkworth," Elektra said. "Fisk's errand boy?"

"You'd know better than me," Dakota said. "Didn't you work for Fisk?"

"That was a long time ago," Elektra said. "Continue."

"That's it, really," Dakota said. "He was gonna take on this Arranger guy, I offered to help, he declined, fin."

Elektra looked down at her hands. What was she doing? She kept saying it—Matthew could take care of himself. Why was she suddenly so interested in his life? She knew why. She was worried. Matthew was strong but also strong-headed. He was still recovering from that explosion. If he took on the Arranger, and the mob boss had something up his sleeve—it could prove deadly. It was unlike him to go quiet for so long. Not when it came to her—they went months without talking. But not talking to Foggy and his new lover—he wouldn't do that.

If he could help it.

Dakota looked at her phone display.

"Police band is talking about some kind of attack at Penn Station—sounds bad," Dakota said. She looked up at Elektra. "Sounds like the kind of thing your type should be handling."

"My type?" Elektra asked.

"Yeah, super heroes. Need a lift?"

Elektra smiled. "I'll see you there."

TWENTY-SIX

WHEN MATT MURDOCK awoke he was in darkness.

Not that he could see that, but rather his radar sense couldn't pick up any sign of light. There was a stillness to the tiny room—no sound. Wherever he was, it was meant to be quiet, calm.

He felt around. He was on a tiny, rigid cot. The sheets felt old and worn—used often and smelling of bleach and starch. His head was pounding. His mouth felt dry. He felt for his mask—for his costume—and realized it was gone. He was wearing a simple T-shirt and sweatpants. They were newly cleaned as well. He tried to sit up, but the headache got worse—sharper. He tried to remember how he could have gotten here.

Bullseye. The Arranger, and his knowing, evil smile. The pen slashing his side.

How long had he been out? He remembered swinging through the city, purely on instinct, trying to get somewhere. But where was he?

Then he heard the organ.

The unmistakable chords of a song he'd heard so many times as a child, holding his father's hand as they walked down the aisles of church to find a seat. The smell of incense.

Then the soft beeps of a hospital room.

The darkness, the all-encompassing darkness.

And a voice. Gruff and low.

"You got your work cut out for you, kid."

Stick.

His mind flashed back. A rooftop in the Kitchen. His face covered by a black scarf, the wind hitting him as he leapt to the next building. A figure waiting for him. That gruff voice again.

"The Natchios woman—she's trouble," Stick said, not looking up, not wasting the energy to move when it wasn't required.

"Elektra?" Matt said, removing the scarf, his radar sense scanning the rooftop before settling on Stick again. "She needs me, Stick."

Then the older man looked up, his eyes wide and empty.

"You gotta stop thinking with your privates, Murdock—use your head, doofus," Stick said. "You wanna learn how to use these abilities? You want to do some damn good in this inside-out world? You need to stop worrying about your social calendar. Elektra has a darkness in her. She'll only drag you down."

Matt didn't hear the last part. He'd already leapt to the next rooftop.

His mind shifted again. A luxury estate. Empty. Only one person waited for him—in her room, staring out into the distance on her balcony.

This is not a home anymore, Matt thought.

He tried to hold her, but then he heard her breathing, flat and unaffected. The sounds coming from her—not a sob. Nothing. Matt knew grief came in different shapes and sizes, but he couldn't shake a deeper feeling. That she had become something else. He reached for her, but she pulled away.

"Elektra, I'm so sorry—"

"Go away, Matthew," she said, her voice distant and empty, like a recording. "You don't want to be here. You shouldn't have to be here."

He grabbed her this time, but she was limp to the touch. He pulled her close to him. She didn't resist, but that blank stare . . .

"I want to be here for you," he said.

"There's nothing to be here for, Matthew," she said, pulling away from him. She motioned for the door. "I'm returning home tomorrow, to tend to Father's affairs—and to figure out my own."

He's somewhere else now. Stepping outside his brownstone. Her voice—shaky and fading—calling to him. He senses her shape, crawling up the steps to his door. He can smell the blood, can hear her heartbeat faltering.

"M-Matt . . ."

He's somewhere else again . . . the location familiar, but the details feel wrong. His brownstone. Except it's not there. Rubble, dirt, concrete . . . everything destroyed. His fingers run through the debris of his brownstone. He's screaming. He's enveloped by panic. Someone is after him—his law license suspended, his home destroyed. Someone knows the truth about Daredevil. About Matt Murdock. And nothing will ever be the same.

A cold cloth on his forehead. A soothing voice. Maggie. *Mother Maggie . . . where are you?* He calls out to her, but the world shifts around him.

Matt is walking down a long hall, a woman next to him. He senses her heat—the chemistry is almost palpable. But he feels so bad. Knows this is wrong. The fleeting glances, the smiles. He feels her hand slide into his perfectly, warm to his touch, like a cup of tea. He smells her scent—Mary. Shy, sweet, thoughtful Mary. But he knows this is wrong. Is screaming in his head that this is wrong. What about Karen? Where is she? Then Mary kisses him and it all melts away—the shame, the guilt, the fear, dissolves into something else—something dark and bad and addictive. . . .

He shifts again, his temperature rising. He's in a church—*that* church. He tries to stop the memory, but it comes anyway, as if alive itself. He's cradling Karen. She'd yelled his name as Bullseye tossed Daredevil's own billy club at her—killing her instantly. Daredevil felt the life leave her. Felt everything leave with her. Every ounce of fight, every desire to live left him then.

No more fighting, he thought.

He'd never stopped fighting.

As a kid, before the accident that left him blind and gifted him with an array of unexpected abilities, Matt's father Jack Murdock had been clear with his son: No fighting. No roughhousing. He had to study to get out of the slums of Hell's Kitchen, and nothing else mattered. Battlin' Jack didn't want his only son to end up like him. So, Matt stayed home—studying, reading, exploring every dank corner of their tiny, cramped apartment on Tenth Avenue. But it didn't help him avoid the wrath of his classmates. Most days, as those kids went off to play when the final school bell rang, Matt would try to slither in the other direction—back home, to his room, his books, and his solitary life. But he rarely made it without a few dings.

"There goes Daredevil, fearless Matt Murdock, hidin' behind his apartment door," Nestor Tate would shout, over the din of the school emptying out. "Too much of a badass to come out and play with us kids, huh?"

"Yeah, Murdock's got his own stuff to do—can't be bothered to hang out with us."

"Have fun, you risk-taker," another would say. "Beware the Daredevil! Protector of Hell's Kitchen!"

The kids had no idea how prescient their barbs would be.

The realization hadn't come quickly to Matt. After he gained his powers, he struggled to control them: the literal sensory overload of hearing every conversation within a mile radius, the overpowering array of scents and tastes that were part of the commerce of New York City drove him to the brink—to a place where a nice padded room felt like a welcome escape. But his life was saved by Stick—mysterious Stick, who understood his abilities better than anyone. Training with Stick had felt almost like trying to become a soldier—long hours, dogmatic ideas, and a menacing foe lurking in every shadow. But like Jack Murdock, Stick had rules, too—Matt was to listen to him, no one else. He had to follow his dictates to the letter, or risk losing all the control over his new abilities he'd built up with Stick's guidance. For a while, that seemed to work, until—like most things—it didn't.

Matt could still remember pulling the suit out, years later. Marveled at how it'd come together, how he'd created it as if in a trance. The yellow-and-black jumpsuit was in the duffel bag he'd brought to Manhattan to see his dad's final fight, tucked between a few T-shirts and boxers. As if he'd known this would be the time to debut it. As if he'd expected all his fantasies and ideations would come to a head that weekend. He ran his fingers over the thick bodysuit, over the yellow sleeves and down to the cloth that would cover his heart. With the dark red "DD" on the chest.

Daredevil.

A nod to the crude nickname his classmates had thrown at him when they were kids. Would they be laughing now? he wondered. It fit snugly, wrapping around his chiseled abs and chest—the product of years at the gym, but also easily masked by rumpled clothes and business suits that ran a size too big. His fingers wrapped around the billy club—part bat, part nunchakus, all useful. The kind of weapon Matt had grown accustomed to while training with Stick. It could do it all—serve as a grappling hook between rooftops or as a weapon to stave off an attacker.

He pulled the mask up to his face, his radar sense wrapping around the yellow hood's shape: the tight eyeholes, the tiny "devil" horns protruding on his forehead, the opening for his chin and mouth. It felt almost silly if he allowed himself to sit and think about it. But that time had passed, Matt realized. The time for pondering and debating was over.

His father was in a morgue somewhere in the city. He would never get up again. He'd never put on his gloves and fight. He'd never playfully rib Matt. He'd never get that one last shot at redemption he'd pinned all his hopes on. Jack Murdock was dead. But someone else was rising from the ashes to continue fighting for what was right.

((((( )))))

"How are you feeling?"

Sister Maggie's voice hovered over him as he awoke. Had he drifted off to sleep again? He must have. He was in the same room he'd sensed before, somewhere in the church's basement. Maggie's voice, familiar and soothing, covered him like a comforting blanket. In his heart, he'd known he was here before he'd realized it.

He reached out his hand into the darkness and felt her worn palm take his. She felt warm. Old and warm. He choked back unexpected tears.

"Maggie . . ."

"Yes?"

He felt the weight of what he'd been dealing with reassert itself now. The questions. The fear. Perhaps he was in this place for a reason.

"What do you do . . ." Matt started. "What do you try to do—when it feels like there's no right choice?"

He knew Maggie was watching him intently. Waiting for him to elaborate. But he wasn't sure there was more to say.

"A terrible man died—in a brutal, painful way," Matt continued. "He was my enemy. He'd done me great harm. You remember. He destroyed my life. Left me in ashes. But he's dead now."

"May God rest his soul," Maggie said reflexively.

Matt nodded. "His killer, the person accused of his murder—is also a bad man," Matt said. "A killer who decides who lives and dies. I've dealt with him before. We are not friends, but we respect each other. Though his methods are wrong. No one should have that power alone. He is not well."

Matt paused. He waited for Maggie to speak, but nothing came. She was giving him space.

"But this killer—he's a man, too. Flawed. Complicated. A child of God. A sinner," Matt continued. "Doesn't he . . . like anyone else . . . deserve a defense? Why should he be thrown to the wolves, even if he is a wolf, too?"

Mary coughed softly.

"He's a man. He may have done great evils, but he is still a man," Matt said. "Is it wrong for me to want to give him the same chance everyone deserves? Even if I hate him? Even if I hate the man he killed? Even if I take joy in this man's death, and have found myself praying for the death of the other?"

"Your sins can be cleansed, Matthew," Maggie said, sounding distant and sedate. "You can confess your dark thoughts. We are all sinners in the eyes of God. We all seek his blessing and guidance toward eternal life. You are a servant of justice. Let that—and God himself—lead you down the right path. Even if it is dark and dangerous. You know what the right thing to do is—but the right thing is often the hardest. This man hurt you. Both men have hurt you. It would be easy to celebrate a death and ease the other's path toward their own oblivion. But what would that mean for you? For your soul?"

Matt rubbed his eyes. He reached for his glasses, propped on a small nightstand near the bed.

"I don't know what's better. The easy path is so tempting. Why do I always have to choose the path of pain and hardship? When can I just be safe?"

"Matthew, you're safe now," she said. "But there is no such thing as complete safety always. We pray for guidance and ask for forgiveness of our own trespasses. We serve in the light of the Lord and hope to be humble and good in our efforts. That is all we can do. All we can do is try."

Matt felt his body relax. He let the air between them grow silent—as it had over the years, the unspoken words doing more work than the ones said aloud.

Sister Maggie had always been there for Matt when he needed refuge. When the Kingpin had shattered his life and destroyed his reputation, when he'd foolishly taken the battle directly to Wilson Fisk, he'd crawled to this very same basement, bruised and battered. Maggie had helped himself pull out of the abyss and back to life.

Matt knew the truth. She was his mother. The same woman who'd left his father, unable to bear the stress of being a parent. The woman who had forced Matt's well-meaning but pugilistic father to learn how to be a sole parent. Matt had resented her for years during his childhood. Had particularly resented her after the accident—until a few days into his hospital stay he'd heard her voice—his augmented hearing making it sound like someone was yelling into his ear before he'd learned to manage and master the gifts he'd been given.

"I'll always be near you, Matthew," she'd said.

They'd never discussed the truth out loud. Had never argued about it. He'd never gotten the chance to ask her why. Why she'd left him. He understood why Jack Murdock wasn't the best husband. But Matt had been a child. He'd been *innocent*. And she'd left him alone with a man she couldn't even bear to be around herself. He wanted to reach for her—to ask her what had been running through her mind when she walked out the door for the last time.

Even now, alone with her in this dank, small room, he couldn't bring himself to.

But that didn't mean he couldn't appreciate what she'd done.

"How long have I been here?" Matt asked, sitting up slowly.

"You've been asleep for over a day—you were feverish at first," she said methodically. "The sisters and I . . . well, we were worried . . . so worried. When that man brought you here, he said he did all he could for you, that it was in your hands now. Told us to let you rest. But your fever broke late last night. Whatever happened to you . . . could have killed you."

"Man?" Matt asked.

"An older man, blind," Maggie said as she poured water into a cup and motioned for Matt to drink. "He did not look well. He was shaky, but somehow strong. I felt a great presence in him. I told him I would call once you awoke—but he didn't leave a number. He said if anyone could survive this, you would. And if not—that was just how destiny worked. Then he laughed and left."

"Stick," Matt said in a croaked whisper.

Had he heard Stick's voice in the present, pushing for him to fight? Or was he reliving his past? Was his old mentor watching over him? He wasn't sure he'd ever know.

"Stick?" Maggie asked.

Matt shook his head.

"Don't worry about it . . . I'm feeling better now," Matt said. It was true. Whatever headache he'd had seemed to be fading. He didn't feel well—he'd still been recovering from the bomb when Bullseye poisoned him—but he felt well enough to be on his way.

"I need to go, Maggie. Thank you. For everything."

She gripped his hand.

"Be safe, Matthew," she whispered. She knew he could hear her. "Even with us . . . with God . . . watching over you . . . there are no guarantees."

Matt held her hand for a moment and then let go.

She motioned toward a pile of clothes on a chair across from the bed. Matt grabbed the bundle—his costume—and put it in a small duffel bag he spotted on the floor. He hooked it over his shoulder and turned to Maggie as he reached the door.

"Thank you, Maggie," he said softly. "I'm lucky to have you."

She tilted her head slightly.

Matt could hear her heart beating faster. Could sense the tears forming around her eyes and sliding down her face. A long intake of breath.

Before she could say anything else, Matt was gone.

TWENTY-SEVEN

ELEKTRA MADE IT to Penn Station in five minutes—a best for her, coming from the Kitchen. The scene was bad. Travelers were rushing out of the transit hub in a panic and she could hear the sound of automatic gunfire even from Broadway. She was the first on the scene, from what she could tell, but she would certainly not be the last.

She stopped an older man running up to street level.

"What's going on down there?"

"Lots—lots of shooting . . . these men . . . metal . . . look like they're half-robots. . . ." Out of breath, he didn't wait for Elektra to respond, sidestepping her and continuing to flee toward safety.

She ran toward the main escalators that led to the Long Island Railroad terminal, sliding down the median between two of them, past the swarms of people rushing up to escape. The terminal seemed mostly clear now, but she noticed the threat right away. A handful of men, men who would've looked nondescript at first glance, standing in the middle of the area, large guns drawn. It was only when she looked closer that Elektra realized these were not normal men—the glint of metal under their coats, the red light coming from one of their eyes.

Cyborgs?

This was new, she thought.

She leapt at one of the men firing into the crowd—sending a kick into his neck. Normally, this would be more than enough to disable someone, but she felt more resistance.

Definitely more than just thugs.

She sent a punch into the man's face—he groaned in response. So, there was some humanity there. Even a robot could cry.

She kicked the gun out of her foe's hand and sent a jump kick into the two men approaching her from behind. From what she could tell, there were only a few of them, but they were trying their best to cause the most damage possible.

She caught sight of a few people scurrying to safety, then focused on the handful of augmented attackers. The men circled her cautiously, waiting for her to make a move. They didn't know her very well, she thought. She could do this all day.

"Who are you?" she asked.

One of the men stepped closer. "We're staking a claim for the boss."

That explained it. She'd wondered once she arrived what the play was here—there was no loot to rob, no target to kill, no purpose—but there were cameras. She saw a few brave people—cell phones out and recording—inching forward on the margins, trying to get a glimpse of the killers attacking Penn Station.

Elektra jumped toward the talkative one, sending another kick into his chin and spinning him backward. His sidekicks looked on in surprise. As she landed, she turned to face the remaining men.

"Tell me who your boss is," she said, her voice calm and focused. "I want to talk to him."

"You won't have to wait very long, Elektra," someone said from behind her. She turned toward the voice. Male. Gravelly. Familiar.

She felt the men backing off and turning alongside her.

A figure walked toward them from the E train, as if he'd just arrived at Penn Station to make a transfer. Average height, he wore a tailored suit and looked as relaxed as a single person on vacation.

Silvermane.

Silvio Manfredi was one of the old-school mob bosses, part of the five Maggia families that claimed dominion over New York City. But those days were long gone. Wilson Fisk had usurped the Five Families and become the boss of bosses—the Kingpin—years before. So, while goons like Manfredi still had power, they had to pay a tithe up the food chain to Fisk. They were far from bosses who could make unilateral decisions for their "families"—in fact, they'd become glorified underbosses by the time Fisk was done. Elektra had learned this the hard way—when she'd worked for the Kingpin as his chief assassin, she'd seen him exert power over the likes of Manfredi, stamping down dissent and making it clear the "Maggia" lived to serve him, and would never attain the heights of power the organized crime gang had enjoyed decades before.

But now things had changed again.

Manfredi had changed, too.

As the mobster stepped into the light, Elektra held back a gasp. The person who stood before her was still the man dubbed Silvermane for his silver hair—but he was now arguably more than a man. Underneath the suit, a silver chest plate shone through. While she knew Silvermane had augmented himself somewhat with cyborg technology years before, whatever had happened recently had pushed things even further. There was very little, aside from Silvermane's head and face, that seemed human.

"Like what you see, Elektra?"

Elektra got into a fighting stance. She was sure she could handle the man—and his goons—but the threat level had just increased significantly. She wasn't just brawling with a handful of clunky cyborgs now.

"I decided to treat myself to a few . . . upgrades. Especially since we lost dear Wilson not long ago," Silvermane said, his head and body moving in a strange, mechanical way—motions that would seem natural to any regular person were stilted and stiff. Someone's idea of how people should move or act. "The boss of bosses must be powerful, you see. Especially when filling such big shoes."

"You must be getting senile, Manfredi," Elektra said, pulling out both her sai and crouching in front of the aging gangster. "Unless I missed your promotion."

Silvermane swung his metallic arm toward Elektra, but she was able to flip backward and dodge the blow. Still, she was surprised at his speed. This wasn't just a slight power-up. Somehow Silvermane had a completely new body—and it meant he was strong, fast, and deadly.

"I don't want to hurt you, Elektra." He stepped toward her. "In fact, I'm quite glad you were the first to respond to my show of power. I could use an ally like you."

Elektra didn't hesitate. She lunged forward and sent a sai into his knee. Sparks flew as the blade connected with his cyborg leg, and she took some pleasure as the hybrid monster shrieked in pain. Apparently his sensors were working fine.

She stepped back as he reeled in anguish.

"You'll regret that," Silvermane said. Elektra watched as the leg seemed to repair itself in real time, the hole she'd created closing itself. "I'm not just a two-bit gangster you can push around anymore. I've been given a gift. We all have."

Silvermane motioned toward his men, who were tightening their circle around her. That's when she saw it—their faces melting away, replaced by horrific metallic skulls that were beneath the flesh all along. These were not humans, Elektra realized—they were abominations. People twisted and contorted by science to serve some evil end.

One of them reached for Elektra, but she pivoted out of the way, sending a kick into its midsection—a hit that barely seemed to affect the creature but which shot pain through her foot.

This was not going to be easy.

"Let it be known," Silvermane said, his voice booming now, his cyborg body creating some kind of microphone effect, "that the underworld answers to me now. To the *new* Kingpin of Crime—*Silvermane.*"

The mob boss laughed with a fervor that was more than unsettling.

Elektra scanned the area around her. The station was truly a dead zone now—only Elektra, Silvermane, and his cyborg stooges remained. She could make an escape without worrying about bystanders—this was pure performance by Silvermane, and it was clear he wasn't planning on killing anyone.

But what was the fun in that?

She jumped, unsheathing the long katana blade holstered on her back, and swung the sword widely—connecting with three of the four men, sending them all reeling backward. As she landed, she heard the metallic thumps of their bodies hitting the Penn Station linoleum. Then she heard something else—the rapid thump, thump of the last cyborg's feet as he approached from behind.

She didn't even look; instead, she leapt up and sent her feet backward. She connected with the assailant's head—hard, knocking him back awkwardly.

Now it was just her and Silvermane.

She got into a fighting stance, bouncing gingerly on her heels as the mafioso stepped closer—his air of invincibility gone. He was cautious now, wary. Good. That's how she liked it. She had learned over the years, when trained by Stick, and years later by the deadly collective of ninja assassins known as the Hand, to make every movement count—to strike clearly and with focus, rather than waste energy or time on subterfuge. If you know what to do, it's best to do it once and well, rather than overwhelming an opponent with distractions or trickery. Battle was a game of strength and guile. If you had both, you used them, period. She was not in a hurry to battle Silvermane, but neither was she afraid of the wired-up old man.

But then something happened.

Behind Silvermane, a burst of light—the explosion blinding Elektra.

She could only make out shapes, Silvermane's big form turning toward the light. Then a strong, deep *thunk* sound, followed by a low moan. Silvermane's voice. As the explosion died down, Elektra's vision cleared, and she saw the cyborg mobster leaning over, a giant sword thrust through his chest and heart. He was clutching at the weapon. And he was bleeding.

Perhaps he was not all metal after all.

"Help . . . help me . . ." Silvermane muttered in a low, fading voice.

Elektra didn't move, just watching as the man crumpled to the ground, moving slightly before stopping completely—his body crashing down to the floor, a growing puddle of dark blood forming under him.

But that didn't interest Elektra. What interested her was what happened beyond the body. The bright light had faded, leaving only a figure, running quickly toward the E train on the opposite end of the Penn Station platform, in its wake. Elektra spared a final glance for Silvermane and sprinted toward the culprit.

She could barely make the person out from this distance, but the fact that Penn Station was basically empty gave her a clearer view. They were lithe, had another sword—and were fast as hell. Elektra was no slouch, but she knew she wouldn't be able to reach them on pure speed. But how?

"Elektra!"

She spun around at the sound.

Matthew.

Daredevil caught up with her—already looking winded. His costume was dirty and torn, as if he'd fallen from a skyscraper and walked over to meet her.

"We have to chase that person," she said, motioning with her head. "Or I do, at least."

Daredevil placed a hand on her arm. "No, we need a plan."

Elektra shook free of his grip and glared at him.

The figure was gone by now. There was no point running after them. But they were gone because Matthew had intruded.

"Where have you been?" she asked. She found herself feeling less concern—and more judgment. She was angry with him now, no longer worried.

"It's a . . . it's a long story."

He was sweating. He looked like shit.

"Matthew, you're not well."

He smiled. More of a wince than a smile, actually.

"Uh, Elektra . . . can we talk somewhere?"

TWENTY-EIGHT

THREE PEOPLE STOOD in the offices of Nelson & Murdock: Elektra, no longer in costume but dressed in what passed for regular clothes—long black leggings and a gray workout shirt; a seemingly alive Matt Murdock; and their guest—reporter Ben Urich, who had just walked through the door.

"Ah, Matt—good to see you. Didn't expect—"

"Hello, Ben," Elektra said.

Ben looked as if he'd been shocked by a frayed wire. Eyes wide. Moves skittish. He and Elektra had a history. When she first reappeared in Matt's life—reborn as an assassin for hire, working for the Kingpin—she'd shoved a sai blade into Ben's back, injuring him badly. They'd met a few times since then, but that injury was the kind of thing that was hard to fully get over.

Ben slid over to Foggy's desk, where he could watch them from a safe distance.

"There's Chinese food over there, on Becky's desk," Matt said, motioning with his chin. "Dakota North will be here shortly."

"The whole gang is coming together," Ben said with a smirk. "But I don't think I should have to remind you—I'm no super hero. I can play with you all being off the record up to a point, but if you say something newsworthy, I'll follow up on it."

"Did you consider, Ben," Elektra said, giving him a sly smile, "that perhaps you're here exactly for that reason?"

Ben looked at her but didn't respond.

Matt stood up. He winced slightly. He was still banged up—from the bomb, from the fall, the poison.

"Silvio Manfredi is dead," he said to his friends. "Stabbed viciously while battling Elektra in the middle of Penn Station. The Owl is still in a hospital bed, under twenty-four-hour surveillance. When I spoke to him in the hospital, he claimed he was also sliced and diced. Both men have one thing in common—they're former employees or underlings of Wilson Fisk. In the wake of the Kingpin's death, they were hurt or killed for trying to step into their dead boss's role. What does it mean?"

"Richard Fisk, too," Ben said, flipping through the pages of his notebook. Elektra and Matt turned toward him. "The Kingpin's son basically said he was scared for his life. He has security tailing him wherever he goes."

"Did he say why?" Elektra asked.

Ben looked at Matt. "He seemed to think the Arranger knew something—and that he was scared, too. Had even pulled Bullseye out of mothballs to serve as his security detail."

"Yes, discovered that one firsthand. . . ."

The front door swung open and Dakota North stepped in. She stopped a few paces into the office. "Wow, didn't expect the Street-Level Avengers to be having a meeting, Matt. You sure you want me here?"

Matt motioned for her to come inside. She closed the door and took a seat near Elektra. The two women exchanged slight smiles.

Matt turned to Dakota. "You said you had news?"

The P.I. pulled a notepad out of her back pocket and flipped to a page as she spoke. "Depends on your definition of news, and I realize we're in the company of an actual journalist, so take it with a grain of salt. . . . But yeah, I've got something newsworthy. It's about the gun."

"The gun?" Elektra asked.

Dakota nodded, not looking up. "The shell casings found on the scene match a gun Frank Castle liked to use—a subcompact Glock 26," Dakota said. "There are even some partial prints that match Castle on the gun the police have in custody."

"That feels pretty damning," Urich said.

"I would tend to agree, Ben," Dakota said. "Except for one thing. Castle didn't have that gun in his possession at the time of the murder. And that gun's casings don't match any of the other crimes linked to Castle with a Glock. But there is a gun that matches those crimes."

"What do you mean?" Matt asked, mouth agape. "Where's *that* gun?"

Dakota reached into her purse and pulled out a plastic bag. A plastic bag that contained a Glock 26, a model Matt could sense by its shape.

"It's right here," Dakota said.

Matt stepped toward Dakota, still unable to shake the surprise from his face.

"But how—who . . . ?"

Dakota put the bag back in her purse.

"I talked to Punisher's old friend Micro, who said he'd recently chatted with Daredevil," she said, giving Matt a knowing look. "He was kind enough to let me visit a few of Castle's more recent drop sites—places where he stashes hot weapons, reloads, recharges, and generally stays off the grid. I'll tell you, the guy could use an interior decorator, for sure."

"And this gun was there?" Matt said, beginning to pace around. "But it's not the gun the police claim shot the Kingpin?"

"And even if there's two guns—are we surprised the Punisher has more than one Glock?" Urich asked, forever the detail-oriented reporter. "The story doesn't fit perfectly."

Matt nodded. He started pacing again.

"Right, but I get what Dakota is hinting at. If Castle had some kind of sentimental connection to the gun she found, why would he suddenly use another here, to off Fisk?" Matt asked. "Are you following me?"

"Sure, Matt, I am—but it's a flimsy case, and I'm not a lawyer," Urich said. "You're expecting a jury to believe that Castle wouldn't use another gun to kill Kingpin, but he'd touch it and leave prints on it? And we should trust a gun someone found in Punisher's own drop site . . . ?"

"No, we are looking at a deception, not a cover-up," Elektra interjected. "The gun that killed Wilson Fisk is a Glock 26 and is the one in custody. It's just not the Punisher's, though he has handled it. So the question becomes—"

"Why would Castle use a new gun to kill Fisk, or—even worse—why would he touch a gun that eventually killed Fisk . . . ?" Matt said, still pacing. "It's not airtight, but it's something. A little daylight, barely. But it does poke a big hole in the prosecution's theory that it's one of his reliable weapons."

Dakota leaned back and sat on Matt's desk.

"Not a magic bullet, but something," she said. "Now, what about this Arranger guy? He's got Bullseye in his corner now?"

"Yes, he was clearly in the Arranger's employ when I went to talk to him. And I didn't get any information from Silkworth," Matt said, rubbing his chin. "Which means our next step is obvious."

Dakota grabbed a spring roll and took a bite before speaking. "So, we should all roll up on this Silkworth? Hell kind of a code name is 'Arranger,' anyway? What's next? The Coordinator?"

"That's exactly what I'm suggesting," Matt said. "But I'm going to be honest—I'm not up for doing it alone. If that psychopath is at his beck and call, I'm going to need all the reinforcements I can muster."

"Bullseye is not to be trifled with," Elektra said, staring down at her feet. She would know best. The assassin had killed her, once upon a time. "But I'm not sure if the Arranger is the mastermind we want him to be. The person who gutted Silvermane, and perhaps the person who hurt the Owl, didn't strike me as an old man. They were too fit, too fast."

"Maybe the Arranger is spending that retirement cash?" Dakota said. "He could've hired someone to do the deed, like he hired Bullseye."

"It's possible," Ben interjected. "Or he could think he's a target as well."

Matt looked at his watch. "It's getting late. Our visit to the Arranger might have to sit. I have to prep for opening arguments in the Castle case—"

"Uh, Matt—"

Matt turned to Ben, who was looking up at him, phone in hand. He didn't like the sound of the reporter's voice.

"What is it?"

"Check the news—it's not just the Owl and Silvermane anymore. Hammerhead's down, too."

Matt walked over to the television and flicked on the screen. The visuals would do little for him, but he could hear better than anyone in the room. He scrolled the channels until he got to NY1. The anchor's soothing voice took over.

"—the latest victim in a series of attacks targeting local mob leaders, the Maggia underboss known as 'Hammerhead' has been rushed to the hospital after an apparent attack while having dinner with colleagues in Little Italy. The gangster, who has never revealed his true name, was one of many organized-crime figures vying for power in the wake of alleged Kingpin of Crime Wilson Fisk's death. The attack, at famed Little Italy restaurant Umberto's, was brazen and targeted, according to bystanders—as a gang of armed gunmen stormed the eatery's entrance and opened fire on Hammerhead, who was enjoying a few dozen oysters with his colleagues. One eyewitness, who refused to identify themselves, claimed that another hooded figure entered the establishment and bludgeoned the Maggia strongman with a 'fiery blade.' Police have cordoned off the area and are not taking questions at this time. . . ."

Elektra flicked the screen off.

"Perhaps your preparations for the Punisher's trial will have to wait."

TWENTY-NINE

"HE'S WAITING FOR YOU, Counselor."

The guard motioned for Matt to enter the small interview room. He stepped in, breathing the stale air—the smell of dust and smoke and cheap paint. He could make out the shape of his client, and heard his heartbeat—calm, methodical. Matt heard his fingernails tapping on the faux-wood table. Heard the clink of the chains holding his legs together, and his arms. He didn't say a word as Matt rested his suitcase on the table and sat down.

"Is this what you wanted? What you hoped would happen?" Matt asked, without a trace of emotion. "This bloodshed. You must have known Fisk's death would lead to this."

"You give me too much credit, Murdock," Castle said after a long pause, looking down at his hands. He let out a breath. "And if I was a normal, average convict, I'd think you were backing out of your job right now. Can't defend someone you think is guilty, right?"

"I didn't say that," Matt said. "But you've given me nothing to work with—so I have to go by what I find myself."

Matt opened his briefcase and passed a manila folder to Castle. The Punisher didn't look at it. Didn't move to touch it.

"Forensic reports from the murder scene," Matt said. "And an accounting of the evidence collected. The bullets found in the Kingpin match the ones in the weapon you routinely carry, and the one you had that night. Same can be said about those in the cop, Sheehan."

Castle didn't even shrug. "What's your point?"

Matt slammed his briefcase shut.

"I'm saying, *Frank*—I need something. I need a sliver of hope if you want to get out of this," Matt said, standing up. "Unless this scenario is what you want. You somehow knew the killings and attacks would play out this way. But how can that be?"

"How can that be, huh?" Castle said with a chuckle, still not meeting Matt's gaze. "Funny how these things all just happen."

"You know what else is funny, Frank?" Matt said, leaning forward, his palms on the table. He could smell the sweat and dirt on Castle. The grime of incarceration. The grime he'd collected over the years—sleeping in flop houses, vans, cheap motels, and now, prison. Always running and gunning, murdering the people he perceived as evil while evading those entrusted to protect the law. "You didn't have that gun on you."

Matt heard it then. The spike of his heartbeat. He'd been caught off guard.

But he recovered fast. Castle looked up at Matt for the first time since he walked in.

"Hell you talking about, Murdock?"

"You may not want to beat this rap, Castle, but when you hired me, you hired the best. And I don't like to lose," Matt said, still standing. "And I think there's more going on here than you're willing to say. Someone was paying that cop—Sheehan—who was with you and Fisk a lot of money. So much money, they'd rather blow up a building than reveal the connection. These reports"—Matt motioned to the file—"they say the gun and bullets match. But I have my own investigator. She searched your last known drop site, and your last known crash pad. Your gun—the one that you used in your last dozen incidents, from dead dealers to murder suspects and white supremacists, the people you gunned down during your own crusade . . . *that* gun was still at your drop site. Kind of weird that the gun the police claim they have isn't your gun. Strange, don't you think?"

"Confusing, at best. What are you getting at?"

Matt picked up his suitcase and started toward the door.

"I'm getting at something complicated. I'm getting at a bigger conspiracy that isn't just about you gunning down a criminal, like you always do," Matt said, looking at Castle from the doorway. "And I'm trying to figure out where you fit in, Frank. And why . . . But I'll get there. Because I know one thing—you might be a cold-blooded killer, you might have a twisted, bloodthirsty sense of justice. But you didn't kill that cop—and I'm not sure you killed Wilson Fisk, either. And I want to know why you're risking taking the rap for both; you could've sent word out that you took them both out and not turned yourself in. It's not like they would have ever captured you. No, not you. So I have to ask myself: What's so important that you'd risk your life like this?"

Castle seemed to turn inward, his response a muted bark: "I don't have to answer any of this," he said, almost petulantly.

"You're right, you don't," Matt said. "But that won't stop me. I believe in justice, even for you. And you might have to brace yourself for being on the outside before you planned. What does that do to your grand scheme?"

The door thudded shut as Matt walked down the long hall toward the front desk and the parking lot. He listened the whole way—hoping to catch something. A curse. A muttered response. Instead, he was met with dead silence.

THIRTY

SIX MONTHS AGO.

Daredevil let himself drop down to the floor in front of Wilson Fisk's sprawling desk. He could hear the mobster's slight intake of breath. Surprise, but not panic. The sounds of the city were muffled even to him because of the thick glass surrounding the massive penthouse space Fisk reserved for his business dealings. Fisk's haven felt apart from the living, breathing metropolis that was New York, and every time Daredevil stepped inside, he felt detached from the place he sought to protect—like he was being dragged underwater. Like he only had so much air left.

It was past midnight, but Daredevil knew he could find his adversary here. Though Wilson Fisk exuded confidence and ease, the Kingpin had reached the top of the New York underworld—a few times, by his count—by sheer force of will, hard work, and cunning. No one put in more time than Fisk. Certainly none of his underlings, like his son Richard, Jimmy "the Whale" Sabini, or the various Maggia family chiefs Fisk had stomped down and forced to kiss his ring. Even at the top, Wilson Fisk was showing his lieutenants how it was done.

"Daredevil," Fisk said calmly. "I assume you have good reason to enter my private office after midnight . . . on a school night, no less."

Daredevil walked toward the desk, casual and relaxed.

"Don't you have law books to study?" Fisk leaned back in his chair. "Now that you're practicing again, I suppose. It's quite amazing how you built yourself back up from nothing. It was just a few years ago that you were disbarred, homeless, and missing in action. Kudos to Matt Murdock."

Daredevil didn't respond.

"The funny thing, though," Kingpin said, standing up and walking around his giant desk, his huge, hulking frame dominating the room, "to me, at least—is that downfalls can happen again. I know quite a lot about building myself up from nothing. I did it once before, when I established my rule over this city. I did it again, when you and your trickery pulled me back down into the dirt. And while I don't hold grudges, *Man Without Fear* . . ."

The mobster smiled. The hiss of his breath, sharp and quick, through his teeth, sent a chill through his visitor.

". . . I never forget, either," he continued. "And you crossed a line that no man should ever cross. You hurt me, Daredevil."

Daredevil knew exactly what Fisk was talking about. He'd orchestrated it. A multipronged effort to not only discredit Fisk as the self-styled "small businessman" who happened to luck into great wealth, but also to bring him down to the level of the petty criminals and thugs he ordered around like a five-star general. Daredevil had managed to implicate Fisk in a murder while also unraveling his business dealings—pointing to connections with white supremacist organizations like HYDRA—to the point where Fisk had become a pariah, an outcast from the socialite echelon he'd become so used to walking through. Since then, Fisk had meticulously rebuilt his empire—one might argue stronger than before. It was a testament to his iron will and canny sense of survival. It had been the latest step in what felt like an endless cycle of collapse and rebuilding, of two men in constant combat, desperate to destroy the other—but walking parallel paths. Destroying each other, body and soul, over and over again.

But it was something Daredevil didn't want to stomach further. And he had the kind of evidence that just might drive the Kingpin back into his hiding spot forever.

They were less than a foot apart. Daredevil hadn't come to fight, but that didn't mean he wasn't ready to brawl if it lined up that way.

"Tell me now, Murdock," Kingpin said, taking another step toward him. "Why are you here? And make it fast. You're not welcome in my home. You never were."

Daredevil smiled. He noticed Fisk stiffening at the sight.

"Edgardo Salazar . . ." Daredevil said and waited. Fisk didn't react further. Not externally. But there was a slight uptick in his heartbeat. An acrid smell of sweat forming on his brow. "He's missing."

"Is he?" Fisk said. "That explains much. I was hoping to—"

"Spare me the *golly, gosh, gee* routine, Fisk," Daredevil said, shaking his head. "You knew as well as I did that Salazar was about to go into protection. That's why he's gone."

The giant figure shrugged slightly—an almost imperceptible movement.

"Protection? What was Edgardo so afraid of?"

Daredevil took in a long breath.

"Salazar worked for you. Oversaw parts of the Bronx and Queens. Was a point man. He even spoke to you directly a few times, not just Silkworth. He could testify to your crimes. And now he's gone." Daredevil tried to remain calm, clenching his fists to temper his voice. He knew Fisk noticed it and hated himself for showing just how angry he was. "You took him out the second the news found its way to your desk."

Fisk let out a low, humorless laugh.

"We're more alike than you think, Daredevil," he said with a dry laugh. "Two men scraping and pushing and clawing to get what they deserve. Eager and hungry to impose their beliefs on a world fraught with chaos, hatred, and stupidity. You seem to think you're some glimmering beacon of justice—I'm merely looking to take care of myself. My family. My justice is different than yours, but is it that different from the mayor you voted for? The police commissioner? I'll keep an eye out for Edgardo. I like him. He has a lovely family. How is that reporter friend of yours, by the way? Urich? Or that blowhard, Foggy Nelson? It's a dangerous city out there."

Daredevil understood what the last comment meant.

But Daredevil hadn't played his last card yet.

"It's over, Wilson. I'm not here trying to bully you into an inadmissible confession. I'm a lawyer, remember? I'm here to tell you we don't need it."

A flutter of the criminal's heart. The rumble of his stomach. A screeching tire a few blocks away. The curses and screams of two drivers immediately following a fender bender. He felt himself connecting with the city again—past the Kingpin's defenses. His own senses were more powerful than anything Fisk could erect to disconnect him from the Kitchen.

Daredevil focused his senses back on Fisk. On his breathing—faster now. He was curious. Angry.

"You come here to toy with *me*? I thought you were smarter than that."

"I'm not toying," Daredevil said, tossing a USB drive onto the desk behind Fisk. "Consider this an early peek at discovery. My treat. Salazar gave his closed-circuit confession—as much of it as he could—a few days before he disappeared. It's over, Wilson. Whatever smoke and mirrors you used to reclaim this life—this place—isn't going to get you out of this one."

Fisk laughed. The laugh of confidence and hubris. But it couldn't mask the truth. Wilson Fisk, the Kingpin of Crime, was scared.

"You think a jury is going to believe the fictional ramblings of a convicted drug felon over me?" Fisk scoffed. "Surely you know better than that, Murdock."

"She's going to testify as well, Wilson," Daredevil said, in a hushed tone. He took a step back, then another—he was inching back as Fisk turned toward him. "She knows all your secrets."

Fisk paused a beat. "It's not possible," he said flatly at last.

"Imagine the breathless new anchors when the story breaks," Daredevil said, motioning across his body, as if suggesting a name in lights. "'Vanessa Fisk, wife of alleged mob kingpin Wilson Fisk, reveals an array of underworld secrets—implicating ex-hubby.' She's the perfect witness, Wilson—because I know, better than anyone else, you can't bring yourself to kill her. She's Teflon. Surely you know what that's like."

Daredevil could hear the mobster's teeth grinding. Could feel the threads in Fisk's expensive shirt straining as his chest swelled with rage.

"It's time for you to leave, Daredevil," Fisk said, in a muffled, angry tone Daredevil had never heard before. "I will not ask you again."

Daredevil backed away and gave Fisk a wave before he turned around. "See you in court, Willie."

((((( )))))

In the coming days, Daredevil would make the rounds. He'd visit Kingpin's various underlings—and the few remaining opponents he had. It was a wide array of criminals. From the savvy and competent, like Black Tarantula on the Upper East Side, to the mostly inept, like the Owl in eastern Long Island. But his message was the same: Wilson Fisk was going down; it was only a matter of time.

The responses ranged from the muted to the definitely intrigued. But Daredevil didn't need to rely on surface reactions. He could sense something deeper. The universal response was excitement. These men, who'd toiled for Wilson Fisk for years, who'd absorbed every kind of humiliation in the service of Fisk's unilateral control of the New York underworld, were primed to help him fall—even if it meant stepping out of their own criminal comfort zones to stick their necks out.

"You'll have to decide," Matt told the various gangsters, "whether you want to go down with Fisk, or hang on to your own shingle for as long as you can."

The message was clear: *Don't get in my way.*

It felt good; it felt like there was some real momentum. With Vanessa Fisk's affidavit, and the evidence about Edgardo Salazar, it felt—to Daredevil—that this might truly be the time for Kingpin to fall.

But as he had these thoughts, these optimistic visions, he'd think back to that night in Fisk's office. To moments after he left the Kingpin's sight, as he sat perched in an air vent, above the entrance to the office—he could still hear his nemesis talking, pacing. The quick intakes of breath. The hurried tapping of a burner phone. The mobster's tongue hastily licking his lips. The ringing of the phone. Two rings. Three. That familiar voice on the other line. The hard swallow of saliva, followed by a hasty wiping of his sweat-soaked forehead. The slight smell of fire and brimstone.

Daredevil savored the words Fisk whispered into the receiver.
"We have a problem."
The Kingpin had been scared, and that was worth something.
Daredevil should have known it wouldn't last.

((((( )))))

Daredevil hadn't heard the whoosh of the bo staff until it was too late. He fell forward, into a roll that stopped a few feet short of the edge of the rooftop. He sprang to his feet, hands raised, ready for a fight. He hadn't been expecting to face him, though.

"You dumb clown," Stick said, shaking his head as he leaned on the staff. Everything Stick did belied a calm and grace that Matt knew he could never attain. His mentor, blind like him, gifted with powerful senses like him, had achieved a command of his abilities that—paired with his own mental training and discipline—gave the impression that everything was easy for Stick. Matt knew it wasn't true, but also understood just how hard it was to get to the point where you could fake it.

"Stick," Daredevil said, not hiding his surprise. "Where have you—"

"No time for small talk, Murdock, no time for those stupid regular-people things," Stick said with a smirk. "Bad things are coming your way, so you'd better get your head out of your ass, because it's not going to announce itself like the clowns you punch."

Daredevil took a step toward Stick. He wanted to hug his teacher—to just sit and listen to him. To learn more from him. But he also knew this would not be a long visit. This was a warning, a brief detour from the new life Stick had chosen for himself.

"What is it?"

"It's you, dim bulb," Stick said. He tapped Daredevil not very gently on the head with the end of his staff. "You always think too hard. Play the game too much. But life isn't a game, Murdock. It's a mess—of feelings and senses and everything else. You're playing with fire again."

Daredevil bristled.

"With Fisk? He's going to pay for his crimes," Daredevil said.

Stick's loud laugh surprised Daredevil enough for him to jump slightly.

"His crimes? You're a real one, Murdock—tweaked in the head. If you'd stuck with me, ignored your heart, used your mind, you'd understand that all this stuff"—Stick waved his staff out toward the noise and smell of Hell's Kitchen—"it's nothing. There's a bigger battle going on. For the soul of this burnt-out planet. Bigger stuff than con men and thugs. But you think small, Murdock. Always worrying about a few blocks of Manhattan, not the real thing."

Stick leapt toward Daredevil, landing a few inches in front of him. His old teacher stuck a finger up at Daredevil's face, waving it hastily.

"This cycle's never gonna end for you, Murdock," Stick said. "You've been battling Fisk since you first got your gift. You think it's gonna end now? You're dumber than I thought."

Daredevil was losing his patience.

"What do you mean, Stick?" he asked, tapping his hand away. "Why do you think you can come here and lecture—"

Stick laughed again.

"*Lecture?* You're beyond lecturing, Murdock," Stick said, shaking his head. "But I've got a soft spot or you—just like with Elektra. Had high hopes for both of you. Being brain-dead asidc, I don't wanna see you go down like that. You put stuff into motion you can't even imagine. You've disrupted the balance. All for another shot at Willie Fisk? It always ends the same. One of you gets knocked down, then you dust yourself off and do it again. Insanity. Defined. You're an idiot for that. I thought I taught you better, lunkhead. Did you forget that girl you sent flying through that window?"

Stick's words, while offensive, were also not chosen at random. And Daredevil felt himself being pulled back into his own past. The night of his father's greatest—and final fight. He'd come to cheer Battlin' Jack on. But it'd become something else. Matt had chosen the path of revenge—had stood over the man who'd ordered the death of Jack Murdock. But he'd gotten careless. Cocky, almost. He wanted to take down the Fixer's last henchman—a man named Angelo. To make him pay for what he'd done to his father.

But instead, Matt had made a grievous error—had accidentally sent an innocent falling to her death. Matt had dragged himself over the coals numerous times—reliving each moment, trying desperately to figure out what he could have done differently to save her. Each time, coming up short. Stick knew this. The words were meant to be more than cutting. They were meant to draw blood.

"No, I didn't mean to," Daredevil said, more to himself than Stick.

But who would know better, Daredevil thought? Stick had also known what happened—had been the person Matt ran to, screaming, in the wake of the accident. But why was this all coming up now?

Another not-so-gentle tap on the head.

"Is it clicking for you yet, Murdock?" Stick asked, exasperated. "You putting the pieces together yet, you idiot? I'm trying to help you—trying to spare you years of pain and hurt. But I can't spell it out anymore."

Daredevil remembered Stick, after the accident—taking Matt aside and trying to impart some knowledge, trying to center him. *Part of the gig is avoiding the darkness,* Stick had said then. *Avoiding the bad energy that can consume us, trickle into our lives, into our bloodstream.*

Even when you make mistakes, kid—you know who you are. I thought I taught you better, lunkhead.

Then he remembered the woman's presence, revealing something new and strangely familiar at the same time. Still, even then, Matt couldn't place her. But he knew it would cost him.

THIRTY-ONE

"WHAT ARE YOU DOING?"

Matt heard the words before he spotted Melinda Torres standing outside of the offices of Nelson & Murdock. It was a little before eight in the morning and Matt was balancing a latte on a stack of case folders while struggling to reach his keys with his other hand.

"Melinda, hey, I'm sorry—"

"This isn't a personal call," Melinda said, crossing her arms. "Though we have plenty to discuss on that subject."

Matt wasn't surprised. He'd been so busy traipsing around the city in red tights he'd barely made time for Melinda. It wasn't an ideal look for a sort-of-boyfriend who'd just spent a while in the hospital for some strange, undisclosed reasons. He'd had a lot on his mind, but it's not like he could exactly vent to her about cyborgs running rampant in New York, or battling Bullseye.

Instead, he'd just sealed himself off.

Not the best idea.

But that wasn't why she was here.

"What do you know about Mezinis and Charleston?"

Matt froze. His mind whirred. He knew the name, of course. But only because he'd overheard it while spying on Melinda Torres having a conversation with an officer in the Internal Affairs department. The clue had eventually led Matt, as Daredevil, to Terry Sheehan, brother to the officer the Punisher allegedly killed along with the Kingpin. The rest had gone nowhere—aside from a massive Staten Island explosion that had left Matt hospitalized. Why was she asking about this now?

"Nothing. . . . Is that a law firm?" Matt said. He could tell from Melinda's heartbeat she wasn't buying it at all.

"Don't lie to me, Matt," she said.

Matt opened the office door and prayed Foggy and Becky weren't in yet. Melinda followed him in. He motioned for her to step into his office and closed the door behind her. He dropped the case folders on his desk and took a long sip from the coffee. He was going to need it.

"Melinda, look, I know I've been—"

"Focus, Matt," Melinda said, refusing his proffered seat. "Where did you hear that name?"

"I have no idea. What does it matter? What is this even about?"

Melinda crossed her arms. He could smell her office deodorant on her—the one she kept in her desk. Had she slept at the precinct? It didn't matter now.

"You're interviewing people—Sheehan's family and friends—and you're asking them about a company named Mezinis and Charleston. My question stands. Where did you hear that name?"

Matt flipped open one of the folders and hastily turned a few pages.

"It must have come up in one of my interviews or research," he said. "Can you tell me why this matters?"

Melinda walked up to Matt and tapped him on the chest.

"You're a terrible liar, you know that?" she said, not a hint of affection in her voice. "But I will be very clear with you, okay? The only people who are talking or should be talking about that company are me and my staff. If you somehow have a leak there, I need to know about it. Because I know of only two people, counting myself, who have heard that name uttered in relation to Sheehan, and the other one *isn't* you. So if you're using information you got unfairly, not only are you in deep shit, but I've lost a lot of respect for you, Matt. And that's a big problem if you expect to spend more time with me."

"Melinda, please—"

She turned around and walked out of his office, slamming the door behind her. Matt plopped down on his chair. The door squeaked open and Matt straightened, hopeful it was Melinda, eager to fix things. But it was Foggy, looking sheepish and confused.

"Your friend seems pretty mad," he said with a shrug.

"You still pissed at me, too, Foggy?" Matt asked.

"Not as mad as she was, no," Foggy said, stepping inside Matt's cluttered office. "But, honestly, still not over it. Got a minute?"

Matt motioned around his office.

"I think I have more than one," he said with a smile.

Foggy sat down across from him and folded his arms.

"We've got a big problem," Foggy said. "And honestly, you're lucky you never bothered to take me off the case in the eyes of the court, because otherwise, you might be looking at some kind of disciplinary hearing."

Matt stiffened.

"What is it?"

"The prosecution is moving to have you removed from the case," Foggy said. "They claim you have a personal vendetta against Wilson Fisk, which creates a conflict—you defending Frank Castle is a problem for them."

"A conflict?" Matt asked, exasperated. "Fisk is dead. There's no conflict in wanting someone dead. And even if I wanted him dead, what does it matter if I'm defending the guy they think did it? If anything, it makes it easier—"

"Matt, I get it, trust me," Foggy said, interrupting. "But this is the game. Motions, delays, hearings—you know as well as I do this is how we play big-ticket cases. They want you off the case. They think because you also seemed to want Fisk gone, that's going to twist how you defend Castle. . . . It's a long shot, but for some reason they want to kick the can down the road."

Matt rubbed his chin. The prosecutor, James Sprenger, was an old hand in the DA's office. Matt had faced off with him often. They shared a mutual respect. Sprenger played by the rules and was an old-school attorney. He put the time in and didn't get too creative with how he prosecuted cases. This instance felt the same—in Sprenger's view, the case against Frank Castle was irrefutable: Castle was at the scene of the crime, if you believed the forensic evidence the prosecution was building their case on. Castle had a track record for being a murderer of criminals and corrupt cops. There were two dead bodies—a criminal and a cop. Case closed. Matt knew it was a tricky case to defend, not just because the state was alleging Castle was on the scene, but because of the huge public awareness surrounding the case. You'd be hard-pressed to find a NYC resident who didn't know Wilson Fisk. He was John Gotti in overdrive. You either feared Fisk because you worked for him, idolized him because you admired his defiance of the norms of society, or hated him because he stood for everything wrong with the world. Everyone knew him. Everyone had an opinion of him. It was a recipe for a challenging jury pool, and even more challenging for a fair trial. So, Sprenger didn't have to get complicated with his prosecution. Which made this move baffling. Someone wanted Matt off the case.

"Matt? You there?"

"Yes, I'm just . . . processing. This doesn't feel like Sprenger."

"Well, it is. I have the filing on my desk. We need to respond. I know there's no *there* there, but we have to do the work," Foggy said.

Matt started to pace behind his desk. He could hear Foggy's fingernails grating on his tailored pants.

"Jesus. You gotta talk to me, Matt, or this case is going to blow up in both our faces," Foggy said, his warm expression now a frown. "I know I told you to take the case and, well, shove it—but it doesn't seem like you're doing anything. It's falling apart around us. I'm hearing from the prosecution almost every day, and they don't seem to know I'm not involved."

Matt shook his head.

"Foggy, I'm sorry—there's been a lot going on. . . ."

"Matt, there's *always* a lot going on with you," Foggy said, leaning forward in the seat, elbows on his knees. "But this isn't a simple case. We have a client who doesn't want to work with us. We're up against one of the best prosecutors in the DA's office. We have a prominent underworld figure gunned down by a vigilante a lot of people identity with for some reason, and a lot of people hate. On top of that, he allegedly killed a cop, too, which isn't exactly popular. I've got reporters calling me a few times a day, desperate for any kind of clue as to what kind of defense we're gonna present, and I have nothing to tell them. And I also have no idea what evidence you or Dakota have gathered, and I don't think you've gone through any of the discovery evidence, either. The trial starts in a few weeks, and—"

Matt raised a hand, a sign of surrender.

"I get it. We need to figure this out," Matt said. He could hear the defeat in his own voice. "Will you help me?"

He knew Foggy would—knew before he responded. Could hear the slow intake of breath. The calming of his heartbeat. The quick double-tap of his left foot. Foggy Nelson was like a brother to Matt. Had seen him through peaks and valleys. Had helped pull him out of the gutter the Kingpin had shoved him into not long before, and had helped him send the Kingpin into exile. An exile they hadn't expected him to crawl out of.

"I know this is personal for you," Foggy said, looking up at the ceiling, as if desperate for some clue. "I remember what Fisk did to you. How could I forget? I was the one who spent my days and nights trying to get you out of it—up from that clinic and practicing law again. He crushed you into dust. But you can't let that cloud anything."

"I'm a lawyer. Before anything else, I'm a lawyer. It's not about Fisk," Matt said, locking eyes with Foggy. "I'm not going to pretend that I didn't grapple with it. That I didn't struggle. I didn't cry a tear for Wilson Fisk. I think he probably deserved to die. But not like that. And I'm not the person who gets to decide that. I'm also not even sure Frank Castle is innocent. But in this country, it's innocent until proven guilty, not the other way around. And no one was stepping up to give Castle the fair shake every person deserves. He would've eaten any public defender alive. We owe him that much. I'll type up a response to Sprenger. Then you and I can get our ducks in row on this case. Jury selection is around the corner and I don't want to drop the ball."

He felt a pang of guilt as he finished his speech. To Matt, the words were true. Technically. But he couldn't shake another feeling, one he'd tried to bury deep inside. A feeling that he was doing this—defending Castle—not to ensure he got a fair shake, but to figure out what the hell the vigilante was up to, and what it meant in relation to Wilson

Fisk. Was he lying to his friend? Matt wasn't sure. But it didn't feel good either way.

Matt walked past Foggy toward the main office area.

Foggy clapped.

"Now we're talking," Foggy said, getting to his feet. "That's the Matt Murdock we need."

Matt hoped Foggy was right.

((((( )))))

"Who leaked it, Ben?"

Daredevil tried to keep his voice level, but he knew he was failing. He felt the flimsy newsprint crunch in his fist, the ink staining his red gloves. A few hours after his impromptu meeting with Foggy, Matt Murdock had decided to walk over his response to Sprenger's spurious motion—only to feel his own familiar features on the cover of the *Daily Bugle*'s afternoon edition:

STAR DEFENSE ATTORNEY HAD
VENDETTA AGAINST FISK, SOURCES SAY

The headline alone was enough to send Matt reeling, but it was the byline that served as the gut punch—Ben Urich.

"You know I can't tell you that," Ben said, wheeling his office chair around and leaving Daredevil perched on his windowsill.

"You couldn't be bothered to call me for comment?"

Ben sighed.

"Matt, give me some credit, will you? If you ask Becky, I'm sure she'll tell you I called," Ben said, his voice sopping with annoyance. "Four times."

He was right. Becky had been after him as he left Foggy's office, but Matt had waved her off. It wasn't her job to take messages either. This was on him. He should've listened. It felt like everything was raining down on him at once.

"But you know it's not true—why write the piece at all?"

"Do I, though?" Ben said, exasperated. "Where's the lie? The Sprenger filing is public, for all to see. Your response will be, too—and I'll update the piece to reflect that."

"It's smoke and mirrors. Someone is trying to distract from the case itself," Daredevil said, stepping into Ben's tiny office. "They're feeding you this story."

Ben slammed a hand on his desk.

"When are you going to learn, goddammit, that I'm a reporter first? I'm your friend, sure—and hell, you know as well as I do the secrets I've kept to protect you . . . but this? I got the filing from a verifiable source. And it's true, Matt. You hate Fisk's guts. Have said as much publicly on a number of occasions. What am I supposed to do here? Put an iron dome around any press that might tie into you or your life? You're defending a guy that most of the city thinks killed the Kingpin—and a cop on top of it all. It's the hottest story in town, and people want to know more about it."

Daredevil took a deep breath.

"Someone is trying to tear this all down," Daredevil said. "Someone is trying to kill off or hurt anyone who might step on the Kingpin's throne. Someone is trying to derail this defense. The pieces are there."

"What do you think is happening, then?" Ben said, spinning his chair around, his back to Matt. "All I can do is report the news. If you have intel, I can chase it. The second you figure out who's behind all this—if such a person exists—slide the folder under my door. Lord knows you've done as much before. But I can't do it all myself."

"Ben, I—"

"Spare me, Matt—I'm not mad at you. But we all have to live our lives. Not everything hinges on how it affects Daredevil, all right?" Ben said, some sympathy in his voice. "Do I think someone nudged Sprenger to make the filing to make you look bad? Sure. Could I prove that? No. But someone's got your number—and they're doing everything they can to shake your foundation. I'll help you if I can, but you have to jump first."

Daredevil leapt back out the window without another word.

THIRTY-TWO

DAREDEVIL SENSED the sleek sedan pull up to the Long Island mansion. It was well past midnight, and the suburban streets surrounding the giant house were empty. It was oddly quiet, too. He wasn't used to venturing this far out from the city, but duty called.

He leapt down from one of the balconies and felt the soft grass as he landed. He positioned himself just to the left of the house, blocked from view by a set of giant bushes. He didn't need to see the two men talking, but they needed to see him. He'd heard the conversation from a few blocks away.

"You sure you're up for this, boss?"

"I said I'm sure, Cicero—quit your yappin', all right? I want to be home. I want to be where my guys are. If there's someone going around gunnin' for us, I want to be behind the gate."

Hammerhead sounded out of breath and muffled, his words wheezing out of his mouth. His breathing was jagged, and he smelled of antiseptic and the giant chicken parm he'd wolfed on his way back to the Island. No matter how injured he was, Hammerhead needed a nice meal to cap off the night.

Daredevil heard the engine shut down and Cicero put the car in park. Then the mob underling got out and dashed to the trunk. The sound of thin rubber tires on asphalt—a wheelchair. Cicero pulled it next to the passenger side and opened the door. Hammerhead winced and groaned as he stepped out of the car and onto the seat of the wheelchair.

The billy club connected with Cicero's temple, knocking him backward with a yelp. The thud of skull and concrete signaled to Daredevil to move in.

"Hey, Cicero—what the hell? What's goin' on?"

"Heard your thick skull took a beating, Hammerhead," Daredevil said, crouching in front of the injured mobster. Hammerhead tried to move away, but realized the car was blocking him.

"Daredevil . . . what gives? I ain't got no beef with you. I need to get inside, to rest. Doctor's orders," Hammerhead said. "You gotta gimme a break, y'see?"

Daredevil could sense Hammerhead's temperature rising. Hurt or not, Hammerhead was not someone to be trifled with. After an accident, the man who'd take the moniker "Hammerhead" had most of his skull replaced with a powerful metal alloy by an underworld scientist named Jonas Harrow. The operation left the top of his skull flat and wide—hence the nickname. In the intervening years, Hammerhead had carved out a slice of the underworld pie, and created a persona ripped from the Twenties gangster serials Hammerhead loved. The act was no longer one to the gangster, who dressed the part and talked like a mediocre Edward G. Robinson impression.

"Someone's got major beef with you," Daredevil said, not moving, "and I need to know who it is, Hammerhead. You're gonna help me."

"Help you? Whaddaya think, I'm some kind of yellow-belly?" Hammerhead exclaimed. "Some kind of rat? Fisk might be gone—but the rules ain't changed."

Daredevil grabbed one of the wheels and yanked back—hard. The pull sent Hammerhead spilling out onto the ground. Part of him landed on his underling, Cicero, who'd been on his way to getting back up to his feet. Now both gangsters were sprawled out in the driveway.

"Hey, what was that for? You make a habit of hurting the suffering, Daredevil?" Hammerhead yelled, pulling himself to a sitting position. "You think just 'cause I'm laid up now I won't remember this?"

Daredevil stepped toward Hammerhead and leaned forward, his face close to the gangster's exaggerated cranium.

"The only thing I care about you remembering, Hammerhead," Daredevil said, "is who did this to you."

Hammerhead looked at Daredevil, then at Cicero, who was pulling himself together.

"You repeat any of this, Cicero, you're done," Hammerhead said, his voice like gravel.

He turned back to Daredevil.

"Someone's trying to shake things up, Hornhead—and I got caught in it," he said.

"Who was it?"

"No idea," Hammerhead said, shrugging. "Wish I'd seen their face. All I remember is I'm shoving a few oysters down the gullet and suddenly it's raining bullets. We all duck down, thinkin' it's the Triads or some other gang, but next thing I know, the dust is clearing and I'm crawling over my own men—my own dead men. And this cloaked guy walks in, swords drawn. I can barely make 'em out before I feel one of them blades shoved into my guts, and I'm screaming, screaming, I tell you—never felt anything like that, and I been shot, you know? Last thing I remember before I black out, is the guy taking another poke at me, then sayin' something . . . something I don't think I can shake from my mind."

"What did they say?" Daredevil asked, trying to keep the curiosity from his voice. The aging gangster let out a croak of a laugh before continuing.

"He said . . . it was weird, I remember that much . . . didn't think I'd memorize it, but the guy said, 'The ministers of kings should learn to moderate their ambition . . . the higher they elevate themselves above their proper sphere, the greater the danger that they will fall.'"

THIRTY-THREE

LOUIS XIV. Whoever was going around killing and injuring the Kingpin's former lieutenants had a fondness for French monarchs. They also wanted to send a message. To the mob, and, Daredevil thought—to him, too.

He'd left Hammerhead splayed out in his driveway and made his way back to Manhattan. Specifically, an apartment building on the Upper East Side. He changed in an alley next to the building and tried to casually make his way to the doorman. He scanned his cane a few paces in front of him and walked into the building's lobby.

"Can I help you?" the doorman asked as Matt entered.

"I'm here to see Melinda Torres," Matt said with a smile. Whether she wanted to see him was another story, but Matt was stubborn, above all else.

The doorman nodded and walked to an inner office behind the front desk. Matt heard him place a call. Heard Melinda's voice on the other end. Angry, frustrated—but relenting. The doorman returned and motioned for Matt to head up. The doorman walked him over to the elevator and offered to ride up with him, but Matt waved him off.

He wasn't sure what he was going to say. Melinda had caught him in a lie—a lie he couldn't talk his way out of. He'd overheard her conversation with Gunderson, had plucked the name of the company funneling money to Sheehan, Mezinis & Charleston, and used it to gather info. That much was true. He couldn't pass the buck and blame Gunderson. So, he really had no other explanation, aside from the truth—that he'd spied on her somehow. A huge violation of trust. Especially in a relationship that was still figuring out where—

He heard it as the elevator approached Melinda's floor. Feet hurrying down the hall. The sound of a cold blade sliding against leather. The loud thump of boots kicking down a door, followed by a surprised, angry voice.

Melinda.

The elevator froze in place, a shrieking sound signaling something going wrong. Matt jabbed at the buttons, but there was no response. The elevator car was stuck between floors. He tried to breathe—to calm himself. And to listen. He heard Melinda order the assailant to back away—to put the sword down. Then the whoosh of air as the blade swung out. A pained scream. Matt couldn't make out the heartbeats—could barely make out Melinda's. There was a struggle. Then a whispered threat.

"If you only knew who you were sharing a bed with . . . Officer," the voice said, low, and angry. Seething. "Perhaps you'd realize what a criminal truly stands for. . . ."

Matt poked at the buttons again and, finally, after a moment, the elevator began to creak upward. The door opened on Melinda's floor and he leapt out, all pretense of being Matt Murdock gone. He rushed right—toward her apartment.

The door was ajar—there was the slight scent of smoke and burning paper. And a low moan. Melinda was on the floor, clutching her midsection. Matt stepped in and reached for her.

"Melinda—what? Are you okay? What happened?"

"They came in . . . stabbed me . . . losing blood . . ."

Matt pulled out his phone and hastily called an ambulance. There was blood everywhere—his hands were slick with it. He prayed she'd be okay.

"Tarantula . . . said his name was . . . Black Tarantula . . ."

Matt gritted his teeth. He hadn't expected that. Hadn't heard it, through the noise and chaos. But he should have.

In moments, the sirens from a pair of ambulances filled his senses. He guided the EMS personnel to Melinda's apartment, holding her hand as they loaded her on a gurney and sped her downtown to the nearest hospital. She was fading in and out of consciousness. Matt followed them into the emergency room. He watched as they wheeled her through a series of double doors. A few moments later, he was stopped—she was going into emergency surgery. He'd have to wait. Matt found himself in a sterile, quiet waiting room. He paced around. But he also listened.

He opened his senses. His hearing. His smell. His touch and taste. It was a trick Stick had taught him—though he doubted his old master would call it a "trick." It was a different way to use the powers he'd been gifted. Instead of hyper-focusing a single sense on one thing, he was casting a massive net, spreading out for city blocks. Listening, smelling, reaching for two words:

Black Tarantula.

It was akin to downloading thousands of gigabytes of information at once. Matt could sense things that were blocks, perhaps miles away. He thought back to Stick, to what he'd taught him—how to open himself up, his mind and body, and allow his senses to reach out. The strain was palpable. He could already feel a headache forming. Beads of sweat dripping down his head. He pushed harder. There had to be a clue nearby, and if he waited too long, that clue would be long out of his range. He felt it all. A conversation in the back seat of a rideshare. A steaming slice of buffalo chicken pizza. A body being slammed into the side of a police car. A muttered threat. The loud beats from someone's portable speaker. A bike tire screeching. Change jangling in a plastic cup. Lips sliding off each other. A nervous laugh. It was overwhelming—a complete sensory overload. But it was Matt's only option. He had to stay put—had to make sure Melinda was okay.

Then something. A low grunt. The voice was familiar. Matt focused. It was in Midtown somewhere. A hotel nearby. A sheepish voice. Hurried Spanish.

"¿Por qué me querrían a mi?"

Why would they want me?

Black Tarantula.

Carlos LaMuerto was the head of the small but powerful Argentinian mob in New York. They mostly stuck to trafficking—drugs, people, stolen goods. He didn't have territory in the traditional sense, like the Italian mobs or the Triads, all who answered to the Kingpin before his death. LaMuerto was an in-betweener. He dealt with everyone, but didn't carve out a space for himself. The kind of middleman organized crime needed. And Matt Murdock just located him.

Matt stepped out of the hospital waiting room and walked toward an orderly he recognized. The man spun around, surprised by Matt's appearance.

"Excuse me, but is there any word about the Torres woman?" Matt asked. He tried to give off an air of authority, but it didn't seem to be working. "She was wheeled in a few hours ago—"

The man shook his head. "I can't tell you anything about a patient, sir, you'll have to keep waiting," he said, motioning toward the room Matt was just in. "I'm sure her doctors will keep you posted."

Matt nodded.

There was no time. He listened in on the operating room. Beeps and muttered commands. Melinda's labored breathing. But something felt different—her heartbeat was cloudy. It was an experience Matt hadn't had before. He wondered if the Black Tarantula had somehow laced his blade with something. Had touching Melinda made a poison rub off on Matt? Was it tied to the poison Bullseye had used on him?

He thanked the staffer briefly, then walked toward the exit. He hoped Melinda would forgive him if she ever found out.

THIRTY-FOUR

"YOU CAN COME OUT NOW."

Carlos LaMuerto's voice shook Daredevil from his crouch, hidden behind the hotel room's large, built-in bar. LaMuerto, clad in his Black Tarantula costume, mask removed, stepped forward, the balcony door behind him, and looked straight at Daredevil.

"I wasn't expecting to see you tonight," he said.

Daredevil stepped toward LaMuerto and put up his fists.

"You have a lot to answer for, Carlos," Daredevil said, his voice coming across like an angry hiss. "Didn't take you for a killer."

Black Tarantula stopped mid-step.

"Killer? What are you talking about?" he said. His heartbeat remained consistent. He was genuinely confused. It gave Daredevil pause. "You come lurking into my room like some kind of stormtrooper and I'm supposed to know what the hell you're talking about?"

"Melinda Torres, the Internal Affairs officer—you broke into her house, stabbed her . . . why?"

Tarantula's heartbeat. Still keeping pace. No sign of anything.

What is going on here?

"You need to get your skull checked, Devil," Black Tarantula said, shaking his head. "I'll humor you for a second, but now I'm getting annoyed. I don't know any woman named Melinda Torres, much less an Internal Affairs lady. If your tomato-red ass needs to know, I was out to dinner with my family before coming here. How would I have time to—"

Then the lights went out. Followed by a loud crashing sound.

Daredevil felt the small shards of the balcony door scatter around him, slicing at him as they zoomed by.

The dark didn't matter to Daredevil, but he realized the switch wasn't for him. He felt the shapes—bodies, at least a dozen of them—appear, swinging into Tarantula's large room from the gaping hole in the balcony door. Small, lithe figures leaping down from the ceiling, swords and knives drawn. Then a larger, giant figure seemed to fill the space between the room and the open balcony. It didn't take long for Daredevil to recognize them—or her.

The Hand—and one of their fiercest warriors, Izanami.

Izanami was massive. Thick and tall, the assassin resembled an ancient oak tree—if it also moonlighted as a professional wrestler. Izanami's shape dominated Daredevil's radar sense. He tried to focus on the attackers, but he couldn't shake a question:

What was a mystical collection of ninjas doing here, in the hotel of a mid-level mob boss?

There would be no time to find out.

"Eliminate them both," one of the smaller figures said, motioning toward Izanami, who seemed to nod in response.

"The hell is happening? I can't see sh—"

Daredevil heard the whoosh of the blade as it entered Black Tarantula's midsection, followed by the pained and surprised gasp. His radar sense picked up the mobster's collapse, first to his knees, then completely to the floor. Daredevil could hear the blood gurgling up through his throat and spreading out over his face and the floor. He wouldn't last long in this state.

Daredevil took a few paces back. He was surrounded. The Hand were everywhere. Izanami seemed to step toward him haltingly.

"What is this?" Daredevil asked.

"This is *revenge*, Daredevil," a voice said. Daredevil recognized it: the Jonin, small and compact—field general to the Hand. "And the dawn of a new day."

The Jonin was Izanami's commander. This wasn't some errant operation; this was an official action. The Hand—the deadliest assassins Daredevil had ever faced—were back in New York City. But why were they targeting him?

There was no time to ponder. Daredevil swept his leg under the nearest three Hand members, sending them backward. Another approached from behind. Daredevil moved backward and grasped the ninja by his tunic, sending him hurtling forward toward Izanami, who sidestepped the body easily. Daredevil heard the tossed ninja scream in surprise as he fell over the balcony. As it connected with the street below, Daredevil heard the familiar hiss of the Hand assassin's body turning to dust. The same brimstone-like smell. The Hand were not your typical gang. They were fueled by a potent mix of mystical black magic and Nazi science—not dead but certainly not alive, so Daredevil didn't have to pull his punches battling them. But he still had to land them.

"Jonin, why are you here?" Daredevil asked as he yanked a sword away from another assassin and sent the blade back toward its user. The ninja hissed out of existence almost immediately. Down to eight, Daredevil thought as he continued. "I have no quarrel with the Hand now."

"How novel for you," the Jonin said. He was riding on Izanami's back now, pointing his lead attacker toward Daredevil. "But we cannot say the same for you—and your allies."

So, this was the play, Daredevil thought—the Hand was making a move to take over the New York underworld. And they were systematically taking out their foes—those that served Kingpin or dared step into the space he'd once filled—in order to do it.

Things were much worse than Daredevil could have ever imagined.

He felt a slash behind him—the sword barely grazing his back. The pain was immediate and sharp. Then an elbow to the face from another direction. He was having trouble keeping up with the swarm. Izanami hovered in the background, laughing to herself, Jonin barking out orders.

His radar sense was blurring a bit. He punched wildly, connecting with someone. He gripped an arm nearby and flung it in the opposite direction. He couldn't survive like this. But at the same time, his mind started to piece things together. The attacks on the various bosses. The attack on Melinda. The Hand was trying to fill the Kingpin's void, but also looking to eliminate anyone that might be a threat. Melinda knew about Mezinis & Charleston, perhaps a front for the Hand—that made her a threat, too. Daredevil had to clear out of here, recover, get his bearings. But he was feeling dizzy, groggy, losing a lot of blood. A punch hit his midsection. A kick to the face. Daredevil felt himself being tossed backward, crashing into a table on the other side of the hotel suite.

Daredevil looked up. The Hand assassins were stepping back, parting to either side as Izanami approached, Jonin by her side. The giant ninja grabbed Daredevil roughly, like a mother cat yanking a kitten up by the scruff of their neck. She slammed Daredevil into the far wall. He felt his body stiffen, pain shooting down his back.

"This is the great Daredevil," Izanami said. "After so much time . . . I had thought you'd get stronger. Better. But you're weak. A desperate man. You will be easy to break."

Daredevil didn't think. He let his strategic mind fade into the background as he tapped into instinct, training. The lessons learned over months with Stick, his mentor—leader of the Chaste, an order of warriors hell-bent on destroying the Hand. What would he do here?

I'd focus, stupid. Get your head on straight. Stop thinking and start doing for once, Stick would've said. Daredevil wasn't sure if he was hallucinating or disassociating, but Stick's voice was clear—booming through his mind. He sent a kick out, and felt the heel of his boot connecting with Izanami's face. Heard the crunch of cartilage. The squeal of pained surprise. The whoosh as he fell back to the floor.

That's it, kid, that's it—now keep it going. Don't lose the momentum. Listen to what's happening around you. Feel the world around you. Don't plan. Don't overthink it, stupid. Just let your body do the work.

Daredevil bounced on his feet, then leapt forward, sending an elbow into Jonin's throat, the thump as he connected with the ninja's neck—followed by the choked scream. Daredevil sent a spin-kick backward, connecting with at least two of the Hand. The clatter of swords hitting the ground. He fired his billy club into the darkness—smiled as the short end connected with Izanami's mouth. The crunch of broken teeth. A groan, pieces of bone being choked down. The Hand were stepping backward now, the four or five still standing.

"You wanted a fight?" Daredevil said, his voice raw and gnarled. "You wanted to brawl, Jonin? You wanted to come into the Kitchen and take *me* on?"

A flurry of hesitant steps backward. A desperate command from Jonin to his attackers.

"Well, you know how the saying goes . . ." Daredevil said, stepping forward. He felt a trickle of blood slide down his chin. "Be careful what you wish for."

((((( )))))

Matt Murdock pushed the hospital double doors open in a panic. He looked around the large waiting room. An employee looked up, concerned by the sound. Matt, blood seeping through his shirt, hobbling visibly, reached the front desk. He'd managed to stave off the Hand—barely. But Matt couldn't shake the feeling that they weren't there to kill Matt. Just to delay him. But from what? Matt couldn't dwell on it now. Getting Black Tarantula into an ambulance had eaten up valuable time. Time during which Melinda might realize Matt Murdock wasn't by her side.

"Sir, do you need medical assistance? I can—"

"No, no, not now," Matt said, waving her off. "Melinda Torres. How . . . Where is she? How is she?"

"Are you a relative of Ms. Torres, sir? If not, I may have to ask you to leave the premises. . . . Wait, is that blood?"

Matt could feel the blood from the wound on his back sticking to the shirt he'd hastily draped over his costume. His head was throbbing. He wasn't sure how he'd made it here. But he needed to see Melinda, make sure she was fine

"Ms. Torres doesn't want to see you, Murdock," a voice said from behind.

Matt spun around. He made out a tall, burly shape moving toward him.

Gunderson.

"Detective, I know Melinda, I found her—"

Gunderson approached the desk, flashing his badge at the staffer, who backed away with a nod.

"I heard. Torres came out of surgery a little while ago. She's gonna be fine. The blade missed anything serious. She bled a lot but she's good. At first, she asked about you, said to let you in. Then she realized you were gone," Gunderson said before pausing. "Where were you, Murdock?"

Matt could sense Gunderson looking him over. Heard the sharp intake of breath as the Internal Affairs officer noticed Matt's bloodstained shirt.

"That from the scene? From when you found Melinda?"

Matt nodded.

"Yes, it must've been, I—"

"You left," Gunderson said. "Why?"

"I had to take a call. . . . I'm working on the Castle case. . . ."

"Matt, you should go home. Clean up. Take some time for yourself," Gunderson said dryly. "I'll say it again: she doesn't want to see you now. Not for a while. I'm sure she appreciates you bringing her here. You probably saved her life. But then you left."

Matt started to respond.

Gunderson shook his head slowly.

"Don't bother, Matt. Try harder next time."

THIRTY-FIVE

"ARE YOU WITH US, Mr. Murdock?"

Matt looked up at Judge Sonia Porras, a staple on the New York bench. When Matt had learned she'd be presiding over Castle's case, he almost let out a yelp of joy. She was fair, progressive, and consistent. But that felt like a lifetime ago. Before Matt had melted down in her chambers, which probably played a big part in every motion Matt submitted being denied. Now, early in the morning, as he sat next to Foggy and waited for her word on Sprenger's motion to have him removed from the case, all Matt could think about was Melinda—and the swarm of ninjas that had brutalized both of them the night before.

"Yes, Your Honor, I apologize," Matt said. He could feel Foggy's eyes boring into the side of his face.

"I've read Mr. Sprenger's motion, and while I find that it has some merit—it is very clear, Mr. Murdock, that Wilson Fisk is not someone on your holiday-card list—I don't think we need to disrupt Mr. Castle's representation, considering Mr. Murdock is defending him for murder, not a minor crime that can easily withstand a change of counsel. Though, Mr. Murdock, I will be crystal clear: If you perform this way at trial, you'll be guaranteeing your client only one part of his rights—that he receives a swift trial. I wouldn't say he'd get much of a fair one," Porras said, slamming her gavel down. "Motion denied. I'll see you both in a few days for jury selection. Let's keep things moving."

Matt sighed as he stood up and felt Foggy's hand clasping his shoulder. He could hear Sprenger whispering orders to his paralegal. He was angry, but not surprised. This was the game. Matt let a brief wave of relief wash over him.

"Now we gotta get to work, Matt," Foggy said. Matt nodded. "We don't have much time to give Castle a defense—and the judge is right. He deserves it, even if he is the Punisher. Right?"

Matt nodded half-heartedly. Castle did deserve it, Matt mused. But was he going to get it?

Matt followed Foggy out of the courtroom, exchanging brief pleasantries with Sprenger at the door. He felt the weight of the last few weeks on his shoulders. His body and mind felt bruised and battered. The Hand had apparently cut a path of blood across the city—murdering and wounding underworld figures in an effort to take over the Kingpin's city-wide operation. Was it just a coincidence that Castle had killed Fisk first—using a different gun than his usual weapon? How did Sheehan play a part? And how did the company Mezinis & Charleston fit in?

"Follow the money," Matt said to himself.

"What?" Foggy asked.

"Foggy, let's meet back at the office, I need to check on something. Why don't you grab a pizza? It's gonna be a late one," Matt said.

Foggy smiled, more at the thought of pizza than Matt leaving, but it was enough.

"Sure, Matty, but don't take forever," Foggy said, turning toward the elevator. "To say we're behind on this case would be the understatement of the century. You good with anchovies?"

((((( )))))

Matt Murdock stacked the manila folders on the table. He was in a small reading room in the New York City Department of Records. He'd spent the better part of the morning trying to find any kind of lead on Mezinis & Charleston, with Becky's help—reading from each file until he said "no" and asked her to move on. Despite their efforts, Matt had come up with nothing.

Until he'd asked the clerk to look a little deeper.

Matt had assumed Mezinis & Charleston was an actual company, or firm. But what if it was meant to be, but never realized? He'd scoured piles and piles of incomplete forms for LLCs looking to form in New York. Most, if not all, were off—Menendez & Charleston. Nicieza & Champagne. Mozingo & Charlemagne. It took hours. But eventually, Matt discovered it. Mezinis & Charleston. The application had been completed. Had even been filed. But for some reason, the person behind the filing had never paid the fee—despite doing everything needed: account, address, and . . . a contact person.

Matt made a set of hasty photocopies. He put them in a thick folder that also contained transaction records between Sheehan and the incomplete Mezinis & Charleston "company." What did it prove? Matt wasn't sure yet. But at least he knew who to talk to.

THIRTY-SIX

SIX MONTHS AGO.

"I don't deal with vigilantes. I don't care what Murdock told you."

Assistant District Attorney James Sprenger frowned at Daredevil. It was well past midnight, and he hadn't expected a red-clad superhero to waltz into his office. What he'd offered him was even further off his radar.

"Murdock told me you're one of the good ones," Daredevil said. "Which carries some weight with me."

"Well, I feel blessed, I guess," Sprenger said, taking a sip of his large soda. "I always liked Matt. Felt like he got a bum rap a few years back. It was clear someone was out to get him. Glad he's back to practicing law. We're all better for it."

Another sip.

"And look, I want as much as anyone else to take down that son of a bitch Fisk. It's a career-making moment," Sprenger said. "But what do you want me to do? A split on my desk? Could she bring him down? Sure. But the second he gets—"

Sprenger paused.

"You didn't *tell* him, did you?" the district attorney asked.

Daredevil didn't respond.

Sprenger put his head in his hands.

"He needs to be *scared*, Sprenger," Daredevil said. But he could hear the assistant district attorney's breathing quicken with each second. "He doesn't rule this city."

"That was a hothead move. Now he knows our play."

"He can't get to her. Trust me."

"Trust you?" Sprenger said with a laugh. "I don't know you from Adam. You wear a mask and red spandex. No, I don't trust you. But if you serve up Wilson Fisk on a platter, well, then maybe I'll like you."

"She's got a signed affidavit," Daredevil said. "It's real."

"To you, maybe," Sprenger said. "I'll believe it when I see it."

Daredevil started to back away. "We'll talk soon, Sprenger."

"And hey, this is none of my business, but Daredevil?" Sprenger said. "The second you let Wilson Fisk know what you were doing—the minute you show a card shark your hand—you just opened yourself up to a world of hurt. Fisk is a planner. He doesn't act rashly. You should know that."

Sprenger took another sip.

"And Fisk? The fat man doesn't strike me as the type to tell you when he's coming for you."

THIRTY-SEVEN

THE AIRTRAIN TO JFK airport pulled into the Jamaica station. Daredevil scanned the area intently from above as a handful of people boarded the mass-transit car toward the airport. One person, in particular, was pulling up the rear. Daredevil jumped down and landed in front of his target and the rest of the group. As the man backed up in surprise, Daredevil motioned for the others to keep boarding.

"My friend and I need to talk," Daredevil said. The commuters complied, eager to be on their way and avoiding whatever was about to go down.

Gotta love New York, Daredevil thought.

He turned to face his target. "Long time no see, Richard."

Richard Fisk weighed his options. Daredevil sensed his head turning toward the long path that would lead back to the Jamaica LIRR station. He turned to face the other direction—which was a dead end. Daredevil knew Richard Fisk was not a dumb man. He couldn't outrun Daredevil. He couldn't out-fight him, either. But he might try.

Daredevil grabbed Fisk by the collar and yanked him forward. He watched as the Kingpin's son dropped his luggage and tried to pull away. Another pull and he brought the younger Fisk's face close to his.

"Heading somewhere?"

"Just—uh—j-just going on vacation," Fisk stammered.

Daredevil yanked his right glove off hastily then pulled the printed-out ticket from Fisk's front suit pocket and rubbed it between bare thumb and forefinger.

"Montenegro, huh? I've heard it's nice there," Daredevil said. "Also, coincidentally I'm sure, doesn't have an extradition treaty with the US. But I'm sure that's not the big draw, is it? You running from the feds, too, Fisk? Worried something's going to bubble up now?"

Fisk tried to pull free.

"What do you want? I'm a target, from all sides—you know what's going on here," Fisk said petulantly. "They're gunning for anyone that worked for my father . . . it's only a matter of time."

"I bet you're real worried," Daredevil said, unable to hide the rage bubbling under each word. "Fear makes us hasty. Can put us in strange positions . . . with strange bedfellows."

Fisk's heart rate was increasing. He was flailing around more. Daredevil tightened his grip.

"I dunno what you mean, Daredevil, look—I don't have beef with you, you had an issue with my father, but he's long gone," Fisk said, desperately. "I'm not in charge. I wouldn't do that to you. Just lemme go—I'm small fry compared to him, all right?"

"Talk to me about Mezinis and Charleston, Richard," Daredevil said, leaning in closer. "Talk to me about it now, or you're gonna be missing more than your flight to Montenegro."

((((( )))))

"You got punked, Castle," Matt Murdock said as he entered the interview room.

Frank Castle looked up and raised an eyebrow.

"You been brawling lately, Murdock?" Castle asked. "Nice shiner."

Matt instinctively touched the bruise under his left eye—a gift from Izanami.

"It's been a busy few weeks."

Castle shrugged and went back to looking at the wall across from him, ignoring Matt.

"I have enough evidence to get you off, Frank, but I need your help," Matt said, positioning himself in front of Castle, forcing him to at least recognize his presence. "The forensics evidence isn't enough. Sprenger will push back on that. But I also have this."

Matt slid over a photograph. He waited as Castle scanned it. His heartbeat stayed in rhythm. He wasn't nervous. His heartbeat had spiked when Dakota passed on the intel from her investigation. Footage and photos.

"Congratulations, Murdock. You have a picture of me walking into a bodega," Castle said with a shrug. "Do you want a prize? I can tell you I got a strawberry Pop-Tart and Vitamin Water."

Matt tapped the photo.

"Check the timestamp. This is from Fiesta Supermarket in Queens. Around that time, someone was blasting a few bullets into Wilson Fisk," Matt continued. "How do you explain that?"

"You're the lawyer. You tell me."

Matt cleared his throat. "The camera timer is off."

"There you go," Castle said. "Then why ask?"

Matt steepled his fingers under his chin.

"Because, Frank, we both know you didn't do this," Matt said. "The bullets were wrong. You were probably in Queens. So, my question becomes—why do you want people to think you did? Why is the prosecution so eager to kick the can down the road on this case? Why am I having a helluva time getting evidence about money being paid to the cop you allegedly killed along with Fisk?"

"I didn't murder a cop," Castle said. "You know that."

Matt could hear his heartbeat now. Fast. Angry. He'd struck a nerve. Sheehan was outside of Castle's comfort zone. Matt pushed.

"To believe the prosecution, you did. You murdered them both in cold blood," Matt said. "How many newspapers do you get in here, Frank?"

Castle shrugged and cracked his knuckles.

"You're a smart guy, Frank. Anyone would admit to that. So why would a smart guy like you let yourself get captured? Why would a smart guy like you sit here and bide his time, and never push back when the prosecution wants to slow down the trial, never even *really* talk to their attorney?"

Castle narrowed his eyes.

"Maybe if you got offered something to make it worth your while," Matt said. "But something tells me you didn't know all this was going to go down."

"What are you talking about, Murdock?"

"The Owl is broken. Hammerhead is hospitalized. Silvermane and Black Tarantula are as good as dead."

Castle laughed. A laugh packed with gristle and glass. "Am I supposed to be sad about that?"

"No, I think a guy like you would be happy—so happy, that you'd be willing to sit back and carve lines on a cell-block wall while you waited for the New York underworld to get gunned down. But I also bet you didn't know who they'd be clearing the decks for."

"Does it matter?" Castle said, a vein bulging on his neck. He slammed a fist down between himself and Matt. "They're dead or close to it, aren't they? That's what counts. Those criminals are six feet under. The others are waiting in their beds for the next boss to walk in and put a bullet between their eyes. Should I shed a tear for them?"

"You made a bad deal, Frank, that's all I came to tell you," Matt said, smiling. "You thought they would lock you up, spill blood all over the city, and then you'd be able to ride a good defense out of here? Did they tell you everything?"

"Spit it out, Murdock," Castle growled. "I don't have all day. Even if I am locked up."

"The gun they do have?" Matt said, trying not to sound gleeful at getting something—anything—over on Castle. "It's got your prints on it. Partials. We can argue that. No prints that show you were handling the trigger . . . but still. It's bad. I'm gonna take a wild guess that you didn't sign up for that part, huh?"

Castle didn't respond. His ice-cold stare locked on Matt.

And he was surprised.

"Prints?" Castle finally said.

"Yes, your prints," Matt said.

Matt could hear Castle's teeth grinding from across the table. He pressed on.

"And now, because you took the fall, the Hand has a clear path back into the city. A path they're already taking. They're here. So, sure, a few dime-store bad guys are dead or hurt. But the new boss? They're much, much worse than the old boss."

"The *Hand*?" Castle asked.

For the first time since he'd become his attorney, Matt heard uncertainty in Castle's voice.

This was no longer a classic New York gang war. It had gone not only international, but supernatural. If the Hand was making a play to enter the New York underworld, and was eliminating any threats to the throne, it would be much more complicated to balance the scales—especially for people like Daredevil and the Punisher. Instead of sitting back and watching their problems solve themselves, they were both witnessing things getting much worse.

"They're here," Matt said. "We're not in some old gangster flick now. If the Hand are here, and not just visiting to kill someone but actually setting up shop, all bets are off. And it's your fault. You sat back and let this happen."

Matt got up and motioned for the guard.

"You're a smug son of a bitch, you know that?" Castle said, spittle flying out of his mouth. He was mad now. "You think you know all the pieces? You think I'm stuck here?"

Matt kept walking. He could still hear Castle as he walked to his car.

"You think I'm trapped inside this pit? You don't think I can get out of here any time I like?"

Matt smiled to himself.

No, Frank. I know you can.

"You think I'm stuck here?!"

PART FOUR

THE KILLERS

THIRTY-EIGHT

GAME TIME.

The jury had been selected. All motions had been exhausted. The moment of truth had arrived.

Matt Murdock did not feel ready.

He thought back to the night before, when he'd entered the empty Church of the Sacred Heart on the edge of the Kitchen. He'd lit the candle almost instinctively. Force of habit. Matt did it before every big trial. Before any challenging moment he could see coming. And this definitely fell under that umbrella.

The odds were not in his favor. Matt knew this. The Punisher was a bit of a cult figure, sure—but the charges were clear. Two counts of first-degree murder, one tied to the death of Fisk, the other to an NYPD police officer. It was a challenging needle to thread during jury selection. You could only have so many anti-police jurors, and that didn't mean those same people would sympathize with a rich businessman who was allegedly the deadliest crime boss in the city's history. The press painted Sheehan as a good cop caught in the cross fire of Castle's psychotic crusade. Lost in the shuffle were his alleged targets. Over time, Fisk had created an air of invincibility. Nothing stuck to him—even the charges that Matt had thought would bring him down just a few years prior.

So, now, Fisk was dead and it became two staples of New York lore pitted against each other in court: the misunderstood millionaire and the bloodthirsty urban vigilante. Caught in the middle was the truth.

The investigation into the crime itself had turned up little, though little could prove to be enough, especially without Castle taking the stand. His client had been silent throughout the process, providing Matt and Foggy with little they could actually use. But two pieces of evidence stood out for Matt: the forensics showed the bullets in Fisk's and Sheehan's bodies were from a gun that was not the same as the one the police claimed it was. A weapon that wasn't traceable to any of Castle's many drop sites or flop houses. Was the gun similar to one that Castle frequently used? Yes. But that didn't mean he fired it.

The big revelation, comparatively, that Matt had in his back pocket was one that would—at best—raise some doubt. But it was that incremental doubt, the little bits of evidence that gave jurors pause, that could add up to something more meaningful—an acquittal. So there was a glimmer of hope for Castle. Surveillance footage, from a bodega in Queens, showed Castle, at the same time as the murders took place, browsing the aisles and buying a drink and a snack before heading out into the night in his van. Could the timestamp have been faked? Certainly. Could it just have been someone that looked like Frank Castle, a dark-haired middle-aged white man? Possible. But Matt hoped it would be enough to raise a reasonable doubt. That was the only burden on the defense. It had to be enough.

Matt knew that even if Frank Castle wasn't convicted of *these* charges, he would be remanded to custody to face charges in dozens of *other* murder cases, which featured reams of evidence against him. Equally as important as not sending a man to jail for something he did not do would be the fact that the police would have to continue to look for the *real* killers and not let those people terrorize the streets further.

James Sprenger seemed to bound out of his seat as he approached the jury box. Matt felt a pang of remorse as he sensed Sprenger's form move. He liked the guy. He respected his methods. Matt had hoped, deep down, that his opponent would be someone he disdained—a hack, a career government attorney. Instead, he got one of the good ones. Sprenger was smart, detail-oriented, and fair. He wouldn't press a case if he didn't have one. And Matt knew he did have one. He said a silent prayer as the veteran prosecutor spoke.

"Members of the jury, let me be clear," Sprenger said. "Frank Castle is a murderer. Frank Castle killed Wilson Fisk and Ed Sheehan. Whatever you learn about either man is irrelevant. Murder is murder—and Mr. Castle is guilty. It doesn't matter how much the defense tries to sully Officer Sheehan's reputation. It doesn't matter how many old stories they try to dust off to make you feel glad Fisk is dead. What does matter is that Frank Castle used a Glock to shoot them both, a weapon he has become known for—a weapon that bore his prints and was found on the scene."

Sprenger cleared his throat and motioned toward the defense table.

"My opponents, Mr. Murdock and his partner, Mr. Nelson, will make hay about the weapon. They'll say it wasn't Castle's 'usual' gun. They'll point to the prints and note they weren't clear, or full. These things happen to be true, but these things are also not enough. Let me ask you this—why else would Frank Castle's prints be on a gun that was fired? Are we to believe Castle gently handled the weapon, left it somewhere, and then, unbeknownst to him, that weapon was used to murder two men in cold blood? Are you expected to believe that Frank Castle is so sentimental, he'd never use another gun except for one, trusty Glock?"

Sprenger let out a dry laugh. He couldn't help himself, Matt thought. He thinks this case is closed.

"Frank Castle is a war veteran. He is used to weaponry. He is used to violence. And he is conniving and smart," Sprenger continued. "In his wake, he has left a community without a valued officer and he has murdered a man before he could be charged or face trial for anything relating to his supposed criminal activities. He has circumvented the very system you, today, are a part of. Again, it does not matter who Wilson Fisk is. The law is blind. It does not matter if Ed Sheehan was a nice cop, a bad cop, or not a cop at all. Both men are dead—shot by a gun that was held by Frank Castle, a man who is no stranger to violence and death, a man who has a vendetta against criminals and police officers that is in the public record."

Sprenger paused. Matt could tell the man knew he was dancing close to a contentious part of the trial: Frank Castle's track record. Matt had moved to strike Castle's criminal record from the proceedings, but thanks to his own outburst in Porras's office, that motion had been denied. Sprenger had reached a fork in the road. Would he double down and remind the jury of who they were dealing with, potentially risking an appeal on the grounds that Porras made a mistake? Or would he play it safe? Matt knew the answer before Sprenger spoke.

"Frank Castle is a cold-blooded killer, many times over," Sprenger said gravely. "This is a fact. To think he is an innocent, a situation of the wrong place at the wrong time . . . is patently absurd. You, the members of the jury, are smarter than this. I exhort you to do what is asked of you. Look at the facts. Look at the people involved. Understand that Frank Castle's guilt is clear, beyond a reasonable doubt. And then, using the power entrusted in you, come to the only verdict that makes sense: guilty."

Sprenger glanced at Matt as he turned away from the jury box. Matt looked down at his hands.

After Sprenger took his seat, Judge Porras looked at Matt.

"Mr. Murdock, we will now hear opening arguments from the defense."

He felt Foggy's hand clench his shoulder as he stepped up, scanning his walking stick gently in front of him. He could sense the anticipation from the jury. He could also sense the blank calm coming from his client, Castle, seated right next to Foggy and seemingly disconnected from the proceedings.

He might not care, Matt thought, *but I do.*

Matt had grappled with this case. With the idea that justice had any role in an internecine war between two monsters. So what if Castle hadn't killed this particular man? Wasn't it better to bring him in, and force him to pay a price that was long overdue, after years of bloodshed, murder, and rampant destruction? Frank Castle was a man who'd decided the systems of justice did not apply to him. That he was better suited to be judge, jury, and executioner when it came to crime in New York. Matt couldn't deny the feelings he'd felt. That perhaps this was God's way of clearing the decks—eliminating two bad actors in one fell swoop.

But Matt also knew the world didn't work that way. And he knew, in his heart, that Frank Castle was innocent—at least of this crime. Did he deserve to spend his life in prison? Did Wilson Fisk deserve to die for his crimes? Perhaps. But that wasn't Matt's call to make, no matter how much he hated Wilson Fisk—or despised Frank Castle's methods. He'd struggled with this since he'd first heard Castle was a suspect. Could he, Matt Murdock, defend a man who stood in opposition to everything he believed, for the murder of a man Matt loathed more than the actual devil himself? He could. And he did. In this instance, Frank Castle deserved a fair shake, and Matt was going to get it for him—whether he liked it or not.

Matt approached the jury and let out a quick breath. He let his senses scan the twelve people sitting before him. He could hear the ticking of Ramon Mencia's watch. The clicking of Yasmin Peppard's tongue as she waited impatiently for Matt to start. He could smell the maple syrup and pancakes on Sam Wolven's breath. These were people from all over. A waiter. A postal worker. A temp at a crypto company. A freelance artist. All pulled together for this short span of time to determine if a known murderer like Frank Castle deserved to be in prison for the crime he was on trial for, or the crimes he'd managed to avoid capture over.

Matt tapped his walking stick absentmindedly.

"People of the jury, I am going to ask you to do the impossible," Matt started. "I'm going to ask you to forget everything you know about two men: my client, Frank Castle, the man accused of two murders, and Wilson Fisk, one of the people gunned down on that night a few months ago. This is a big ask—and it will not be easy. But you must. You must open your minds to what you learn about those men here. The *facts* of the case are relevant, and nothing more. No person living in New York City has had *no* contact with the idea or reputations of Fisk or Castle. We have all been touched in some way by their stories and actions. But I must warn you: Not all of that is materially relevant to what happened on February twenty-third of this year. The prosecution will tell you this is an open-and-shut case. That, because of what we presume—*presume*—to know about both is enough to determine not only what happened that night. but who was behind it."

Matt took a step forward.

"But that's not how the justice system works. Your duty, as jurors, is to take the evidence—the facts—that you collect during this trial and determine if you can conclude, *beyond a reasonable doubt*, that Frank Castle gunned down Officer Sheehan and Wilson Fisk. That he had motive, and that evidence places him on the scene and using the weapon the NYPD collected from the scene and tied to the injuries sustained by both Fisk and Sheehan. I am here to tell you, off the bat, that such evidence does *not* exist. Could Castle have handled the gun that shot Wilson Fisk and Edward Sheehan? Yes. It is safe to say that Frank Castle has handled many weapons in his life, not all of which he then fired himself. In the coming weeks, my colleagues and I will not only show you that the gun used to kill Fisk and Sheehan was not, and *could not have been*, in Castle's possession and that the prosecution's purported forensic details are thus irrelevant, but that, in fact, Castle himself, all aspects of his reputation aside, was nowhere near Midtown Manhattan at the time of the murders."

Matt felt one of the jurors take in a sharp, brief breath. The heart rates across the board were ticking up. They were listening.

"What happened in Wilson Fisk's large, multimillion-dollar penthouse office was a crime. That cannot be discounted. Someone shot and killed two people violently. But as the defense reveals its case, it will become plainly clear that the NYPD rushed to judgment, at the expense of catching Fisk and Sheehan's true killer. Desperate to find an easy solution to the death of one of the city's most recognizable figures, they leapt at the opportunity to bring in Castle and pin the crime on him, rather than do the due diligence and investigating that a murder of any magnitude deserves. You, as jurors, need to separate yourself from the tabloids and the rumors. You need to digest the facts as they are presented and remember—guilt must stand beyond a reasonable doubt."

Matt paused.

"Castle's guilt does not exist. The defendant is innocent of this crime. Is he a good man? Was Fisk? That's immaterial. What matters is the crime he is here to defend himself against today. And he was not involved in that crime, nor should he pay the price for it."

As Matt turned and walked back to his seat, he heard one of the jurors—Yasmin Peppard—mutter under her breath, so softly that no one but Matt could hear.

"Damn. This is gonna get interesting."

THIRTY-NINE

THE FOLDER MADE a flopping sound as it landed on Ben Urich's desk.

The reporter spun his chair around and glanced at the stack of papers, then looked up at Daredevil.

"Glad we're still on speaking terms."

"We're old friends, Ben," Daredevil said. "What kind of friends don't argue from time to time?"

Ben tapped the folder. "What's this?"

"Read it. Wish I'd had this when I gave my opening, because I think the information exonerates Frank Castle. It also connects Richard Fisk to a shell company that was paying off the cop, Sheehan. Not airtight evidence that he was involved in his dad's murder, but it certainly raises enough questions," Daredevil said. "Might be nice color to accompany your story on Castle escaping."

Ben's eyed widened.

"Hasn't happened yet," Daredevil said. "But it's a matter of time."

"How can you tell? He's been in there for weeks."

"Let's just say his lawyer presented some . . . irrefutable evidence," Daredevil said with a smile.

Ben rubbed his chin.

"Strange timing," Ben said. "My sources tell me there's some kind of underboss meet happening tomorrow night. Upstate—not sure where, exactly. Some big hotel near a lake, everyone's gathering. Trying to decide on a path forward."

"Who's left?"

"Good question. My guess is it's guys like the Lobo Brothers, Jigsaw, Tombstone, Don Fortunato, Count Nefaria, Mr. Negative . . . Hell, we might even see the Slug, or a new Rose pop up. Word is everyone is showing up for this one," Ben said. "To be a fly on the wall at that meeting . . ."

Daredevil put a hand on Ben's shoulder.

"Ben, if you hear where—I need to know."

Ben looked up at Daredevil.

"Matt, we talked about this."

"It's not about the story, Ben, I'm not trying to scoop you," Daredevil said. "But if my gut is right—everyone walking into that meeting is coming out in a body bag."

FORTY

"THE PROSECUTION CALLS Tamika Briggs to the stand."

Matt sensed Briggs's halting journey to the witness stand. He could hear her thumping heart as she was sworn in. She wasn't just nervous. She was scared.

Sprenger calmly walked toward the witness stand, a notebook in hand.

"Miss Briggs, could you explain to the jury what your role is in the medical examiner's office?"

Briggs cleared her throat.

"I'm a pathologist for the ME, uh, the medical examiner," Briggs said haltingly. "I help the medical examiner with—well, everything."

"Including autopsies?" Sprenger said, trying to nudge her along.

"Yes," she said flatly.

"Could you walk us through the forensic evidence as it relates to the deaths of Wilson Fisk and Ed Sheehan?"

Briggs straightened up. Matt could sense this was the easy part for her. The recapping of a rcport.

"Both victims suffered multiple gunshot wounds resulting in death, pronounced dead on the scene before being transported . . ." Briggs hesitated. Matt could sense her breathing picking up. "Before being transported to the ME's office for a full autopsy."

Sprenger nodded.

"Based on the autopsy report, could you elaborate at all on how the victims were killed? Would it be safe to say that it was a . . . painful way to die?"

"Objection," Matt said curtly, loud enough for the judge to hear. "Ms. Briggs's extrapolations of the facts are not relevant."

Sprenger spun around, eyebrow raised, but spoke in the direction of Judge Porras.

"I beg to differ," he said. "This is an expert witness. She is up here for that very reason."

Porras nodded.

"Overruled, Mr. Murdock," Porras said. "Please proceed, Mr. Sprenger."

Matt frowned. He knew the objection had been a reach. But it also opened the door for what he was going to do next.

Briggs let out a brief sigh.

"They were both shot multiple times. Nothing painless about that," she said, eliciting a few quiet chuckles from the audience.

Porras's gavel came down fast.

"Order," Porras said. She looked down at Ms. Briggs. "May I remind you you're in a courtroom, Ms. Briggs, not a comedy club?"

Briggs, chastened, continued—her voice shaky.

"By my estimation, their deaths were very painful," Briggs said.

"No further questions, Your Honor," Sprenger said as he moved back to his seat.

Matt stood up calmly and made his way to Briggs.

"Ms. Briggs, is it safe to say you're often in charge of autopsies for major cases?" Matt asked.

Briggs hesitated. She was smart. She knew what was coming.

"Well, I guess it depends."

Matt gave Briggs a warm smile.

"Let me help you then," he said. "Would you say that when there's a big murder investigation, that you usually end up handling the autopsy?"

Briggs nodded slowly.

"Well, yes," she said. "I've been with the department for a long—"

"Is it true that you didn't personally handle the autopsy of Wilson Fisk?" Matt asked, his tone light, as if asking a meaningless trivia question during game night.

The air in the courtroom seemed to fill with an electrical charge. Matt could hear Sprenger shuffling his papers. A hushed whisper to his second chair.

"What the *hell* is he talking about?"

Matt tried not to smile.

"That is true, yes," Briggs said.

"Is that uncommon?" Matt said before sliding a finger over his notes. He faced Briggs again. "Was this signed off on by your supervisor?"

Briggs swallowed hard. "I can't do them all."

"Did your supervisor okay this?" Matt asked, a little more persistent. "Sam Weingarten, right?"

Briggs nodded. Matt motioned for her to speak.

"Yes, Sam Weingarten is my boss. He signed off on it. I had a high caseload. He said he was trying to help ease my burden, if that's what you're asking."

Matt smiled again—that humorless, knowing smile. Like a bird of prey circling an errant mouse.

"That's not what I'm asking, Ms. Briggs, but let me clarify," he said, his tone flat, all humor gone. "If you are usually the person that handles high-profile murders, if you're the one often charged with doing autopsies for major cases—was there a reason beyond you 'not doing them all' for not handling the murder of someone like Wilson Fisk?"

Briggs squirmed, shifting her weight in the chair. Matt could feel the heat emanating from her body. She was sweating now.

Tamika Briggs was a good woman. Matt Murdock knew this. He felt some shame over using this intelligence—a detail culled from his conversations with her as Daredevil—to roast her on the stand. But he had no choice. He would deal with the aftershocks later.

Melinda Torres flashed in his mind. A company name whispered among colleagues.

The shame felt sharper now.

This is who I am, Matt thought.

He tucked the thought away. Life was messy. He could only control the moment.

Briggs shook her head slightly. The pause was dragging on now.

"I must remind you, Ms. Briggs, that you are under oath," Matt said, as softly and gently as he could.

"I wasn't assigned to the Fisk case," Briggs said. "So I didn't perform the autopsy."

Matt pulled a paper out of his folder. He'd anticipated this moment. He placed it in front of Briggs, who scanned it. Her shoulders seemed to slump as she realized what it was.

"Can you confirm to the jury what this document is?" Matt asked. He spun briefly toward the jury and spoke. "Noting for the record that I've placed Exhibit XM-137, the Fisk autopsy report, in front of the witness."

Briggs bristled, then snapped. "What you just said—it's the Fisk autopsy report."

"Thank you," Matt said, taking the document back. He tapped at it absentmindedly before moving his face toward Briggs again, brow furrowed. "One more thing, though—and maybe this is common, but can you read who signed the autopsy form?"

Briggs frowned.

"I signed it."

Matt gave Briggs—and then the jury—a bemused look.

"Huh," Matt said. He had to remind himself to step gingerly, to not seem like he was savoring the fact he'd just unveiled to the jury. "Is that common? For you to sign autopsies you didn't perform?"

Briggs sighed.

"I'm a supervisor, so I often have to sign off on other work—when another pathologist does a procedure and that sort of thing," Briggs said matter-of-factly. She had quickly graduated from miffed to pissed off.

Matt nodded, tapping his finger on the form.

"That makes sense," Matt said. "Is this that kind of instance?"

He looked up at Briggs.

"I mean, were you signing off on the work of someone that reported to you, or worked in your department?"

Briggs's eyes narrowed. Matt didn't need to be a telepath to know what she was thinking, and it wasn't kind to him.

"I was signing off on the report, yes."

"Did you examine the body to check the work?" Matt asked.

"I did not," Briggs said, not meeting Matt's gaze.

The courtroom was buzzing. Matt heard Sprenger cursing under his breath.

Matt tapped his chin with his pen and frowned.

"I have to ask again—is that common, Ms. Briggs? To sign off on an autopsy report you did not perform or double-check?"

Briggs slumped in the seat.

"It's not," she said. "It was not . . . a routine situation."

Matt let the words hang over the courtroom for a moment before proceeding.

"Ms. Briggs, for clarity and for the record, can you please let us know who performed the autopsy on Wilson Fisk?" Matt asked. Now his heart was thumping.

Briggs's hands moved up to cover her face. Matt could hear her choking back a sob.

"It wasn't my call, all right? I didn't decide to use Fisk's private doctor—I didn't agree to it. But I signed it. I did what I was told, okay? God dammit, I told them this was messed up," Briggs said, her tears streaming down her face, anger fueling her words. "You have the biggest murder in New York history and you let his private doctor perform the autopsy? How messed up is that?"

Matt gave Briggs a somber look before turning to the jury.

"No further questions, Your Honor."

((((( )))))

Matt couldn't shake the feeling, like a thick cloud over him.

Was he cheating, he wondered? Was he using his powers—his abilities and other identity—as an unfair advantage? He knew he was, he thought to himself as he sipped coffee outside the courtroom. After Briggs's collapse on the stand, Sprenger had zipped through the rest of his case—relying heavily on the facts: the fingerprints, the weapon, Castle's record. But Matt understood momentum—and by poking holes in the prosecution's autopsy evidence, he opened the door to something else, to something deeper: that all of the prosecution evidence was flawed. Was it true? Probably not. But that's why it was called a reasonable doubt. Matt had made a big dent in their case. But at what cost?

Who else had Briggs told about Fisk's doctor besides Daredevil? He would never know. But she probably wouldn't ever trust the vigilante again, with good reason.

Was it worth it?

He had to think yes. A lawyer's job was to get a fair trial for their client. There was no way Frank Castle, a serial murderer and symbol of chaos and anarchy, was going to get anything close to a fair hearing. Not unless Matt used every tool at his disposal. And as bad as it made him feel—he had to do it. Even it if tore him up inside.

He turned to walk back into the courtroom when he heard a familiar voice. A voice he'd been listening to for hours just today.

"You landed a good one there, Murdock," Sprenger said. Matt could hear his footsteps shuffling past him. "But this is a marathon, not a sprint. See you in there."

Matt didn't respond. He didn't have to.

He was up to bat.

((((( )))))

"The defense calls Detective Thomas Gunderson to the stand."

Matt listened as Gunderson walked past him and up to the witness stand, his strong cologne invading Matt's nostrils. He listened for Gunderson to take his oath before getting up and starting to walk toward the Internal Affairs officer.

So much had changed over the last week since Sprenger first started to present his case. The city itself felt aflame—an internecine gang war enveloping the streets and headlines. The Kingpin was dead, and so was the firm control he had over the New York underworld. Matt not only had to win this case before Judge Porras, he had to find a way to stop his city from bleeding out. He wasn't sure how he could do that.

"Detective Gunderson, can you explain to the jury what it is you do for the NYPD?"

Gunderson shrugged and glanced at the jury.

"Sure. I work for Internal Affairs. We're the cops that investigate the cops. Not the most fun, but if we can't—"

"Thank you, Detective," Matt interrupted. "Generally speaking, does your department frown upon officers and detectives from the NYPD fraternizing with known underworld figures?"

"Objection," Sprenger said, moving to stand. "Leading the witness. Mr. Gunderson merely *works* for the Internal Affairs department; he does not set policy."

Judge Porras nodded. "Overruled. I want to see where Mr. Murdock goes with this. But be quick."

Matt nodded, then turned back to Gunderson.

"I can't speak for the leadership of the department, but, yeah, I mean—unless you're working an undercover operation, it's not a good look to be hobnobbing with mobsters," Gunderson said gruffly.

"Would you say it suggests an improper relationship?"

"Objection. We're spiraling into the hypothetical here, Your Honor," Sprenger interjected.

Judge Porras turned toward Matt.

"Please get to the point, counsel."

"Yes, Your Honor," Matt said, chastened. "Mr. Gunderson, can you speak to Officer Ed Sheehan's reputation as an officer in good standing in the NYPD?"

Gunderson seemed to squirm, realizing where Matt was heading with the question.

"I can't speak to any open investigations, if that's what you're asking," Gunderson said defensively. "As far as I could tell, socially speaking, Ed Sheehan was a good cop who was in the wrong place at the wrong time."

"Can you confirm if there is an open investigation relating to Ed Sheehan currently happening at Internal Affairs?" Matt asked, raising an eyebrow.

"I cannot disclose that, no," Gunderson said, through gritted teeth. "But from what I knew of Ed, he was well-liked, did his job . . . family guy. I don't think anyone in the department had a bad word to say about him."

"Are you aware of a company known as Mezinis and Charleston, Detective?" Matt asked, his tone casual and relaxed. He could almost hear the droplet of sweat slide down the detective's forehead.

Gunderson cleared his throat, looked at the jury briefly. "I don't recall hearing that name, no."

"I'd like to remind the witness that he is under oath," Matt said as he walked to the defense table and pulled out two sheets of paper from a folder, then returned to hand them to Gunderson.

"Can you read to the courtroom what you see here?"

Gunderson swallowed hard.

"It looks like a wire transfer. A history of transfers. Between, uh, between that company you mentioned," Gunderson said, "and Ed Sheehan. And then Terry, his brother, I believe."

"Could you read to the courtroom the total amount of money being transferred, Detective?"

Gunderson frowned.

"According to this, it's . . . well it's about forty-five thousand dollars."

"Have you ever seen this document before, Detective?"

"Objection, Your Honor," Sprenger said. "What is the relevance?"

Judge Porras motioned to Matt.

"Please enlighten us, Mr. Murdock."

"Detective Gunderson, is this the kind of document—a document pointing to large amounts of money being transferred to an NYPD detective, then to his brother after his murder—that would raise alarm bells in your department?" Matt asked.

Gunderson's mouth was agape. No sound was coming out.

"Objection," Sprenger said, this time with a little less pep in his voice. "Defense is relying on speculation and I'm still not—"

"Overruled. Answer the question, Detective," Judge Porras said.

Gunderson cleared his throat.

"Well, I can't speak generally for all cases, but yes, something like this would raise some alarm bells," Gunderson said methodically. "It certainly doesn't look good."

"I'll ask you again, Detective," Matt said. "Have you seen this document before?"

Gunderson looked at Matt. His heart was racing. He could hear him cracking his knuckles near his seat. He licked his lips quickly.

"I had not seen that before today, no," Gunderson said softly.

"Are you sure?" Matt asked.

"To the best of my recollection," Gunderson said, then winced.

"No further questions, Your Honor," Matt said.

Sprenger declined to cross-examine the witness, shaking his head as Gunderson walked meekly back to his seat.

As Matt returned to his own chair, Castle leaned forward and looked at his attorney.

"You're pretty good at this, Murdock."

Matt smiled for a moment.

"Let's hope it's enough," he said.

((((( )))))

"What's on your mind, Foggy?"

Matt let his question float between him and his best friend as they stood outside, shoving dollar pizza slices into their respective mouths. They had time for a real lunch, but over the years of their partnership, Nelson and Murdock had made a habit of maximizing every ounce of time. That meant eat fast, work hard.

"Something's bugging me about the evidence," Foggy said as he chewed a piece of his pepperoni slice. "About the gun—mostly."

"What about it?" Matt asked.

Foggy looked out toward the bustling Midtown street, his brow furrowed, deep in thought.

"It's just . . . if the gun is wrong, if someone planted the wrong gun to tie it to Castle, but it actually wasn't his gun," Foggy mused. "Then what else could've been messed with?"

Over the years, it had become too easy to underestimate Foggy Nelson, Matt had learned. He was easy to write off. Just a jolly, nice guy. But Matt knew better. His partner was a hell of a lawyer, the kind of attorney who could zoom out and look at the big picture, coming up with sharp, thematically powerful arguments, but also hyper-focus on glitches in evidence or data. He was witnessing it right now, Matt thought.

"You think we should question their evidence more? I'm not following," Matt said.

"I'm not sure yet, I'm not sure it's something we have time to fix, not here—in the middle of a trial," Foggy said, shaking his head. "But I think I know who might be able to help, even if it's just a thought."

Foggy waved his cell phone at Matt as he tossed his oil-soaked paper plate into a nearby trashcan.

"Gonna make a call," he said. "I'll see you inside."

((((( )))))

"The defense would like to call Detective Melinda Torres to the stand," Matt said, knowing what this would bring down upon him and his personal life.

Sprenger leapt up almost immediately.

"Objection, *objection* . . . Detective Torres is nowhere on the witness list the defense submitted," Sprenger said as he stepped around his table.

Before Matt could move, Melinda stepped in front of him—her stare a powerful mix of betrayal, surprise, and pain. She was also enraged, clenching her teeth to avoid leaping at Matt to rip his throat out. He tried to speak, unsure what to say—but she cut him off with a whisper.

"Go to hell, Matt."

It'd been almost inaudible, the kind of thing you'd struggle to hear even standing next to someone. He couldn't dwell on it, Sprenger's angry pleas in front of the judge distracting him.

Porras shook her head and motioned for the attorneys to approach the bench to sidebar. As they reached her, she shook her head and looked at Matt.

"What's the meaning of this, Mr. Murdock?"

Matt looked up at Porras.

"Your Honor, we had no plans to call Detective Torres to the stand until we heard the testimony of her colleague, Gunderson," Matt said. "We believe Torres's testimony is of the utmost importance to the case and might impeach Gunderson's statements—creating reasonable doubt in the eyes of the jury. We don't think Gunderson is telling the truth about that document, Your Honor. But if Ed Sheehan and his brother were being paid off, it is relevant to the case—and points to a deeper relationship to Fisk. Not only that, it opens up the door to other potential killers, not just my client, Your Honor. My job is to raise a reasonable doubt, not prove innocence. My client is innocent until Mr. Sprenger proves otherwise."

"This is insanity, Your Honor," Sprenger said, seething. "We're in the weeds—talking about bank transfers and memos when two men are dead at the hand of . . ."

Sprenger stopped himself.

"It should also be noted," Sprenger said, trying to calm himself before continuing, "that the defense counsel is believed to be in a personal relationship with the witness being called."

Porras looked at Matt. "Is this true?"

"Yes, Your Honor, but it is not relevant to the case," Matt said.

"It may be relevant to your personal life," Porras said with a quick, dry laugh. "Still, I'll allow it. For now. But keep your questions direct and brief, Mr. Murdock. I won't let you dilly-dally."

Matt nodded and backed toward the defense table.

"Matt, have you lost your mind?" Foggy hissed.

"Trust me, Foggy," Matt said, tapping his legal pad. "Just trust me."

Foggy didn't respond as Matt stood up. He could sense Melinda's familiar shape on the stand. Could hear her wincing slightly as the stab wound in her midsection brushed against the banister of the witness stand. Could feel her temperature—hot. Her fingers were clutching the fabric of her skirt. Her jaw was clenched, her teeth grinding. Matt wasn't sure if their relationship would survive this. And he had to be okay with that.

He stepped forward.

"Detective Torres, can you please explain the nature of our relationship, for the sake of clarity and transparency?"

Melinda's eyes narrowed. "I'd say the nature of our relationship is . . . very precarious."

A stifled laugh cut through the courtroom.

Porras slammed her gavel down. "Order, order. I won't have this courtroom turned into a comedy skit," Porras said. "We understand that you two are an item, or were. I also was led to believe this testimony was relevant to the trial. Please don't make me regret allowing you to call this witness, Mr. Murdock."

"Understood, Your Honor," Matt said before turning back to the stand. "Detective Torres, can you explain your role at the Department of Internal Affairs?"

Melinda frowned. "I'm one of the department heads. A few detectives report to me about their investigations."

"Are you able to say whether or not Officer Ed Sheehan was under investigation?" Matt asked, knowing how she would respond.

"I cannot."

"Did you receive any evidence that Officer Sheehan might not have been performing his duties properly or without undue influence from outside factors?"

Melinda tilted her head, confused.

"I can't say whether or not Sheehan was under investigation," she said coolly. "And I feel like talking about any evidence would jeopardize an investigation, if there were one."

Matt walked over and handed her the same sheets Gunderson had stumbled over earlier in the day.

"Can you give me your professional assessment of what these documents reveal, Detective?"

Melinda looked over the bank transfers for a moment before looking at Matt.

"These are bank records showing money being transferred into a couple of accounts," she said flatly. "From a company named Mezinis and Charleston."

Matt nodded. "Let the records show that the account numbers on the document match those belonging to Ed Sheehan and his brother, Terry Sheehan." He turned back to Melinda. "Seems like a lot of money, doesn't it?"

She shrugged. "It's certainly a decent chunk of change."

"Is this standard for police officers? To receive large sums of money from mysterious corporations weeks before they die?" Matt asked.

"Objection!" Sprenger said, sounding exasperated. "What's the relevance here?"

"Sustained," Porras said. "Rephrase or move on, Mr. Murdock."

Matt nodded and turned toward his maybe-girlfriend.

"Have you seen these documents before, Detective Torres?" he asked. "Had you heard of Mezinis and Charleston before?"

Torres locked her stare on Matt and waited. A few seconds passed.

"I have seen them, yes," Torres said, dejection in her voice.

"Did you discuss them with anyone in your department?" Matt continued. "Like Detective Gunderson?"

Torres looked down at her hands before responding. "Yes, I believe so."

Matt started to pace in front of Torres's seat.

"Detective, was this information—potentially tying Officer Ed Sheehan to an unknown company financially—something you considered relevant to the investigation of the murder of Wilson Fisk and Officer Sheehan?"

"Documents can be faked, and we were in the process of investigating the validity of these documents. The account numbers on the documents matched account numbers on bank statements found in Ed Sheehan's apartment during the investigation of his death, though none of those showed this transfer. If and when we confirmed they were legitimate, we would have brought them to the attention of the officers investigating the homicides, but we had not yet heard back from the banks on verification."

Matt walked to the defense table and came back with another set of printouts.

"Well, strangely enough, we reached out to Ed Sheehan's bank. Once we served them with a subpoena, they very kindly granted us access to Ed Sheehan's and Terry Sheehan's accounts," Matt said. "Let the record show I'm sharing item K-17 from evidence. These are financial overviews for both individuals. Can you look at them along with the earlier document you suggest might be a fake?"

As he stepped closer to Torres, he could hear her harsh whisper.

"What the fuck are you doing, Matt?"

He didn't respond. Sweat from her palms sliding over the paper. The shuffling of the sheets. Her hard swallow before she spoke. Matt waited.

"These seem to confirm the validity of the first document," Torres said.

"Can you summarize, in your professional experience, what these documents reflect?" Matt asked.

Torres looked up, a humorless smile on her face.

"It appears someone was paying Ed Sheehan a lot of money," Torres said.

Matt turned around.

"No further questions, Your Honor."

FORTY-ONE

MATT BUZZED THE DOOR again and waited. He knew she was in there, had learned as much as he overheard the doorman calling up to her place. Before he could look up to tell Matt she didn't want to see him, Matt had darted to the elevator.

Now outside her door, he could hear her heart beating. Her light footfalls on the wooden floors. Melinda Torres was ignoring him, and he was pretty sure he couldn't blame her.

Matt also didn't know if he'd see her again—and as messy as his life could be, he didn't like leaving things tangled up, even if she hated him. Matt had put her entire professional career on display—had publicly pointed out her department's cover-up, or at least slow-walking, of Sheehan's misdeeds. He was probably the last person Melinda Torres wanted to see.

An hour ago, he'd gotten an encrypted text from Ben Urich with an address, nothing more. But it was enough. The Old Continental Hotel in Greenwood Lake was massive from what Matt could tell, and it was secluded—the lakeside town was about two hours from the city by car and boasted a vibrant community of former city-dwellers looking to touch some grass. It was the kind of place where a meeting of this magnitude could happen right under the noses of the residents and, more importantly, law enforcement. Its seclusion also meant it would be very hard to sneak up on the meeting. And so his plan had become to track down one of the attendees—Richard Fisk, who after his run-in with Daredevil had apparently decided to stay local—and shadow them into the meeting itself.

But he wanted to deal with personal matters first. Even if it meant he and Melinda were over.

He buzzed the bell again. Footsteps. More hurried. The door swung open. A stone-cold angry face peeked through the partially opened door.

"Matt, I don't want to see you," she said, no humor in her voice. "I told the door—"

"I understand, Melinda, but please—can we talk? Just for a minute?"

After seeming to consider the pros and cons of the request internally, finally Melinda let out a sigh and opened the door for Matt to step inside.

The apartment smelled of takeout and box wine. Matt's heart ached. He had never intended to hurt Melinda, a woman he genuinely cared for. But even he had to admit the timing had been off. The Castle case had dominated his life, and because Melinda wasn't privy to his alter ego, it was impossible to explain it away without seeming unhinged. He didn't come here hoping to rekindle their stalled romance. Matt just wanted a chance to explain himself.

Melinda hobbled down a long hallway and turned right into a large living room area. She motioned for Matt to sit on the couch and pulled up a chair. She winced slightly as she sat down.

"How are you feeling?"

"I'm feeling great, considering someone stabbed me in the stomach and my boyfriend put me on trial," she said with a scowl. "Seems like whoever was trying to kill me wasn't very good at aiming their sword, so you had to have your shot, too."

"Black Tarantula?"

"Hm?" Melinda asked.

"You told me, when I got here that night, that it was Black Tarantula," Matt said, sitting on the couch.

Melinda shrugged. "Matt, is that *really* why you came here? I should put your name on a list downstairs, so you can never get up to my door again. You basically ruined my career. I look like I was covering up some massive conspiracy just because we hadn't fully cleared some information. And you're here asking me about . . . a Black Tarantula?" she said. "What do you want me to say? I was bleeding out. Some giant dude dressed in black came at me when I answered the door, mumbling something—"

"A Louis XIV quote."

Her heart skipped a beat. Melinda glared at Matt.

"I'm not on the stand here, not anymore," she said. "Save that for the rest of the trial, if you can do it without getting your jollies from roasting me."

Matt nodded a few times. "I came here to apologize, not to criticize. I'm sorry I wasn't there when you woke up. I should have been. And I'm sorry I had to call you to the stand."

Melinda nodded slowly.

"Where were you?"

Matt didn't respond.

She continued, "That's what I keep asking myself . . . this man, this guy that everyone loves and admires, who seems like a good partner most of the time . . . just disappears when I need him most. I'm literally having emergency surgery performed on me to save my life and you go out for a walk?" Melinda put her hand on her temple, as if willing away tears. "Then, out of nowhere, you call me up to the stand—to undermine my own staff and to create smoke and mirrors around your client. I thought you were different, Matt, but you're just like any other lawyer—a slimeball just scraping and clawing to get by. And here, you've got the guts to come apologize, but you can't even bring yourself to tell me what was so goddamn important that you left me dying in the hospital? You treat calling me as a fucking witness like it's some kind of DMV appointment?"

Matt opened his mouth, but Melinda went on.

"No, let me finish," she said. "Where *were* you, Matt? What were you doing?"

Matt had prepared for this question, as shameful as it felt to have a lie at the ready. But now, in the moment, his excuse felt so flimsy he almost stayed silent.

"I got a tip about the Castle case," Matt said. Even he wouldn't have believed himself if he'd heard it. "An informant. I had to go. I wish I'd stayed."

Melinda scoffed.

"An informant, huh? Was it the guy that handed you those bank records? The ones that I was certain were not public?" She blew out a breath. "Okay. Gunderson said you looked like you'd gotten your ass beat—blood on your shirt, bruised all over. Hell, I can see that shiner from here. Matt, you've got some dark shit going on in your life. As wonderful as you can be, you're a secretive dude, and honestly, I'm too old to be playing games. I want to meet someone who wants to be with me, not just when it's convenient. That's the last time you get to treat me like trash. You can leave now."

Matt stood up along with Melinda and tried to reach his arm out, but she backed away.

"Melinda, I'm—"

"You're sorry, I get it. But an apology doesn't mean you're forgiven. See you around, Matt. Hopefully not for a good long while."

His instinct told him to keep talking, to try and end things on better terms—but Matt Murdock was also smart enough to know when a conversation was over. He made his way to the door. As he wrapped his hand around the knob he heard Melinda curse under her breath.

"What is it?" Matt asked.

Melinda was a few feet away, looking at her phone. She looked up at Matt.

"It's Castle," she said, her eyes wide.

"What?" Matt asked.

"He's gone."

FORTY-TWO

HE HATED HIMSELF for doing this, but he couldn't help it.

Her heart had skipped a beat.

As the media and the city spun out in response to Frank Castle's brazen escape from Riker's, Daredevil was perched outside Dakota North's apartment fire escape, listening.

"Remind me never to date you again," Dakota said, not sarcastically. "If this is what you do to your girlfriends."

"It's not like that," Daredevil said.

Dakota tilted her head and frowned.

"Then how is it, Matt? You called me and asked me to look into this Torres woman. I know you guys were an item. Trust me, I did my own little social-media-stalking spiral after you brushed me off. She seems like a great lady. Smart, beautiful, respected . . . Leave it to you to screw it all up."

"What did you find?" Daredevil asked, avoiding Dakota's criticism.

"Don't rush me, Hornhead," Dakota said with a snap. "You had all the time in the world to run a background check on your lady friend. Maybe you should be asking why you let yourself fall head over heels so fast, huh?"

"I deserved that," Daredevil said. "Just tell me. What did you find?"

She shrugged.

"A whole lot of nothing," she said. "Torres hasn't been in New York very long—but her records check out. Born and raised in Jersey. Went to school in California. Law enforcement in South Florida for a few departments, then transferred up here to Internal Affairs when a spot opened up. Her friend, Gunderson, vouched for her and she got the gig. You didn't exactly give me time to do any deep-dive interviews, so all you get is the paperwork I could dig up. But none of that tells me anything aside from the fact that she's a hard-working lady, appreciated at her workplace, and unfortunately another victim of Matt Murdock, serial playboy."

"That's not fair."

"*Life's* not fair, Matt," Dakota said. "You can head back to whatever you were doing before. There's no there-there with this lady. You have to face the truth."

"What's that?"

"That you messed this up on your own. You violated her trust and didn't get away with it," Dakota said. "You might have to sit with that for a bit."

Daredevil nodded. Dakota was smart. Independent. She didn't mince words, either. It's what drew him to her in the first place. But it stung to hear it this way.

"I'm heading to intercept Fisk," Daredevil said.

"Need a hand?" Dakota asked. Daredevil could sense her softening. She'd laid into him—deservedly so. But that's what good friends did.

"Stand by," Daredevil said as he shot his billy club into the Hell's Kitchen air. "I may need all the help I can get."

FORTY-THREE

RICHARD FISK WAS off the board, hooked into a number of wires and tubes at St. Vincent's Hospital. Whatever Daredevil thought he could get from him was far out of reach.

Daredevil looked down at the floor of Fisk's apartment, where the EMTs had found him—three vicious stab wounds cutting through him—and cursed his timing.

Daredevil walked farther into Fisk's Midtown penthouse. Richard Fisk may have flamed out as a mob boss, first as the Schemer and later, and somewhat more successfully, as the Rose, but that didn't preclude him from living in luxury. From what Daredevil could tell, he didn't seem to be wanting for anything.

He crouched down next to the dried pool of blood that had collected under Fisk's body. The potential killing blow had come from behind. Daredevil frowned. After running into Fisk, he'd managed to scare the errant mob boss into sticking around. Was his potential death going to be on his tab?

Daredevil had planned to shadow Fisk to the upstate meeting—a free pass to the biggest underworld convention since the Apalachin raid. But now he wondered if there was a meeting at all.

The apartment was ransacked—sofa cushions sliced open, file

cabinets tipped over, glasses and plates shattered. This wasn't just a targeted murder—there was a search element. He found the note in the kitchen, half underneath the refrigerator. It was in a greeting card envelope. But once Daredevil opened it, he found a twice-folded piece of notebook paper, with a hastily written message on it. A message for Daredevil.

The meet is a trap. I'm out.

It'd never been sent.

And that smell. Brimstone and fire.

The smell was familiar—similar to the smoke that arose when a Hand foot soldier was killed, but not the same. It was a scent he'd picked up a few places before.

"They're making a final play."

Daredevil sensed Elektra standing across the room. Her sword was drawn. He wasn't surprised she'd snuck up on him. Elektra was the best—able to elude even Daredevil's super-senses.

"Who is?"

"That remains to be seen, Matthew," Elektra said, scanning the room.

"You know, Elektra, if I didn't know any better, you'd look like a great suspect for all this," Daredevil said. "But I was with you when Silvermane was taken out."

Elektra spoke without moving. "My days as an assassin-for-hire are over. But the Hand still appreciates my form and old methods. But if I was the one behind all this, Matthew—you'd be the last to know, and the first to fall."

Daredevil wasn't sure if she was joking but he smiled anyway. He needed any kind of laugh at this point.

"Fisk was my best lead. He was the money man. He paid off Sheehan—ran Mezinis and Charleston. But now he's off the grid. So, is it as simple as the Hand stepping into the underworld, or is there more?" Daredevil said, slamming a fist into his open palm.

He felt his phone buzzing and pulled it out. It was Foggy. He picked up.

"Foggy, I'm—"

Daredevil paused. His expression was enough for Elektra to move closer and mouth, "What's going on?"

"You're kidding," Daredevil said. "No, yeah, I'm on my way. Yes. At the office. Of course—you have to represent me. Becky can second chair if we get that far. Dammit."

Daredevil jabbed at his phone display and slid it back into an unseen pocket of his costume. He turned to Elektra, a look of complete disbelief on his face.

"Foggy said the police came by to arrest me," Daredevil said.

"Arrest you? Matt Murdock?" Elektra asked. "On what grounds?"

"They claim to have evidence that . . ." Daredevil trailed off. "That I helped the Punisher escape."

FORTY-FOUR

"WHAT KIND OF evidence do they have, Foggy?"

Matt Murdock paced around the main waiting room in the offices of Nelson & Murdock. Foggy and Becky watched as he ran a hand through his hair.

"Matt, they're not gonna show their cards. But they have enough for a warrant, so a judge saw the evidence and okayed a search of your apartment," Foggy said. "And, I guess, based on that, Sprenger is filing charges. And look, it sure didn't help that you've been AWOL for most of the day. Now you're a damn flight risk. Couldn't you be bothered to check in with the cops when your own client escapes from prison?"

The words sent a jolt through Matt. They'd searched his home. He tried to think about any major evidence—his costume, files on enemies, *anything*—that would tie him directly to being Daredevil. But nothing came to mind. The bulk of his equipment was tucked away in a secret compartment that only he could access, a small structure on the roof of the building that resembled a work shed. It was secure, Matt knew—but hearing that people had wandered through his living space without his consent did not sit well.

"They want to arrest me, then?"

Foggy nodded. "Yup. They're on their way here." He motioned toward the street. "And based on the gaggle of press in the lobby, they're looking for a perp walk."

Becky wheeled her chair between Matt and Foggy and pulled up her phone's messaging app.

"I have a friend in the DA's office—a close friend. They're putting their neck on the line for sending me this," Becky said, reading messages from her phone.

Looks like they found texts between your friend and Punisher.

Tips on how to get out that matched Punisher's actual escape.

Does not look good. Only room is to fight ownership—they have no real way of confirming that it was Murdock texting Castle, aside from them saying who they are.

"This is a setup," Matt said. "And I'm not going to play along."

Foggy stood up.

"Matt, we don't have a choice—I'm sure we'll beat the rap, but we have to play by the rules," Foggy said. "You can't just go on the lam."

"You never saw me tonight, Foggy," Matt said, grabbing his coat. "I wasn't here."

He tossed his cell phone onto the ground and stomped on it with the heel of his foot. Then he crouched down and threw the pieces into the trash.

"I'm not returning your calls, either."

((((( )))))

They wanted him off the board.

Daredevil knew that much, as he swung through the city, weaving between Midtown high-rises and apartment complexes, the sounds and smells of the city pushing to get through to him.

But why?

He landed on a nearby rooftop and let his senses blanket Hell's Kitchen. He let the sounds (the screams, laughter, honking horns, screeching tires) and smells (food vendors, burnt rubber, cheap perfume, stale beer) flow over him. This was his city. It was the place he'd sworn to protect.

Someone knew he was Daredevil. And knew that if you have Matt Murdock in jail, so goes Daredevil.

But whoever knew that would also know that Matt Murdock—and Foggy Nelson—were great attorneys. The rap wouldn't stick for very long.

So what was happening now that required Daredevil to be absent for a while?

He reached for the burner phone in his pocket and dialed the number by memory.

"*Daily Bugle*, Urich. Say your piece."

"Ben . . ." Daredevil let his voice hang over the phone.

"You shouldn't be calling me."

"Then let's say I'm not," Daredevil said. "Someone wants me taken out. I know the stories are already hitting the press. Picking up on the momentum from the last smear campaign. I don't have a lot of time."

Ben remained silent on the other end of the line.

"I need a favor, Ben, and I need you to trust me," Daredevil said, unable to hide the desperation in his voice. "Someone is gunning for the remaining underbosses in the city—under the pretense of a meeting upstate. They got Richard Fisk already. They probably helped Castle get out, too."

A quick intake of breath from Ben. Nothing more.

"I think whoever set this meeting up doesn't want to hash things out with the other bosses, they want to *kill* them, either with Castle's help or some other way. I need to know who got invited. My only thought was your contact. Did they say who was coming?"

Another long pause.

Finally, Ben spoke.

"You'll be getting something in a second."

Then the line went dead.

Daredevil tapped the burner phone and was alerted he had one unread text message from an unknown number. It was a list of names and addresses. He tapped a few keys from memory.

"Thank you, Ben," Daredevil said under his breath.

Then he leapt into the cold Hell's Kitchen evening.

FORTY-FIVE

OSWALD SILKWORTH was scared. Very scared.

Daredevil could hear his thumping even from a rooftop away. Even without powers, he mused, he might still pick up the nervous squelching of Silkworth's indigestion as he zipped around Wilson Fisk's old penthouse office. He could smell his acrid sweat, no matter how desperately he blotted at it, too. The Kingpin's former right-hand man was muttering a soft Hail Mary under his breath as he paced around the room.

"We gotta get goin', boss," Daredevil heard someone say from behind. Bullseye. "Getting there isn't exactly a hop and a skip."

Silkworth turned around and faced his hired assassin.

"Do you take me for a fool, Bullseye?"

"You really want me to answer that?" Bullseye responded.

"We're not going to this meeting," the Arranger said, sitting in a chair in front of the desk that had once belonged to his boss, the Kingpin. "I don't care how powerful the Hand claims to be—or how curious I am to hear who's running their operation. I believe in preserving my life. Don't you?"

Daredevil heard Bullseye's cold, evil laugh.

"Whatever you say," he said. "As long as your check clears, right?

You wanna stay home and watch a rom-com, let's do it. I'll make the popcorn."

"I'll be in my study," the Arranger said, moving toward Bullseye.

"You mean *Fisk's* study, right?" Bullseye said with a wink.

Then came the click of an automatic rifle from a nearby rooftop. The sweat on a trigger finger touching metal.

Daredevil didn't have time for more. He crashed through the main window of the Kingpin's office, shards of glass spreading across the luxurious room—he felt his body slam into Silkworth's light form as a series of gunshots hit the space he'd just occupied. The older man was shaking, glass caught in his shirt and face. Daredevil stood up and turned around. Bullseye was standing across from him, the giant hole Daredevil had created in the windows behind him.

"You got a nasty habit of wrecking these windows, Daredevil," Bullseye said with a smirk. "Shall I put it on your tab?"

Daredevil braced, but their brawl-to-be was interrupted by another hail of bullets, then another body hurtling through the window.

The Punisher.

"Castle—the hell are you doing here?" Daredevil asked.

"Should ask you the same thing," Castle said with a grunt before he sent a new barrage of bullets in Bullseye's direction, barely missing as the deft assassin did a backflip to dodge the spray of gunfire.

Castle turned his gaze back to Daredevil—the machine gun pointed in his direction.

"Need you to step aside," he said, as if he were asking Daredevil to pass the mustard.

Another piece of the puzzle fell into place for Daredevil: Someone had not only clued in Ben Urich on the invitees to the meeting, they'd also clued in Castle. And perhaps helped get him out of prison.

"They say your lawyer found a novel way to get you out of prison," Daredevil said.

Castle chuckled.

"I didn't need Murdock's help, never did—and that guy would never give me any," Castle said, reloading his weapon. "Whoever left the door unlocked knows me well. And that's just fine by me. I want these assholes dead. I don't care who points me in their direction—or who pulls the trigger."

Another wave of gunfire. Daredevil leapt left, feeling the whoosh of the bullets streak past him. Then he heard a muffled groan, and a gurgling sound that could only signal one thing.

As he landed, he rolled to his right and looked at Silkworth, seemingly pinned to the far wall, a handful of bullets in his chest, blood trickling down his off-white shirt, the red matching his tie.

The Arranger was done for.

Daredevil scrambled to his feet and watched as the Punisher approached Bullseye, who'd taken a fighting stance across from him.

"I came for Silkworth, but you can be the bonus," Punisher said.

"That's not the deal," Bullseye said, a sliver of fear in his voice.

The deal.

Bullseye was in on it. Whoever had organized the meeting had also let Castle loose—and framed Matt for the crime. Had they also been using Bullseye to keep tabs on the Arranger, too?

"I don't know about any deal," the Punisher said, opening fire on Bullseye. "Not anymore."

The assassin leapt out of danger and reached for a handful of glass shards, tossing them. The Punisher groaned in surprise as the high-speed chunks of glass embedded themselves into his arm and upper body. As Bullseye rushed toward the doorway at the other side of the sprawling office, Daredevil reached for his billy club and sent one end toward his feet. He felt the shape of the black-clad assassin trip over the wire connecting the two sticks of his billy club, and then he yanked to tighten the hold. Bullseye tumbled forward, his face and shoulders bearing the brunt of the fall.

The Punisher was still rolling around the floor in pain, glass embedded in his neck and shoulder. Daredevil made his way to Bullseye and placed a knee on the killer's neck.

"What was the deal, Lester?" Daredevil said, pinning the killer down. He knew Bullseye wouldn't answer. Not right away.

Then a sound. A strange humming coming from Bullseye. It took Daredevil a moment to recognize what it was.

Laughter.

"The *deal*, Hornhead?" Bullseye said with a cackle. "This was the deal. For Silkworth. For Castle . . . for you. Welcome to the trap, buddy."

Then that smell. Brimstone. Smoke. Singed flesh. Daredevil sensed it coming closer.

The ding of the elevator.

A figure—familiar. Her scent. But not just one. Two of them. Two people. In one form. A shape and feeling he never thought he'd experience again.

She walked through the elevator doors, flanked by a half-dozen members of the Hand. She drew two large, flaming swords from her back. Daredevil felt his heart shatter as he braced for this nightmare to get much, much worse.

And much more personal.

"Hi, babykins," Typhoid Mary said, stepping into the office. "Long time no see."

FORTY-SIX

THE PUNISHER charged at her first.

Typhoid moved seamlessly toward the vigilante, sending one of her swords through his midsection. Daredevil watched as the man slouched over and screamed while Typhoid pulled her sword back out, the *schloomp* sound booming in Daredevil's head as the Punisher crumpled to the floor.

"Oh, what a shame," Typhoid said. "And here you'd just gained your freedom. I hope you didn't make big plans, Punisher."

Daredevil jumped to his feet and assessed the situation.

Typhoid Mary was fully in the office now, a handful of Hand ninjas on either side. The Punisher was down for the count, and Bullseye was watching from the edge of it all.

This did not look good. Not in the least.

"Daredevil, been a minute . . . Or has it?" Typhoid said, stepping toward him. "Don't think I haven't missed you, though. In fact, you could say you were always top of mind."

"Mary, what's going on?" Daredevil asked, scanning the room. "You're working with the Hand now? You've sold yourself out to them?"

Typhoid swung one of her swords in Daredevil's direction. He leapt back easily. But he knew it was just meant as a warning shot.

"Sold myself? Come on now, sweetie," Typhoid said. "This is personal. I didn't make any deals that didn't benefit me. And every fool in this room was helping me—even you."

Daredevil jumped at Typhoid, lunging at her, hoping to take her by surprise—but she seemed to predict his offensive, side-stepped his leap. He was met by one of the Hand, who hit him with a series of punches and kicks that forced him to the floor.

"Tsk, tsk, tsk, Daredevil," Typhoid said. "At least let a girl finish, huh?"

The rest was a blur. He felt an elbow slam into the back of his head. A powerful kick to his stomach. He could hear the Punisher groaning in pain as life seemed to trickle out of him. Then someone grabbing his face—sending a brutal punch into his mouth. Laughter. Loud, booming, shrill—she was watching. Watching these mystical ninjas pound Daredevil into a puddle.

He tried to fight back. He pushed some of them off him, but more came—a shuriken to his chest, a slash in his arm, a kick to the shin.

Just give up, he thought. *You've done enough. Let it go.*

Then Stick's voice, always the loudest.

Don't be stupid, kid. Hold on. Keep fighting. Keep brawling. Use what I taught you. Fight.

Then darkness.

FORTY-SEVEN

"YOU GOT ANYTHING FOR ME, Urich?"

Jonah Jameson's voice echoed across the *Daily Bugle* newsroom and landed squarely on Ben's wobbly desk. They were minutes from the Final Edition deadline, and Ben hadn't filed his story. He couldn't bring himself to do it. It just felt wrong.

Ben looked at his laptop and reread the headline he'd crafted as a suggestion to the copy desk. It still felt wrong, to say the least. But he didn't have anything to refute it.

STAR ATTORNEY MATT MURDOCK WANTED
FOR AIDING ALLEGED MURDERER'S ESCAPE

FINANCIAL RECORDS POINT TO CONNECTION
WITH DISGRACED POLICE OFFICER

"Why'd you do it, Matt?" Ben muttered to himself as he reread the lede to the story. It made no sense. Matt wanted the Punisher behind bars; he just wanted him to have a fair shake. And Matt had been digging around the company funneling cash to Sheehan, not funneling the cash himself.

Sheehan.

Ben rubbed his chin. Then he grabbed his cell phone and called a friend.

Luke Cage picked up on the first ring.

"Ben, my man. How are you? Kind of late for a check-in."

"Matt's in trouble, Luke," Ben said. "And I hate to involve myself in this super-hero stuff, but I don't think he can get out of this by himself."

"Sure is in trouble," Cage said. Ben could almost see him shaking his head. "All over the news. Been trying to get ahold of him, too."

"You got any contacts in the NYPD anymore, Luke?" Ben asked.

A pause.

"I might. What do you need?"

"Ed Sheehan—the dead cop they wanted to pin on Castle," Ben said. "He was crooked. I just don't know how. The facts I have, the facts I need to report on, say otherwise. But my gut tells me they're wrong. Sheehan was making boatloads of money. They're trying to pin it on Matt . . . but what was he really doing? I need to know."

Cage grunted on the other line.

"Lemme make a few calls. I'll ask Jessica to chip in, too," Cage said. "What's your timeline like?"

"Like, now," Ben said, letting out a long breath. "It's not going to make the paper—but it just might save Matt's ass."

"That's what we're here for sometimes," Cage said with a low laugh. "To save Matt Murdock's white ass."

Ben let out a slight chuckle as he disconnected the line, but it fizzled. He felt helpless. But he also felt a gnawing sense that he was missing something. Something major.

He knew the charges against Matt were bogus.

He selected the text of the article on his screen and hit Delete.

Ben Urich was a reporter. Perhaps the best this city had ever seen.

He trafficked in facts and information. Journalism was like an equation. You put in the different elements—dates, quotes, details—and the story was the result. But the story had to be true. It had to reflect the reality. It had to paint a picture.

What picture did the facts—and the lies—paint, Ben wondered?

He pulled out his notebook on the Fisk case and started crossing things out.

FORTY-EIGHT

"MATT . . ." THE VOICE—FAMILIAR. Soothing. Reaching out to him, pulling him back. "Matt, wake up. It's okay."

Melinda. Her shape, blurring. He didn't know where he was. How he'd gotten here. But he could hear her voice. Smell her. But something was wrong.

"C'mon, baby," Melinda said, her voice sharpening. Twisting into something else. "It's time you learn the truth of it all."

Daredevil felt cloudy, a loud buzzing around him—around his senses. He couldn't pinpoint anything. Smells, sounds, touch—all seemed to blur. It sounded like Melinda. Smelled like her sweet, tangy perfume. But also like something else. Someone else's voice. Fire.

And brimstone.

"Melinda . . . ." Daredevil said, his voice a low croak. "How did . . . how did you get here?"

He felt a hand ball his shirt and yank him up. Then that voice again.

"Get here, baby? I've always been here."

It was Typhoid now. But how was that possible . . . ?

"Still not clicking for you, tough guy?" Typhoid said. "Taking a minute to get that brain working again?"

Daredevil could feel her breath, hot on his face. Melinda. Typhoid.

Both of them. In the same place—same space.

But how?

"No . . . it can't be," Daredevil muttered to himself.

Typhoid kissed his mouth tenderly.

"But it is, baby," Typhoid said. "Payback's a bitch, isn't it?"

Daredevil tried to speak, but his mind was overwhelmed. Details seemed to flood into his brain from every direction.

"Thought you were smarter than this, Matt," Typhoid said, her mouth close to his. "Kind of amazing what some mutant pheromones and ninja mysticism can do . . . can make you even forget who you are . . ."

She kissed him on the mouth again, slow, and passionate.

". . . or who you're with . . ."

Daredevil pulled away. That was when he realized he was bound to a large, metal chair. Taut rope wrapped around his wrists and arms. He couldn't sense anyone else nearby—no heartbeats or movements. But that meant little when you were dealing with the Hand. They could be anywhere. They were ethereal—almost ghost-like. But that wasn't the immediate problem. From what Daredevil could tell, they were still in Fisk's building—below the penthouse office, in the cavernous, secret spaces only the Kingpin and his cronies knew about. The room was large—perhaps once a giant meeting space, now devoid of chairs and tables. Just an empty void. But that was the least of Daredevil's concerns.

"What did you do with her . . . ?" Daredevil said, his voice dry and cracking, as if he hadn't used it in years.

Typhoid's tone changed. From romantic and silly to serious and stern. She was annoyed.

"Don't you get it, baby? There is no Melinda. Never was. This was the longest of long cons, and you fell for it like the lovesick dope you are." Typhoid sent a slap across Daredevil's face. "So much for the big bad super hero, huh? The razor-sharp legal mind? Bet you thought you were some A-list alpha calling your girlfriend up on the stand, just to prove a point—that you were better than her. That you were a good guy, sacrificing your personal life to protect a nutjob like Castle, while Melinda Torres was just another corrupt cop."

Daredevil heard the blade unsheathing. Felt the cold wind as she brought it up close to his face.

"Who's laughing now, Matt? The trial of the century is over, your girlfriend never even existed, your rep is in the shitter, and the entire Kitchen is aflame."

"What are you . . . Typhoid . . . What are you even talking about . . . ?"

Daredevil felt his radar sense go foggy. He couldn't think straight. Typhoid had this effect on him. He couldn't pinpoint where she was—could barely make out the room. Where the hell were they? And was what she was saying even possible, Daredevil wondered? Could Typhoid have . . . been Melinda?

His mind raced. He took a roller-coaster ride through his memories. The moments with her. Pulling her close in her bed. Kissing in the rain, each drop a light jolt. Sliding his fingers into hers as they crossed the street. Her sly smile across the table. The sharp perfume that he could locate a block away. Matt Murdock had been on the cusp of falling in love with this woman. Had opened his heart to her in a way he thought forever lost—forever gone. Since Karen. Elektra. How had he missed it?

The smell. Fire and brimstone. Melinda's lack of a past—of connections beyond her resume. Mezinis . . . the name stuck in Daredevil's skull. It came back to him now. Mezinis & Charleston.

Typhoid Mary was Mary Walker. That was her birth name. But she had many aliases. Mezinis had been one of them, long ago. It was under the name Mary Mezinis that Matt Murdock had been able to have Mary committed, during his attempt to sabotage the Kingpin's empire from within.

After battling Typhoid Mary as Daredevil, he'd weakened her defenses—tempting her into an intimate moment with him and coaxing her inner personality of "Mary" out. Matt had manipulated her. Abusing the knowledge he had of her mental illness, her insecurities—to gain intelligence on the Kingpin and, in his mind, help her recover. In the short term, his actions had left the Kingpin isolated, and—he hoped—given Mary a chance at treatment. In the moment Daredevil felt gutted, but in retrospect he realized this had been just one instance in a long pattern—of Daredevil using and abusing the knowledge gained from his relationships to further his own personal crusade, everything else be damned. He'd become a lesser man to try and save her, while also trying to destroy Fisk. He'd done the same to Briggs. To Melinda. Had sacrificed bonds to further his mission, over and over.

He thought Typhoid Mary was gone—better, healing, safe. But he was wrong. Here she was. In complete control of her powers. And if what she said was true, she'd been hiding in plain sight for months—in every corner of Matt's life. Intimately aware of every aspect of it.

"It's not possible," Daredevil said weakly. "It couldn't happen like that. . . ."

"Oh boy, it happened, Matty," Typhoid said. "And hey, I can't say it wasn't fun. I've always thought you were a stud. And what a charmer. For a second there, I almost let myself believe it—here was Mary Walker, head over heels in love with lawyer Matt Murdock. The power couple of the year. But this is the really sweet part, baby. That look on your face. I wish you weren't blind . . . you would've sure gotten a kick out of it."

"Why . . . Why, Mary?" Daredevil asked, still tugging at his restraints. He couldn't get a read on her. She'd always been a cipher to him. Her vitals always changing and morphing. Even now, in this enclosed space, she was a moving target. His radar sense was almost useless. "This isn't you. . . . This is just part of you."

"Oh, you're a doctor now? Please, Matt, spare me," Typhoid said, pressing the blade closer to his face. He felt the cut forming—the sting of pain. "I'm tired of the well-meaning-dude perspective. 'Oh, sorry, honey, I just wanted to hear you talk to me under oath, is all, to be sure.' You don't think I caught that little nosy friend of yours sniffing around me, too? My records were airtight, though. No one raised a single eyebrow when it came to Melinda Torres. Why should they? There was one. I just happened to fit the profile. It was kismet. And to think—maybe somehow, someway, you could have met her? Things sure would've been different, huh?"

"You're a murderer . . ." Daredevil said. "Monster . . ."

A punch in the stomach now.

"We're resorting to insults now?" Typhoid said, standing up and backing away. "Like this is just another brawl for you? Matt, you slept next to me for months. We shared meals. We made travel plans. We were together. How does it feel to know that I only got this close to you—this far inside you—just so I could burst out and tear you apart?"

Daredevil let his head hang down. He felt broken. His entire being felt uprooted. Melinda wasn't Karen. He'd always known that. Who could be? But there had been something there—a glimmer of hope—that even if this woman couldn't match the partner he'd lost, perhaps she could light a new path. A new love. A new life. Realizing it wasn't that—it was something darker and more sinister—left a gaping hole inside him.

"You didn't answer . . . my question," Daredevil said, wincing as he tried to break free. He could hear the end of the rope grating against something metal. Every time he pulled he could hear some of the fibers snapping. He just had to keep at it, had to keep her talking. "Why, Mary? You don't want to be a mob boss . . . you don't like giving orders. You love the thrill. The violence. The bloodlust. I know I hurt you, Mary. Took you out of this life. But I need you to believe me—I wanted to help you. I wanted to get you away from Fisk. Somewhere safe, where you could get the attention you needed. I cared about you, Mary."

An elbow to the jaw. Daredevil felt something crack.

"You selfish prick," Typhoid said. "You didn't *care* about me. You just cared about yourself. You cared about your little brawl with Fisk. About the Kitchen. I was collateral damage."

Daredevil heard her breathing—heavy and weighted. She was pacing back now, her sweaty palm on a doorknob, turning slowly.

"But I'm a survivor . . . I know how to turn your strengths into weaknesses," Typhoid said, each word coming out like a dagger. "Do you remember that feeling, Matty? When it feels like everything is falling apart? You don't know where to turn? That was me that night—after telling me you loved me, when you left me in some dive motel, naked and alone, only to be found by some cops and psychiatrists eager to study me, like some kind of experiment."

Daredevil felt Typhoid's hate. "But now it's your turn," she added.

He started to respond, but Typhoid didn't slow down.

"Right now, beloved local attorney Matt Murdock has a big ol' warrant out for his arrest," Typhoid said. "For aiding Castle—who I think is still bleeding out in Willie's office, maybe someone should check on him—anyway . . . but you're also in deep water for the very thing you dragged me . . . Melinda . . . through the mud over. That shell company? Once your little sidekick Ben Urich digs into the documents you probably slid his way . . . he'll see that Mezinis and Charleston was operated by none other than *you*, cutie."

Daredevil pulled at his restraints again. A few more threads popped loose. But not enough.

"No, that's not possible," Daredevil said. "Fisk . . . Richard Fisk never filed the paperwork. . . ."

"You believe anything that washed-up never-was has to say? How charming. How optimistic you've become in your old age," Typhoid said, her hand still on the doorknob. "You really think Richard Fisk was a player? That strung-out nepo baby served his purpose. But all the big moves were coming from here. From me. And from *him*."

The door swung open, and a massive figure stepped through.

"Matt Murdock," the Kingpin said in his booming, deep voice. "What a pleasure to witness your final moments."

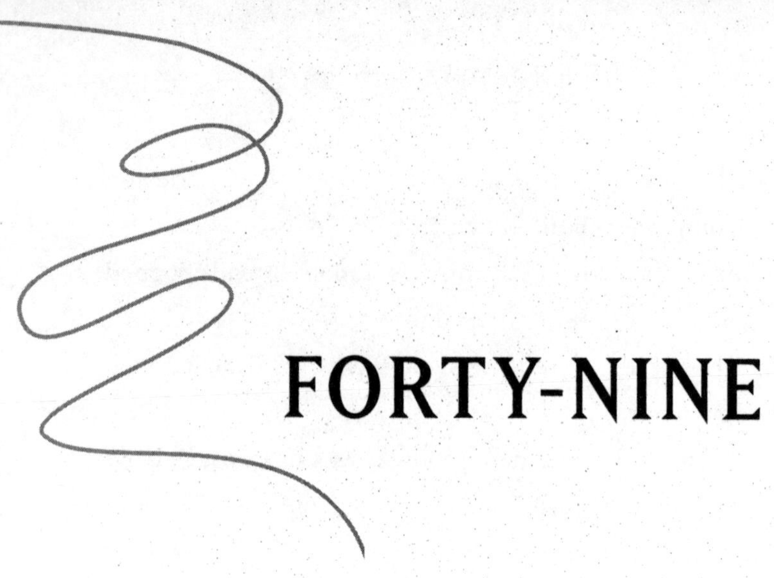

FORTY-NINE

"FISK," DAREDEVIL SAID.

It was him. There was no trickery here. No doubt. Daredevil recognized the heartbeat. The acrid smell of his sweat. The way he moved. Wilson Fisk—the Kingpin—was alive. And Matt Murdock's entire life was unraveling right before him.

"You don't seem all that surprised," Fisk said stepping into the room. A handful of Hand henchmen followed. Daredevil could tell they were dragging the Punisher along with them. "But it doesn't matter. Not now, at least. Everything has gone according to plan—the fortification of my rule over the city, and the downfall of one Matt Murdock."

Daredevil pulled at the ropes again. More threads popped. He was close now.

"A tragedy about Silkworth," Kingpin said, mostly to himself. "He was the perfect custodian of my empire. Never a threat, always loyal. A shame he had to die, and not knowing the truth, either."

But to what end? Daredevil was confident in his abilities—he knew he could fight. But against Typhoid, a swarm of Hand ninjas . . . *and* the Kingpin? The odds were not in his favor.

But had they ever been?

It all seemed to sync up in Daredevil's mind. The "why" of it all. Wilson Fisk had felt threatened. Had felt his own underlings encroaching, tasting blood. Word had spread that he was going down. So, preemptively, Fisk fakes his own death and slowly eliminates his competition, including his failure of a son—while playing a long con on the man he felt was the biggest threat to him of all, Daredevil. Only to come back stronger and deadlier, partnered with the Hand and with both Typhoid and Bullseye by his side.

As far as schemes, Daredevil thought, this was a pretty good one.

"Have you figured it out yet, Murdock?" Kingpin asked. "I'd broken you before. I saw you come back from nothing—from the wreckage of your home and life—to become an even greater thorn in my side. And you began to taunt me, with your threats—about my wife, about my empire crumbling. The one thing I can't stomach is taunting. I will not be bullied. That was when I knew I had to do more than take things away. I had to crush your spirit. I had to crush your heart. You're a man of feelings and drive, Murdock. If I not only broke you from within, but also made it clear to the world around you that Matt Murdock, beloved and respected attorney, was actually just another corrupt criminal bleeding the city dry . . . then I would truly win. Then I could return and sit atop my throne, without any worry. And with Typhoid by my side."

She moved to him. Matt sensed them getting closer, her blurred form blending into his. Their mouths connecting. He felt a strange pang of jealousy. He wasn't sure why. Melinda was gone. Had never existed, really. Just another trick—another trap.

He had to get out. Had to regroup.

Daredevil pulled again. Gently this time. One of the ropes loosened. Then the other. He'd pulled so gently it'd be impossible for anyone to notice. He waited. Positioned his body as if he was still tightly bound. As if the ropes were still taut.

"Wow, dead or not, you sure do love to hear yourself talk, Fisk," Daredevil said with a smile. "Didn't you learn anything in the afterlife?"

Kingpin lunged at Daredevil, expecting him to be incapacitated and unable to dodge—but Daredevil toppled his chair to one side, letting the Kingpin's massive frame and momentum carry him past. Daredevil rolled to the side of the room—which seemed much bigger than he'd first thought. But that didn't improve the odds much—the Hand henchmen were poised and ready to fight, and Typhoid had drawn her swords, aflame thanks to her pyrokinetic abilities.

Kingpin pulled himself up from the wreckage he'd caused and dusted off his suit. He didn't like to get himself dirty like this. Only if he had to.

Still, he walked toward Daredevil slowly, confidently.

"There truly is no point to this, Murdock. Your life is on the precipice of a shambles . . . by this time tomorrow, you'll be broken, imprisoned, and wishing for the death I will refuse to give you."

Daredevil heard her heartbeat. The sound of heavy boots on a windowsill. Deep breaths meant to calm her body and mind.

And for the first time in what felt like forever, Daredevil felt relief.

"You think, Willie, that you'd stop acting like you'd won so early in the game," Daredevil said, raising his fists. "Don't you know by now—"

Then the crash came, and Daredevil sensed Elektra's lithe body tear through an open window, her boot connecting with Typhoid's face. As she landed, sais drawn, surrounded by the Hand, she looked at Daredevil and allowed herself a brief, fleeting smile.

"The Devil of Hell's Kitchen is hard to kill."

FIFTY

"ARE YOU KIDDING ME, Urich?"

J. Jonah Jameson's eyes bored into reporter Ben Urich's skull, spittle flying from the *Daily Bugle* publisher's mouth as he leaned over his desk.

"I'm ten minutes from the final print deadline and you delete your one-A story—and you come at me with *that*?" Jameson said, banging a fist on his desk. "I'll have to redo the entire front page. Not to mention have legal look it over."

"It's legit, Jonah," Ben said softly. "Wilson Fisk is alive."

Ben dropped a stack of papers Jameson's desk.

"Everyone was hyper-focused on Ed Sheehan, the cop, getting paid off. But no one considered that maybe he wasn't just getting paid—he was a funnel," Ben continued. "The reason Matt, when he was defending Castle, couldn't make the facts stick was because they'd been changed. When they wheeled in Fisk's body, the medical examiner faked the report, at least according to a tip I got recently. I didn't have time to dig into it much because of everything going on, but once I did the picture became clearer. Seems he listed weapons he assumed Castle would have on him but didn't. The person who signed off on the autopsy Fisk's people did—lady by the name of Tamika Briggs—was ordered to do it by an ME named Sam Weingarten. Seems Weingarten had a negative gambling balance bigger than some countries' national debt. He was primed to be manipulated."

"How does that mean Fisk is alive?" Jameson said, his growl softened as he scanned the data Ben had tossed his way. "That's a big leap."

"A source in the department tells me Sheehan was crooked through and through—had worked as a bodyguard with Fisk for years when he was off-duty, and he was also his mole in the department. His handler. The Arranger would task him with different police-related assignments all the time. Heard he was running some cybernetics from down south up here to Silvermane's gang too. Another one of the Kingpin's men, apparently, was teeing up Weingarten to fake an autopsy and forensics report. Except Sheehan didn't know it was Fisk's death the coroner had to fake. My guess, and I can't put this in the story yet, is he pushed back on that plan. It would be too big, you know? Tweaking an autopsy on someone that's still dead might be reasonable, but faking a death entirely? That's gonna make some noise, I bet. Sheehan probably balked, maybe stormed over to Kingpin's office with a mad-on. Then he ended up dead, dressing on the fraud salad Fisk and his gang were making."

Jameson shook his head.

"Anything else? Anything we can attribute to a real person . . . a real name?" Jonah said. "You're giving me details about an autopsy and a name, but that's not new. It doesn't prove to me Fisk is alive, or might want to fake his death—just that the ME's office might not be great at paperwork. Tell me you've got something else, Ben. Something bigger."

"I've got an affidavit. Signed and legitimate," Ben said. "It outlines many of Fisk's worst crimes over the last few years, including the death of one of his own capos, Edgardo Salazar."

"Affidavit? From who?" Jameson asked. "Please don't say Matt Murdock."

"Vanessa Fisk."

"The Kingpin's wife?" Jameson asked, incredulous. "Geez. Do I even need to ask how you got this?"

Jameson paused, rubbing his chin.

"But why, Ben?" Jameson said, looking up at the ceiling. "If you're Wilson Fisk, you have endless money, lawyers in every room . . . why fake your own death?"

"This affidavit is full proof, Jonah," Urich said. "Fisk needed to go underground, destroy Murdock's reputation, then come up and explain it all away. He needed to get off the board to reset the game."

Jameson looked at Urich, then he tapped the printout on his desk.

"Can you make this stick, Ben?" Jameson said. "Will this hold up when it hits in the morning? Because you've left me a giant hole on the front page, but I don't want to fill it with the kind of stuff that'll get me sued and sink this paper."

"Aside from the Vanessa Fisk document, I've got two sources in the department—one works in the coroner's office and can speak to Weingarten being crooked," Ben said, flipping pages in his notebook, his hastily written scrawl dominating page after page. "The other is a new hire in Internal Affairs. He doesn't want to be named, but he tells me that IA squashed any investigation into Sheehan—and casts doubt on those funds being linked to Murdock."

"So it was a smear on Murdock?"

"Seems like it," Ben said.

Jameson cleared his throat.

"Ben, this has to be airtight. I know you and Murdock are friendly. This can't look like we're trying to cover for your pal," Jameson said, though his tone was soft. He knew to tread lightly when questioning a journalist's ethics. "Anything else—preferably something that isn't anonymous?"

Ben pulled out another short stack of pages.

"I did some digging on the company—Mezinis and Charleston—that supposedly came from Murdock to Sheehan. Seems like the details about Matt were added recently, after the fact. And the company itself was never fully consolidated," Ben continued. "Fisk's kid, Richard, the guy who used to wear a purple mask and call himself the Rose, was the one filing it. It points right back to Fisk, not Murdock."

"What I don't get, Ben, is why now?" Jameson said, scratching his chin. "Fisk had it all. Murdock's just a fly in the ointment."

"That's the clincher, Jonah," Ben said. "I spoke to Sprenger, the assistant DA—guy who was prosecuting Castle. But he said in no uncertain terms that Daredevil himself had promised him some intel on Fisk, in relation to a murder in the Bronx—Murdock had suggested Daredevil talk to Sprenger. Seems that one of Fisk's capos—a guy who was set to testify against him and enter protection, suddenly disappeared, and there was clear evidence Fisk gave the order. That's in the affidavit."

"Huh. So, that plus his wife's testimony and the bastard would've been cooked just on this Salazar business," Jameson said. "But all of that goes away if he's dead. And if Murdock's rep is shot, he can come back and claim it's all tainted, part of Murdock's vendetta against him. Kind of brilliant, actually."

"Exactly," Ben said.

Jameson looked down at the printout, all his bluster gone.

"Robbie and I will give this a read, then we need to rush it over to Legal, tell them it's nuclear-hot. Get Design to rework the front on your way out, I'll tell the printer we've got a late one."

At his heart, Jonah was a newspaperman. The vendetta against

Spider-Man, that was his twisted obsession. But above everything else, Jonah wanted to put out a good paper. The kind of paper New Yorkers could trust. "Here's the headline: 'The Kingpin Lives.' Sub: 'Reputed mob boss Wilson Fisk faked death to avoid criminal charges.' Prep a version for online, too. I want this up and out there as fast as we can do it. And Ben? Do it well. Go."

Ben Urich ran.

FIFTY-ONE

THEY WERE SURROUNDED. Elektra and Daredevil stood, poised for battle, their backs to each other. Around them was a who's who of evil—the Hand, Typhoid Mary, and the Kingpin himself.

"Just like old times," Daredevil muttered.

"Now is not the moment for humor, Matthew," Elektra said, barely a whisper. She knew he could hear her. "It's time for action."

Daredevil felt Elektra backflip over him, landing between members of the Hand and sending her two sais into a pair of them, turning them both almost immediately into clouds of noxious gas. Then she spun around and did the same to two more. The odds were getting better.

Daredevil sent a pair of billy clubs at Typhoid, knocking her flaming swords out of her hands. A curse escaped her lips as they clattered to the floor.

Typhoid charged, as Daredevil knew she would—running full tilt at Daredevil without strategy or thought. But Daredevil had to let her come at him—even if it meant pain now. Sacrifice. He could feel her rage as she steamrolled toward him. She hated Daredevil. For what he did to her—intentions be damned—and for who he was. There would always be something between them. Even when she'd manipulated him to destroy his relationship with Karen, he'd been complicit in his own way. He was drawn to Mary. Perhaps that's what made connecting with Melinda easy. She had felt warm and familiar. To learn it was Typhoid all along was a surprise, but now, with a little bit of time to process it—it seemed to fit. Perhaps, in another world at another time, Matt Murdock and Mary Walker could have been something together. They both seemed to see that, and they both felt angry about it.

"You think bringing in your girlfriend is going to close this down?" Typhoid said, lunging for Daredevil, her hands scratching at his chest. "Your rep is dead, Matt. You're a broken man—inside and out. I got to see every angle of you. Your demons. Your dreams. And all I can say is . . ."

Typhoid clutched Daredevil's throat, tightening her grip. Her strength was frightening. Daredevil could already feel himself struggling for air. He sensed Elektra's figure moving behind them—had banked on it. Had taken the scratches, the insults, and the pain for it.

"You're just like all the rest, baby," Typhoid said. "Just another man who thinks it's on them to save the world. Just another guy who thinks they know it all, and damn the torpedoes if you get in his way. But I'm here to tell you, Matty, you're not as smart as you think you are."

The sound of air swooshing past a sharp, three-pronged weapon, coming closer. The zipping sound ringing through Daredevil's skull. Then the connection as Elektra's sai bored into Typhoid's back. Her voice a shrill, high-pitched scream, but not of fear—of anger. At the possibility of defeat. Of an opportunity stolen. This was to be her chance. Her moment to revenge herself on a man who'd wronged her. And now it was gone.

"No, no . . . get it off me, get it out of me!" Typhoid shrieked, her arms off Daredevil's neck, now clawing and scraping at her own back, desperate to pull the weapon away. She rolled away and Daredevil watched her writhe on the floor, still screaming, a mix of pain and anguish that Daredevil realized he could not cure himself.

"I'm sorry, Mary," Daredevil said, his voice choking back every word. "I'm sorry I let you down. I never meant to hurt—"

Boots rushing down a long hallway. A clicking sound. The grunt of someone lifting something heavy up to their shoulder. The smell of fresh blood.

The far door slammed open and Frank Castle stood in the doorway, backlit. The smell of gun smoke surrounded him.

A second later, he opened fire.

Daredevil lunged away from the hail of bullets and watched as Castle's attack took down the remaining members of the Hand, creating disturbing clouds of dust where the ninjas once were.

Then Castle started to approach Fisk, his machine gun pointed squarely at the stocky mob boss's chest. He knew what Castle was after. Elektra was too far off to stop him. Frank Castle intended to murder Fisk, in front of Daredevil. To put an end to the madness the only way he knew how.

For good, this time.

"You got away long enough, Fisk," Castle said. "But now I can make your little role-play fantasy a reality. I don't like to be manipulated. Your people promised me a shot at taking out your lieutenants. That's fine. Didn't mean I wouldn't take my shot at killing you, too."

"No, Castle—that wasn't the deal, that was never the deal," Fisk said, raising his hands up—as if those hands, who'd killed so many people directly—could stop bullets. Maybe.

Daredevil watched—as these two men, who'd been in opposition to him on so many things, in so many ways, faced off. And he asked himself: *Do I let this happen? Do I let Castle kill Fisk, then take Castle down—send both away down into an abyss of their own making?*

No.

This couldn't happen. Not after everything else. Everything that had led up to this moment. Daredevil couldn't allow the Punisher to become the decision-maker, even if it was over the life of a corrupt monster like Fisk.

He wouldn't allow it.

Daredevil tossed his billy club at Castle—sensed it as it whipped past Fisk and slammed into Castle's hand. The gun went rattling to the floor, and Castle's surprised expletive echoed in Daredevil's mind.

Then the Kingpin ran. He pushed Castle aside and stormed through the door, leaving it waving in his wake. Castle turned, as if following the club that had prevented him from finishing Fisk off.

"I should kill you for that," Castle said.

Daredevil moved toward Castle.

"You're welcome to try, Frank."

The Punisher let out a dry laugh.

Then he leapt at Daredevil, pushing him through the door Fisk had barreled through. Daredevil could hear Fisk—his heavy, lumbering footsteps, the hurried breathing, the ding of an elevator. He just wanted to catch up to him, to put this all to bed. But his business wasn't just with the Kingpin, Daredevil realized. This had been about the Punisher, too.

Punisher swung first, connecting a fist with Daredevil's jaw and sending him farther into the anteroom outside. He couldn't hear the Kingpin as well, but he could hear enough—Fisk was on the ground, making a break for it toward the Kitchen.

Daredevil wiped blood from his mouth and got back on his feet.

"Your brawl isn't with me," Daredevil said. "Let me do what I need to do."

"What's that, Red?" Punisher said, pulling a Glock from a holster at his back and pointing it at Daredevil. "Find Fisk, hug it out, and see if he wants to go to prison? Not this time. I was part of their scheme—they conned me. Now they'll pay the price and I'll be on my way."

"I can't let you do that," Daredevil said, leaping and sending a kick toward Punisher's gun-hand. The vigilante pulled back, grabbing Daredevil's foot and yanking him forward, causing him to drop to the floor.

"You've got nothing to do with it," Punisher said as he sent his boot heel into Daredevil's midsection. He felt the impact. Guessed it'd cracked a few ribs. "I don't have time to debate with you—or your lawyer friend."

Or your lawyer friend.

Did Punisher know that Matt and Daredevil were one and the same?

Daredevil jumped up, swatting the gun out of Castle's hand with a well-time hand-chop, Punisher letting out a low yelp of surprise. Daredevil followed with a 1-2-3 punch sequence—hook, hook, uppercut. A move he'd seen his father perform so many times before. The gun clattered to the floor but Punisher was still standing, bracing for more. The killer was off-balance, but Daredevil didn't have time for this—he needed to get to Fisk. Now.

"This guy—Fisk—he played us all, Red," Castle said, blood trailing down his face. "The long con to eliminate his enemies—the two-bit thugs like Silvermane and the real threats, like Murdock. And us. You fell right into his trap. You think I'm gonna let you sentence him to a low-security prison, where he can rub elbows with other twisted millionaires to figure out his next big plan? I don't think so."

The knife came out of nowhere, probably tucked into Castle's sleeve. He slashed forward, and Daredevil felt the blade slicing into his chest. He screamed in pain. Punisher kept coming—jabbing at Daredevil, the point of the knife getting deeper with each poke as he tried to back away.

"I'll kill ya if I have to, Red," Punisher said nonchalantly. "I sleep well no matter what. It's gonna be me catching up to Fisk—I owe him a bullet to the head."

Daredevil swung wide, the back of his fist swatting Punisher's arm away. He felt the blood coating his shirt. The dizziness setting in. He needed to get out of this. Fast.

"You're insane, Frank," Daredevil said, his voice booming. "You're also embarrassed. Fisk shamed you. Used you as a toy—a little piece on his board to move as he saw fit."

Daredevil stepped forward, driving a knee into Castle's midsection. He had to stay close, out of the range of guns and knives, just two fighters brawling for inches—tied together and scraping for any advantage. Daredevil felt Punisher's hands clawing at him, desperate for purchase. Daredevil couldn't move his arms. But this had to end. Now.

"Frank, it's over," Daredevil said through gritted teeth.

"You think so, hero?"

"I know it," Daredevil said, seconds before he pulled his head back slightly, then slammed his forehead into Punisher's, sending the black-clad vigilante stumbling. Daredevil shook off the dizziness, shook off the pain and pressed. An elbow to the face. A quartet of body blows. Then the finale. Daredevil grabbed Punisher by his scalp and slammed his face into the nearest wall, the soft crunching sound letting him know if Punisher wasn't completely out, he was damn close. He watched as Castle's body slumped down to the ground, a low moan the only sound escaping his lips.

He heard her breathing before she spoke.

"I'll take it from here."

Daredevil turned around to reply to Elektra.

Elektra placed a boot over Castle's fallen form. Her actions said more than words could.

I've got this under control.

"You could've joined in at any time," he said.

Daredevil thought he heard Elektra chuckle, but couldn't be sure.

"It seemed like you needed this fight as much as he did," she said.

Daredevil sensed Elektra reaching out a hand. He took it. She moved toward him. Their faces close.

"You're hurt, Matthew," she said, placing a hand on his face. Gentle, warm. "Let me help you. You need to rest."

Daredevil shook his head and stepped back. "No time, Elektra," Daredevil said. "I've got a Kingpin to catch."

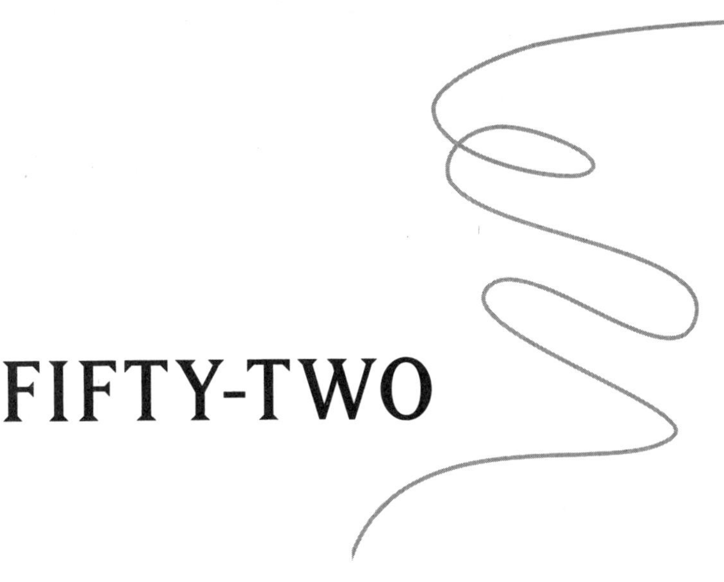

FIFTY-TWO

HE WAS IMPOSSIBLE TO MISS. This hulking, giant figure, off-balance, struggling down Ninth Avenue—pushing past the homeless man on the corner of Fifty-Third St, shoving the single mom pushing a stroller. It was late, but the street was alive. The sounds and smells ever-present as Daredevil tried to keep up. The hot dog hissing as it hit boiling water. The smell of a fresh pour of Yuengling. Two coworkers complaining about their boss. The slap of vomit hitting the street just outside of Josie's Bar.

But none of it mattered. Nothing except that shape. That big, giant creature lumbering down this crowded street, desperate for escape—desperate to go back down into his hidey-hole until it was safe to come up again, safe to come up and exert power. Crush his enemies. Manipulate the world around him and bend those less powerful to his will.

Wilson Fisk had tried to break Matt Murdock. Had tried to destroy Daredevil. Through lies, subterfuge, bribery, and murder, Fisk had built a plan that would have left Matt in ruins. His reputation in tatters and his double life spiraling down into the abyss.

And this wasn't the first time.

Ever since Daredevil had proven to be a meaningful thorn in Fisk's side, he'd put a target on his own back. Daredevil wasn't just Fisk's nemesis. It was personal. Daredevil and Kingpin were two sides of the same coin—two men driven to pull themselves up and out of poverty to become the best of the best. But their paths were very different. Daredevil sought to uphold justice—as a lawyer and man but also as a vigilante, a tool to help the system bring those that had wronged it to justice. Fisk had battled through his traumatic youth to become an even bigger monster—a bully who trafficked in fear and destruction, a conniving tactician who used guile and manipulation to get what he wanted, and to exert power over those who could not defend themselves.

It ends now, Daredevil thought.

"Fisk!" Daredevil yelled. His radar sense picked up the shape slowing down—then turning around slowly. "It's over."

"Daredevil," Fisk said, not even out of breath, his voice calm and serene, as if he'd just walked outside to get the paper. "You mistake my brisk pace for fear. I don't fear you. I pity you."

Fisk took a step toward Daredevil.

"Even if, by some twist, you are able to defeat me here, on the streets of your city," Fisk said, "what do you have to return to, Murdock? Your personal life is a wreck—you'll be a laughingstock. Your word is in tatters. I've destroyed the public's faith in you. You're already dead—and you'll be buried as a corrupt liar, that which you feared the most."

Fisk's laugh boomed through Daredevil's ears.

"You may want to cut the laughter short, Willie," Daredevil said, a laugh escaping his lips. "And check your phone."

He knew the message waiting for him on his own phone—from Ben Urich. Recalled the audio text autoplay from his phone: *FISK IS GOING DOWN.*

Fisk's entire demeanor changed. His body language went from

powerful and dominant to shaky. Daredevil's words had cut through his hubris. It gave him pause.

Ben Urich, I love you, Daredevil thought.

Daredevil sensed Kingpin reaching into his coat pocket. He pulled out his phone. The gasp would've been inaudible to anyone else. But to Daredevil, it was like a bullhorn sounding across a quiet field.

"What . . . what is the meaning of this?" Fisk muttered to himself. "No . . ."

"Feeling the pressure, Willie?" Daredevil said as he stepped closer now. "Feeling the heat? Even from the great beyond?"

Daredevil picked up his own burner phone and clicked the volume button on the side of the phone a few times, listening to the audio read-along of the article.

". . . *Bugle* reports that reputed mob kingpin Wilson Fisk is in fact alive and well—residing in his Midtown Manhattan skyrise. According to *Bugle* reporter Ben Urich's detailed expose, Fisk faked his own death, funneling money to corrupt members of the NYPD's Internal Affairs and coroner's office to make it seem like the supposed businessman had been gunned down by serial murderer Frank Castle, otherwise known as the urban vigilante the Punisher."

Daredevil looked up at Fisk, who was spinning around desperately, trying to find a path out—a way to freedom. There wasn't one.

". . . allegations outlined against Fisk were numerous, including ordering the death of an alleged capo in his organization, bribing a police officer, and trying to frame noted New York attorney Matthew Murdock, who most recently defended Frank Castle against murder charges relating to Fisk's supposed death. But the most egregious claim points to the supposed 'Kingpin of Crime' actually killing disgraced police officer Ed Sheehan himself. As of now, we are awaiting word from Assistant District Attorney Sprenger, who has scheduled a press conference within the hour—where we presume he will announce a citywide manhunt for Fisk. . . ."

"It's over," Daredevil said. "You've got nowhere to run to, Kingpin."

Daredevil rarely wished for his vision back. He'd come to terms with what he'd lost—and also what he'd gained in that accident, years ago. But right now, in this moment, he desperately wanted to see the expression on Fisk's face. The fear. The desperation. The hate. But Daredevil also realized that perhaps now, in this moment, sensing every detail surrounding Fisk's collapse, he was actually experiencing something deeper—more intimate. He was watching a man completely implode.

Kingpin turned toward Daredevil and sent a huge fist in his direction. But Daredevil had expected that. Kingpin was moving in rage, not strategically. He was fighting instinctively. Daredevil let the momentum of the punch carry the Kingpin forward.

Daredevil spun around as Kingpin recovered, his breathing irregular and jagged. He was scared now, Daredevil thought. He was off-balance.

"I don't need to fight you, Fisk," Daredevil said. "It's just time to turn yourself in."

Kingpin lunged again. Daredevil dodged.

Kingpin tried to send an elbow down on Daredevil, but missed. He was off. The air of desperation and panic setting in. Daredevil saw every move—every attack—a few seconds before Kingpin acted on it. After a few more minutes, Kingpin was panting. Sweat coating his body.

And there was a crowd forming now.

"Get him, Hornhead!"

"Take that rich prick down!"

"Is that Fisk? Thought he was dead . . . ?"

"Didn't expect to see a brawl on Ninth Ave . . ."

"Bring him in, DD!"

The crowd was inching closer, phones out. If it wasn't up on social media yet, it would be any minute. Soon the world would have confirmation that Wilson Fisk, the Kingpin, was alive. And he was in Hell's Kitchen.

Kingpin seemed to have the same realization, and bolted through the heart of the crowd, knocking people backward, ignoring their curses and surprised yelps. Daredevil followed, sprinting to keep pace with Fisk.

He was a few steps behind. Daredevil followed Fisk as he cut down an alley, his movements erratic, scared. Daredevil could hear him mumbling to himself.

"Away . . . Must get away . . . Still time . . . get to the jet . . . Europe . . . Vanessa . . ."

But Daredevil knew he wouldn't get to a jet. He wouldn't even get past this street.

"It's a dead end, Willie," Daredevil said, as Fisk stopped, realizing the alley he'd hoped would lead him to an open road was just a pile of trash. Fisk dropped to his knees, his hands clutching his head.

"Vanessa isn't waiting for you," Daredevil said. "It's time to face up to what you've done."

Fisk fell forward then. His hands on his head. He turned to face Daredevil, each breath a pant of desperation.

"You think this . . . is over?" Fisk said, wheezing now. "You think you've won? Daredevil, Daredevil . . . don't you know me by now?"

Fisk remained silent after that. Quiet as the police cars arrived. Silence as the uniformed officers led him to large van. Nothing.

Until he walked by Daredevil. Daredevil could smell his heavy aftershave. The mint mouthwash he used. Heard the words he whispered as he was pushed toward imprisonment.

"Watch your back, Murdock," Kingpin said. "I don't fall that easily. The battle is yours. But the war . . . is far from over."

Daredevil grabbed Kingpin's shoulder, holding him back for a second.

"I'll be waiting, Willie," Daredevil said, smiling at the Kingpin. He listened for the retort, for the snappy response. But he got something else.

Fear.

The smell of sweat on his skin. The sound of him swallowing quickly. And, most tellingly, a hurried whisper, shared between two foes who would forever be at odds.

"Damn you, Murdock. Damn you to hell."

Daredevil laughed. The officers escorting Fisk turned back, confused.

"Hell, Kingpin? That suits me fine. See you there. See you in hell."

Where else could you expect to find a Devil?

EPILOGUE

TWO WEEKS LATER.

Daredevil reached the rooftop with two minutes to spare. They were already waiting for him. The stale Hell's Kitchen breeze swept over the sparse ground atop the *Daily Bugle* building.

"Luke, good to hear from you," Daredevil said as he approached Cage, who was flanked by Elektra, Jessica Jones, and Dakota North.

Cage was hired muscle—but his heroism was never in doubt. An ex-con cursed with superhuman strength an impenetrable skin, Cage used his powers to help those in need, and wasn't afraid to make a few bucks in the process. He'd served as a bodyguard to Matt Murdock a few times, often in tandem with Jessica Jones, a former hero who now used her super-strength, flight, and invulnerability as a private eye. They were a couple, as far as Daredevil could tell—just based on the uptick in their heart rates when they spoke to each other. He could also hear another heartbeat—much softer, much younger—coming from Jessica. She was pregnant.

"Seems like the gang's all here."

"We thought we'd check in on you, Hornhead. Been a busy stretch, to say the least," Cage said with a laugh. "How you holdin' up?"

"I've been worse," Daredevil said. "Seems like the charges against

Fisk might stick this time. Sprenger revealed he found some actual evidence that Fisk himself did the deed on Sheehan. He didn't elaborate, but that's good news in my book. Ben sent me the list of mobsters headed to their doom upstate—I was able to get Punisher's old pal Micro to warn them in time. I owe you all. You guys and Urich really pulled my ass out of the fire more than once."

"Least we could do," Dakota said. "But it was mostly Ben. We gave him some info, but he had a lot of the evidence already, and he worked the phones. Old guy knows how to hustle. He pieced the conspiracy together in record time. If he ever retires from the newspaper biz, he'd make a helluva private eye."

"Don't give him any ideas," Jessica said with a warm laugh, her jet-black hair shining in the moonlight. "I don't want to lose any more clients to you."

"What of Mary Walker?" Elektra asked, her tone dry. She was never one for small talk.

"She's under medical surveillance. They can't hold her forever–though she is implicated in a number of crimes. But it seems she's actually participating in a program, so I'm cautiously optimistic."

"How are you with all that?" Jessica said, an eyebrow arching. "Gotta fuck with your head that she was pretending to be your partner all that time—using her pheromone power to confuse and trick you. You given yourself some grace, Murdock?"

"Are you asking me if I've meditated or gone on some kind of spiritual journey?" Daredevil asked. He'd meant for the comment to be flip and funny, but it came across as defensive. He stopped himself. "I'm sorry. You're worried about me. I appreciate that. Honestly, I haven't given myself time to process it. I think Mary's rage came from a place that existed before me, but I didn't handle things well with her originally—and that's my fault. I need to think about how to do better. How to do more than just punch the bad guys and let the city sort it out. I can't cash out my relationships to be a hero. Part of being a hero is doing it the right way."

"Growth," Jessica said. "What a concept."

Before Daredevil could respond, Dakota interjected.

"No leads on Punisher, eh?" she asked. "Guess he could've left whenever he wanted to. So why didn't he?"

Daredevil rubbed his chin before responding.

"Punisher was content to take the deal—sit in prison and watch the underworld burn," Daredevil said. "But there was another reason to be in there. When Fisk was trying to frame me for getting Castle out, Foggy rushed over to the police to smooth things over. That's where he learned one of the last people Castle talked to was a man named Burchell Clemens."

"Cottonmouth?" Cage interrupted. "The Serpent Society cyborg?"

"Exactly," Daredevil said. "Punisher was looking into something that tied into Clemens—and into the spike in cyborg activity in the city. Makes me wonder if he really was pissed about Fisk planting his prints."

"This part of why you wanted to see me, Hornhead?" Luke asked.

Daredevil handed a thick file to Cage.

"Not sure if Elektra mentioned this to you, but when we brawled with Silvermane, before Typhoid skewered him, we noticed his men were getting souped up with some pretty nasty cybernetics," Daredevil said. "They didn't look like his usual upgrades. And when we dug into Sheehan's role in this, we learned he was supervising some goods being funneled from down south. He was working with Clemens on transferring cybernetics from Virginia, actually—some of the towns you've mentioned when you've talked about your childhood."

"Huh, well damn," Cage said, flipping through the documents.

"Got some family down there, for sure. Interesting. You want me to look into it?"

"If you're up for a trip," Daredevil said. "If someone is using cyborg tech to empower the underworld, and if it ties into the Hand that could be a huge problem."

"Sure could," Cage said. "I'm on it."

Daredevil sensed Jones, Cage, and Dakota North make their way in different directions. He could still feel Elektra nearby.

"All right, say your piece," Daredevil said. "I figured you'd want to talk."

"You're hurt, Matthew," she said. He could hear her walking up behind him. "As someone who is quite familiar with burying feelings and ignoring what they mean, I must emphasize how important it is for you not to do that. I saw you with Melinda. I was tricked in the same way, though not as deeply. You loved her. I know that you love deeply and with abandon, Matthew. Don't lose that. Don't let this muffle that part of you. Let it forge you into a better man."

Daredevil turned around. He could feel the tears welling up in his eyes.

"Why did it have to be like this, Elektra?" Daredevil said, his voice cracking. "I knew I wasn't being my best self—to her, to my friends . . . but did I really deserve to be lied to like that? I realize Mary . . . isn't well. She wasn't able to make the right choices. But dammit. Why?"

Elektra stepped toward him and pulled Daredevil close, his head resting on her shoulder.

"If life was fair, Matthew, we wouldn't even be here."

"We'd be on a beach somewhere, sipping a cold drink, taking risks, laughing . . . enjoying ourselves."

"Perhaps," Elektra said as she pulled him back, her hand gently patting his face. "We can never know. All we can do is be here, and keep fighting. Keep trying to do what we believe is right."

Daredevil sighed.

"It's exhausting."

"It's all we have," Elektra said. "You could have easily let this go—let Frank Castle serve time for a murder he didn't commit. Let Wilson Fisk die by Castle's hand. You had opportunities to guide justice by your own desires and grudges—but you didn't. You're an admirable man, Matthew. I love you for that. We all do. But I also know it's not an easy path we've chosen."

Daredevil pulled Elektra close now. Their faces touching. Her warmth electric.

"The Devil's road never is."

ACKNOWLEDGMENTS

AS SOLITARY AS WRITING IS, there's a hidden truth to any novel—each book has many masters. In the case of the Daredevil crime novel—*Enemy of My Enemy*—you hold in your hand, there were numerous people who helped me on the journey from idea to finished book, and I'm grateful to all of them

To my editor, Adam Wilson, and the entire team at Hyperion Avenue, I'm grateful for your level head, sharp notes, and deft navigation of the process. A good editor helps their author actualize the vision they probably don't know they have for a book, and that was definitely the case here. My high concept—"Punisher on trial for the murder of the Kingpin"—felt really compelling, but it wasn't until we dug into the nuts and bolts of it that I discovered a greater, deeper theme—and one that resonated with Matt Murdock himself. I'm grateful to Adam for his patience and dedication to getting this Daredevil story right. Huge thanks to pal Dan Kaufman, Meredith Jones, and Guy Cunningham—copy editors extraordinaire—and the talented team of art director Amy C. King and designer Henry Sene Yee for making me look good on the outside and inside of this book. Thank you also to Elsa Sjunneson, a superb sensitivity reader.

To the great team at Marvel Comics, including Sven Larsen, Jeremy West, Sarah Singer, and Jeff Youngquist—I am thankful to have been allowed to add a (prose) chapter to the history of Daredevil, perhaps my favorite street-level Marvel hero. Matt Murdock is a complicated, messy, and ambitious guy, and it was a true honor and thrill to showcase him in all his complex glory in this medium. I hope we did him justice.

To those that came before—thank you. I'm particularly blessed in that I've gotten the chance to cross paths with many great Daredevil creators over my own career as a writer. Before I set out to put pen to page on this project, I read every issue of *Daredevil*—from his first appearance to the current run. These stories reveal a man driven by justice, scarred by tragedy, complicated by lust, and haunted by religion. Unlike some of his contemporaries, Matt Murdock is a very flawed person—not a stoic hero with a clear, unmoving sense of justice and right and wrong. Murdock makes mistakes, loves carelessly, and takes risks—and, most importantly, grapples with those choices. His story is one of failure and redemption, of tragedy and hope. So many writers I love and admire have taken time to recount his essential stories, but I am particularly thankful to creators like Stan Lee and Bill Everett, Gene Colan, Gerry Conway, Marv Wolfman, Frank Miller, Klaus Janson, Denny O'Neil, David Mazzucchelli, Ann Nocenti, John Romita Jr., Rick Leonardi, Lee Weeks, D. G. Chichester, Gregory Wright, Scott McDaniel, J. M. DeMatteis, Karl Kesel, Joe Quesada, Jimmy Palmiotti, Kevin Smith, David Mack, Brian Michael Bendis, Alex Maleev, Ed Brubaker, Michael Lark, Greg Rucka, Mark Waid, Chris Samnee, Javier Rodriguez, Paolo Rivera, Charles Soule, Ron Garney, Phil Noto, Chip Zdarsky, Marco Checchetto, Saladin Ahmed, Erica Schultz, and Aaron Kuder. I particularly want to thank Annie,

Dan, and Lee for introducing me to Daredevil and his world. This book would not exist without their work, which hooked me into Hell's Kitchen forever.

Endless thanks to the many readers, reviewers, librarians, and booksellers who have championed this book, often months before even seeing it. Your confidence and excitement means the world to me.

Huge thanks to my agent Josh Getzler and the entire team at HG Literary, the best advocates a writer could hope for. Most importantly, I want to thank my wife Eva, my two wonderful kids, Guillermo and Lucia, and my family and friends for their constant support and love. Without it, I'd be nothing.

Thanks for letting me visit Hell's Kitchen. It's been an honor.

Alex Segura
Queens, NY

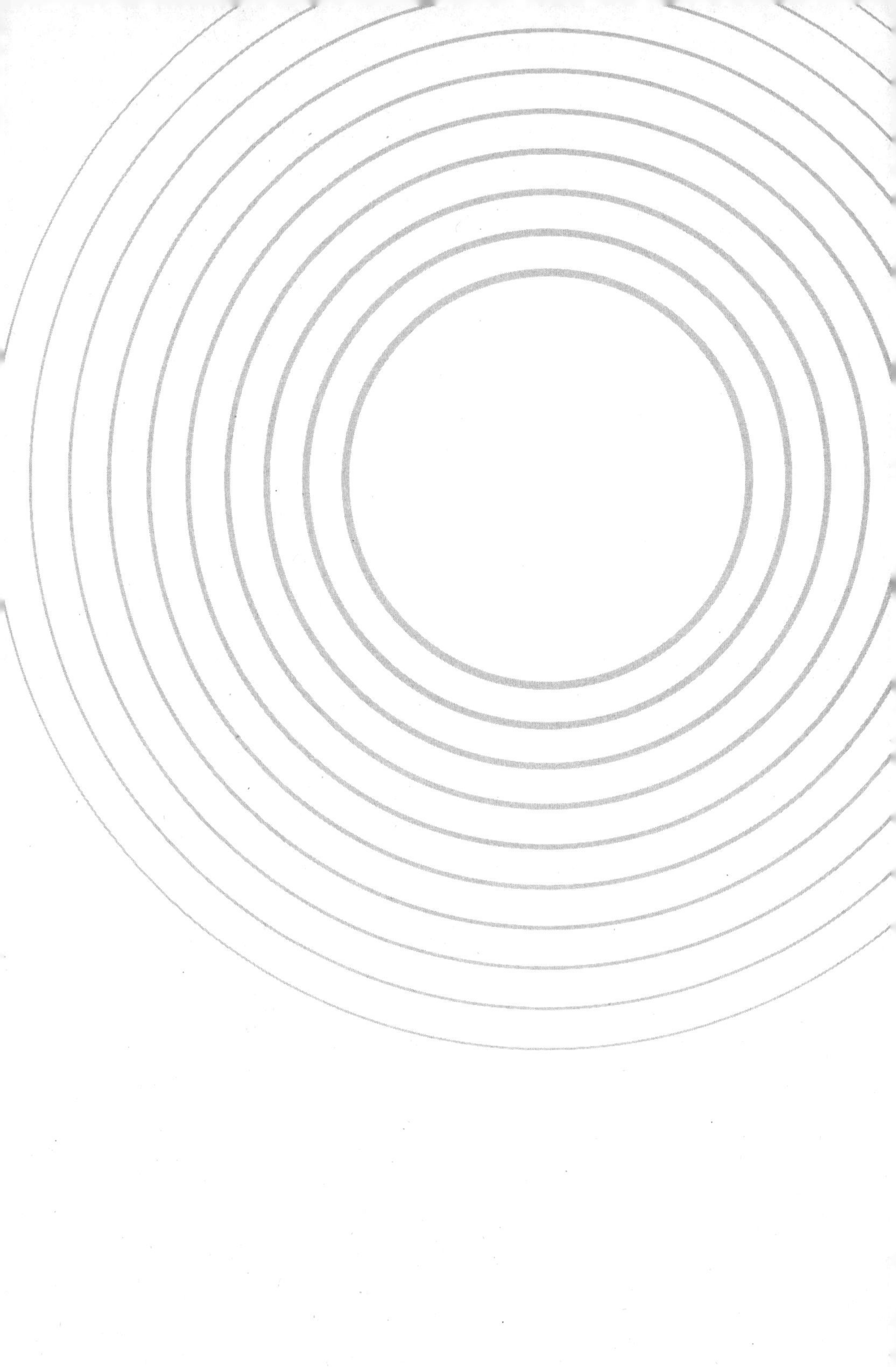

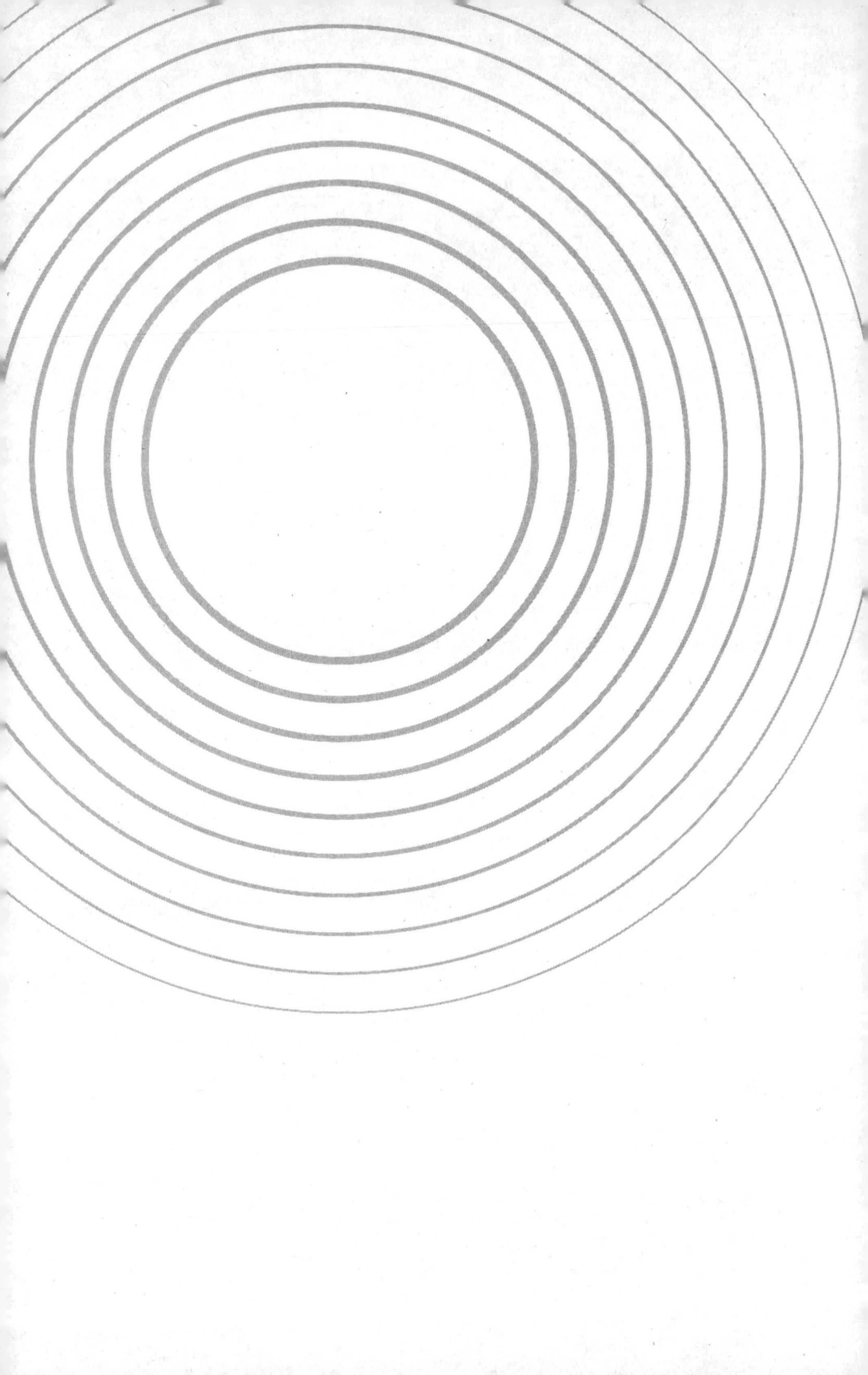

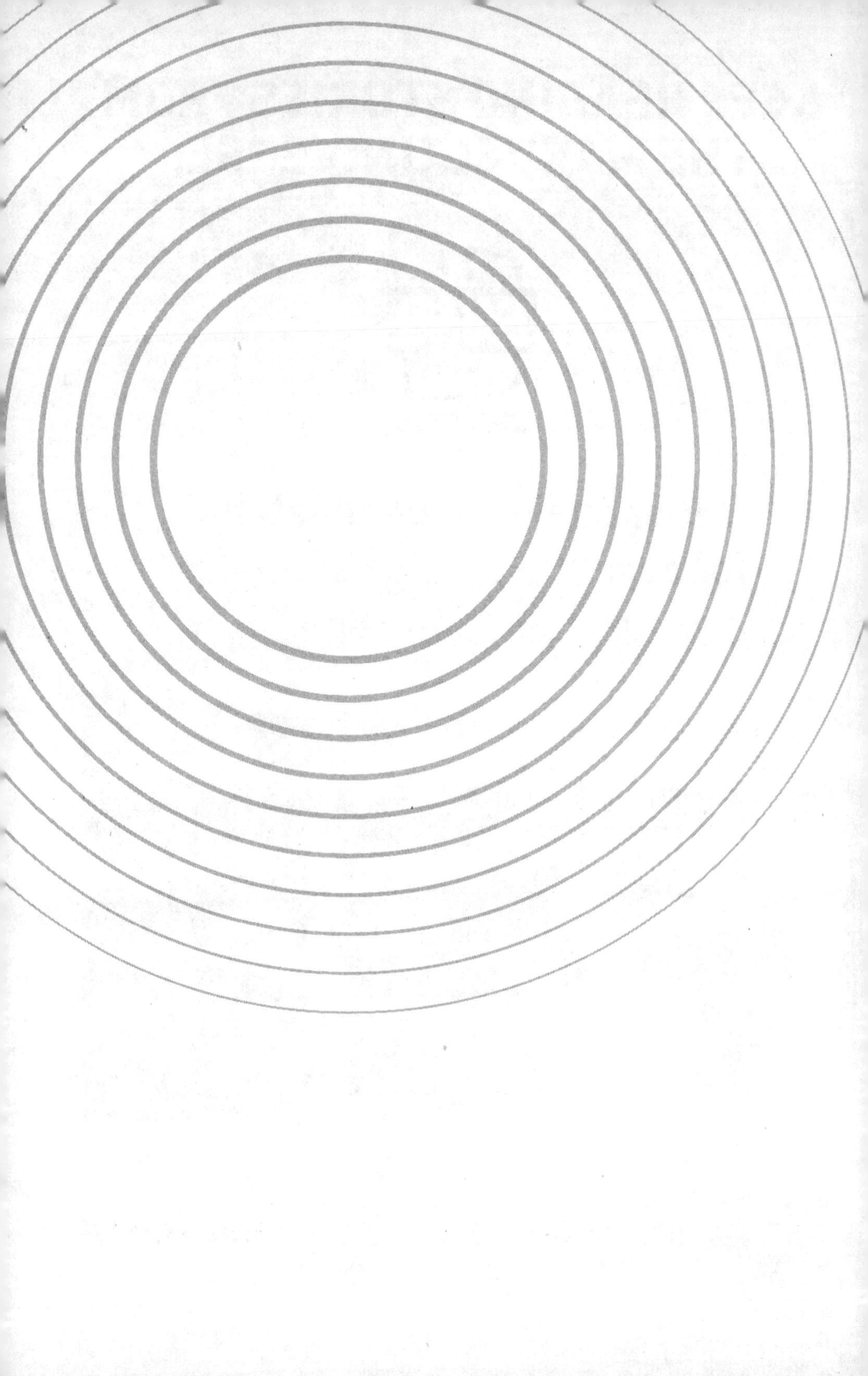

PRAISE FOR *BREAKING THE DARK*

A Jessica Jones Marvel Crime Novel

"Fresh, lively, insightful—from page one, Lisa's take on Jessica owned me. Astonishing."

—A. J. Finn, author of *The Woman in the Window*

"[A] novel that reveals the depth and complexity of one of the most fascinating and indomitable characters in the Marvel canon."

—S. A. Cosby, author of *King of Ashes*

"I was hooked from the start and couldn't turn the pages fast enough. Original, clever, and cinematic."

—Alice Feeney, author of *Rock Paper Scissors*

"Tricksy, endlessly interesting, and pure entertainment; don't miss this one."

—Gillian McAllister, author of *Wrong Place Wrong Time*

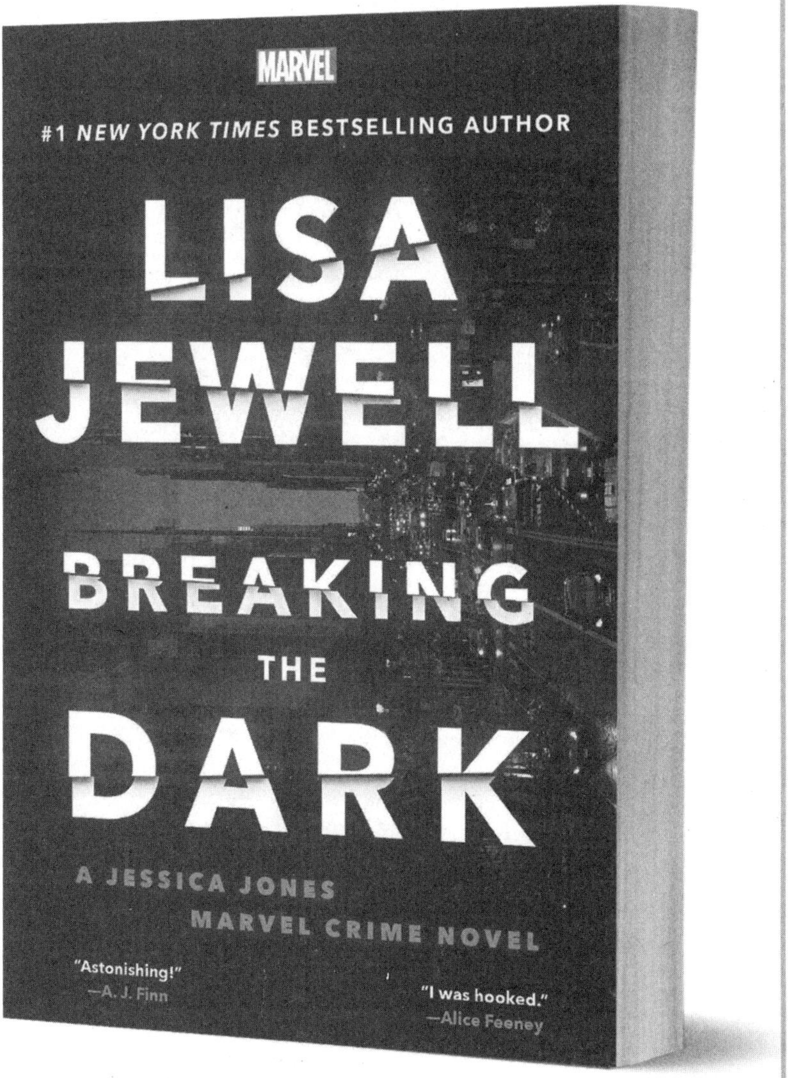

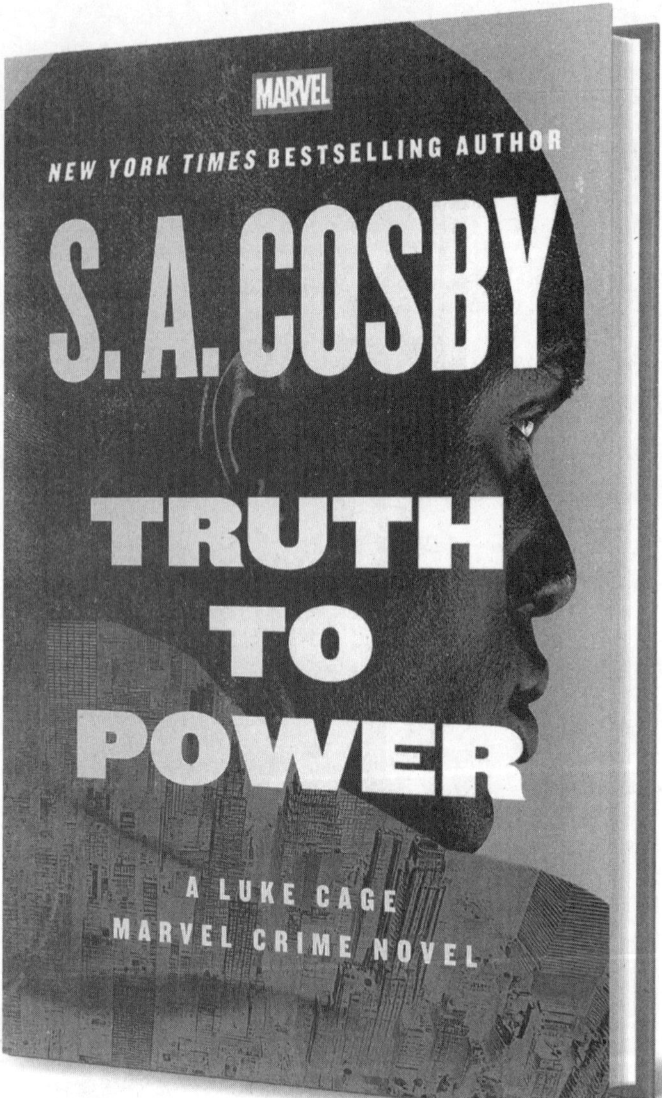